"You're a man with a ... aren't you?"

Wolf's scowl deepened. Panic surged through him. Sarah had unerringly sensed that he was hiding a great deal from her. Well, wasn't he? Hell, he was desperately trying to hide it from himself. His voice was clipped with warning as he retorted, "You've got the curiosity of a cat."

"And that isn't going to stop me from finding out why you think so little of yourself," she answered steadily.

Wolf's gut tightened, and he tasted fear. "If you're doing it for curiosity's sake, don't try to unlock me." Wolf stared at Sarah, the challenge in his gaze backed up by the growl in his voice. "I don't play games with anyone."

Her curiosity warred with the knowledge of potential danger. Despite her head's warning, Sarah's heart demanded to know his terrible secret. "Haven't you noticed yet? I don't play games, either."

Dear Reader,

Welcome to Silhouette **Special Edition**, where each month, we publish six novels with *you* in mind—stories of love and life, tales that you can identify with.

Last year, I requested your opinions on our books. Thank you for the many thoughtful comments. I'd like to share with you quotes from those letters. This seems very appropriate now, while we are in the midst of the THAT SPECIAL WOMAN! promotion. Each one of our readers is a *special* woman, as heroic as the heroines in our books.

We have some wonderful books in store for you this June. *A Winter's Rose* by Erica Spindler is our THAT SPECIAL WOMAN! title and it introduces Erica's wonderful new series, BLOSSOMS OF THE SOUTH. Not to be missed this month is *Heart of the Wolf,* by Lindsay McKenna. This exciting tale begins MORGAN'S MERCENARIES.

Wrapping up this month are books from other favorite authors: Gina Ferris (*Fair and Wise* is the third tale in FAMILY FOUND!), Tracy Sinclair, Laurey Bright and Trisha Alexander.

I hope you enjoy this book, and all of the stories to come!

Sincerely,

Tara Gavin
Senior Editor
Silhouette Books

Quote of the Month: "Why do I read romances? I maintain a positive outlook to life—do not allow negative thoughts to enter my life—but when my willpower wears, a good romance novel gets me back on track fast! The romance novel is adding much to the New Age mentality— keep a positive mind, create a positive world!"

—E.J.W. Fahner
Michigan

LINDSAY McKENNA

HEART OF THE WOLF

Silhouette®

SPECIAL EDITION®

Published by Silhouette Books New York
America's Publisher of Contemporary Romance

If you purchased this book without a cover you should be aware
that this book is stolen property. It was reported as "unsold and
destroyed" to the publisher, and neither the author nor the
publisher has received any payment for this "stripped book."

To the "Wolf Pack"—Ardella Hecht, Marlene
Johnson, Bonnie Birnham, Betty James, Ruth Gent,
Karen Durham, Roni Lee Bell, Karen J. David, Patty
Thomas, Coletta Swalley, Eileen "Tunney"
Lunderman, Laura Dahl, Mary Buckner, Gary Gent,
Glenn Malec, Glorynn Ross and Karen Pietkiewicz

SILHOUETTE BOOKS
300 East 42nd St., New York, N.Y. 10017

HEART OF THE WOLF

Copyright © 1993 by Lindsay McKenna

All rights reserved. Except for use in any review, the reproduction
or utilization of this work in whole or in part in any form by any
electronic, mechanical or other means, now known or hereafter
invented, including xerography, photocopying and recording, or in
any information storage or retrieval system, is forbidden without
the permission of the publisher, Silhouette Books, 300 E. 42nd St.,
New York, N.Y. 10017

ISBN: 0-373-09818-9

First Silhouette Books printing June 1993

All the characters in this book have no existence outside the
imagination of the author and have no relation whatsoever to
anyone bearing the same name or names. They are not even
distantly inspired by any individual known or unknown to the
author, and all incidents are pure invention.

®: Trademark used under license and registered in the United States
Patent and Trademark Office and in other countries.

Printed in the U.S.A.

Books by Lindsay McKenna

LINDSAY McKENNA

After the publication of *Return of a Hero* (SE #541), I received hundreds of letters asking what happened to the story's hero, Morgan Trayhern. Well, in my latest trilogy, *Morgan's Mercenaries*, the question is answered.

I loved returning to the characters of Morgan and his wife, Laura, and am thrilled to give you three very exciting, adventurous and intensely romantic stories about the men in Morgan Trayhern's employ.

Mercenaries have always fascinated me—they are loners in our world, with mysterious pasts and brooding secrets deep within their hearts. I hope you enjoy reading about Wolf, Killian and Jake as much as I did writing about them!

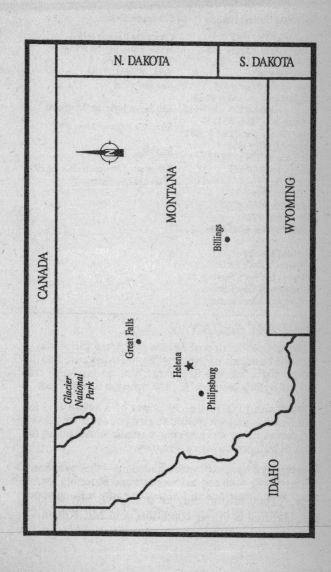

Prologue

"Dr. Shepherd? I'm Morgan Trayhern, from Perseus. You've got two of my men here, Harding and Killian."

Morgan realized he was having trouble controlling his voice. He cleared his throat. Dr. Marlene Shepherd, a pleasant-looking woman whose face was lined with fatigue, looked up at him.

She smiled tiredly and leaned against the nurses' station. "I'm glad you could come, Mr. Trayhern."

"How are they?"

She straightened and gestured for him to follow her to the empty visitors' lounge. At two in the morning, the entire hospital was quiet, with only a skeleton staff on duty. "They arrived only an hour ago, Mr. Trayhern. Mr. Harding is in fair condition, and Mr. Killian is in good condition."

Morgan inhaled a deep, thankful breath. Restlessly he scanned the dimly lit halls, automatically hating Bethesda Naval Hospital's sterile, antiseptic smells. "Then they'll be okay?"

The doctor halted within the spacious visitors' lounge and faced him. She took off her glasses and rubbed the bridge of her nose. "I won't lie to you, Mr. Trayhern. Both men are malnourished, just for starters."

"Starved," he said flatly. It was a statement, not a question. Morgan wondered how much the navy doctor knew about his three-man mercenary team's stint in Peru. Studying her intently, Morgan decided from the worry and confusion on her full, square features that she didn't know much.

"Yes."

"So what's Wolf Harding's condition—specifically?" Wolf had been the team leader in Peru.

"Specifically, Mr. Harding has been, for lack of a better word, tortured extensively, Mr. Trayhern." The doctor's full mouth pursed, and she gave him an incisive look. "So has Mr. Killian—to a far lesser degree."

"You're going to need a microbiologist, a good one," Morgan said grimly. "They've been in the Peruvian jungle for nearly two years. They may be suffering from bacterial infections."

"We've already begun testing for that," Dr. Shepherd said, putting her glasses back on. "No broken bones," she offered.

Broken spirits? Morgan wondered bleakly. The entire Peru venture had been unsuccessful. As he stood listening to Dr. Shepherd continue to list his two mercenaries' lesser medical problems, Morgan forced himself to be patient.

Wolf Harding had been commander of the three-man Perseus team. And his condition was only fair. What had gone wrong? Morgan tried to appear attentive as the soft-spoken doctor completed her analysis of his men's conditions.

"When may I see them, Dr. Shepherd?"

"0800 tomorrow morning, Mr. Trayhern."

"Not any sooner?"

She gave him a sympathetic smile. "I'm sorry. Both men are exhausted and are sleeping deeply right now."

Curbing his impatience, Morgan gave her a curt nod. "I appreciate all your help, Dr. Shepherd."

"Of course. If you'll excuse me, Mr. Trayhern, I have my rounds to complete."

Morgan nodded, then remained standing in the gloomy visitors' lounge as she disappeared down a corridor. The silence ate away at him as his mind traveled back in time. Two years ago, he'd formed Perseus—a security consulting company—and hired twenty mercenaries. His men and women would go anywhere in the world, aiding those in jeopardy who were beyond the help of direct U.S. government intervention. Today, Morgan had more demands for his people's services than he had people to fill those requests. And Perseus had an unblemished record of success—until now.

Rubbing his sandpapery jaw, he decided to stay at the hospital—just in case Wolf took a turn for the worse. He wouldn't abandon his men the way he'd been left—to die alone in some foreign country's hospital. He didn't care whether his men knew he stood guard over them. When he'd started his company, Morgan had made a promise to his people and to himself: He'd treat them the way he'd want to be treated.

Morgan's connections in the upper levels of government meant Perseus lacked for nothing. He had state-of-the-art communications with the FBI and CIA, satellite links, and the eager help of friendly countries. The government had been only too happy to hear he was setting up shop. There were many cases involving American citizens that they couldn't become directly involved in—shadowy political cases that could threaten the progress of diplomacy if the government was implicated. Perseus came in and quietly handled the problem.

Slowly pacing the length of the visitors' lounge, Morgan felt exhaustion tugging at him. He'd had a sixth sense about this long mission, which involved three of his best men. Stopping, he looked around at the gloom and sighed. He was lucky they hadn't been killed. And for that he was grateful. Perseus employees were culled from the top mercenaries in the world. They were at the top of their craft, highly intelligent, loyal, and emotionally stable—unlike many mercenary types, who might have skills, but lacked the stable psychological profile Morgan demanded.

He thought of Laura, his wife, who would still be sleeping soundly in their nearby Washington, D.C., home. She'd become accustomed to him bailing out of bed at ungodly hours to meet his returning mercenaries, arriving from a mission at one of the region's two major airports—or sometimes at the Bethesda Naval Hospital. He'd call and leave Laura a message on the answering service so that she'd know where he was and not to worry.

Frowning, Morgan loosened his paisley tie and unbuttoned his shirt collar. He sank down onto the plastic cushions of a visitors' room sofa, which creaked in protest as he relaxed for the first time in hours. Two of the three men he'd sent to Peru had been injured. Jake, the

third—not requiring medical transport—would be returning on a later flight. Morgan would have to wait to
hear his version of events. Morgan wished he could get
used to this part of his job, but he knew he never would.
Once a leader of a company of men, the old Marine
Corps saying went, always a leader of a company of men.
Well, he'd had his men caught in one hell of a vise. They
were lucky they'd survived at all.

With a sigh, Morgan tipped his head back and closed
his eyes. He needed to talk to Wolf Harding. He needed
to find out what had happened.

A groan pulled Wolf out of his deep, healing sleep. The
noise sounded as if it came from faraway, but as he
slowly forced his eyes open a fraction he realized he was
the one doing the groaning. Pain lapped at the edges of
his semiconscious confusion. Where was he? The room
was quiet, white and clean. The hell he'd lived in for over
a month had been dark, dank and torturous.

I'm alive.

The thought congealed in his groggy mind. Wolf
forced his awareness outward. He was in a bed—un-
shackled. Every muscle in his body felt as if it were on
fire. Widening his attention span, Wolf took in two IV's
dispensing life-giving fluids into both his arms. Blips of
memory from the nightmarish past sped through his
mind.

He saw faces, inhaled horrible smells. He heard
screams. The scream of a woman. *Oh, God...*

The door to his room slowly opened.

Wolf blinked back the tears that had welled up in his
eyes. Though his vision was blurred, he recognized his
boss, Morgan Trayhern, who look disheveled, his face

darkly in need of a shave, his tie askew over the open collar of his white silk shirt.

A wall of emotion funneled up through Wolf. He opened his mouth to speak, but all that came out was an animal groan. He saw Morgan's pale features grow taut as he approached, his mouth thinning. Wolf knew he must look like death warmed over.

"You look like hell," Morgan said by way of greeting as he halted at Wolf's bedside. Wolf's face was bruised, cut and swollen, the flesh around his eyes puffy, allowing Morgan only a glimpse of gray through the slitted eyelids.

Wolf nodded and dragged in a ragged breath. "Where?" he croaked.

"Bethesda Naval Hospital. The Peruvian police called me, and we sent the jet down for you and Killian. You arrived around midnight last night."

At the mention of his Irish friend's name, Wolf tried to speak, but he found it impossible.

"He's in better shape than you are," Morgan said, reading the question in Wolf's bloodshot eyes. "And Jake is fine. He caught a military flight out of the country and will be arriving here shortly." Morgan frowned. "You're the one we were worried about."

"Yeah?"

"You in much pain?" Morgan recalled all too vividly the times after his own surgery when his pain medication had worn off and he'd sweated in agony for hours before some harried, overworked nurse finally came by to check on him.

Wolf nodded once. He saw Morgan lean over and press the button that would bring a nurse with a shot to numb his physical pain. But as much as he wished there was a shot or pills that could dull the raging pain in his heart,

Wolf knew there was nothing to lessen that shattering ache. A clawing sensation tugged at his chest—something he wanted to escape but couldn't. The emotional wall of pain nearly suffocated him as he lay beneath Morgan's concerned gaze. From somewhere, he dredged up the strength to speak.

"Leave," he muttered thickly, his words slurred. "I want to go away, Morgan."

Morgan's eyes narrowed. "Oh?"

"I want to leave the field for a while."

Morgan watched as a parade of emotions crossed Wolf's battered features. "Perseus has an automatic policy to grant returning mercenaries time out of the field after a mission's completed, Wolf—you know that."

"More than a month," Wolf rasped, struggling to speak, struggling to overcome the pain. At least the intensity of the physical pain seemed to temporarily override the emotional pain. That was something.

Morgan looked up toward the window. The bright May sunlight was spilling into the room. "Something happened down there."

Wolf's breath began to come faster, and his heart began to pound, as it thought of— Savagely he slammed the door shut on the too-fresh memories that haunted him. "I...want...time... Need time, Morgan." He forced his eyes as far open as possible. "Get away. Get me a job...any job...away..."

Hearing the desperation in the rising pitch of Wolf's husky voice, Morgan raised his hand. "Just tell me what you need, and I'll make sure it happens, Wolf."

Collapsing against the bed, the tension bleeding out of him, Wolf closed his eyes. His voice was wobbly with raw feelings. "Something safe...quiet... The mountains. Somewhere away from everything."

"People?"

Wolf was always startled by Morgan's insight. Maybe it was because he'd suffered so much himself that he could read Wolf's suffering so easily. "No people. Got...to be alone..."

Rubbing his jaw, Morgan thought for a moment. "Dr. Shepherd said it would be at least three weeks before you can leave the hospital."

"After that," Wolf forced out violently. He had to escape! He had to be alone in order to start dealing with the horrible atrocities he'd managed to survive in Peru—and the emotional ones he feared he hadn't survived....

"Montana far enough away?" Morgan asked.

Wolf nodded.

"I can get you a job as a forest ranger. I've got the connections. You'd be fairly isolated. Working alone in the wilderness. Interested?"

Again Wolf nodded. He was afraid to speak, afraid that if any noise escaped him it would be a sob—and he'd start crying for all those months of hell he'd endured.

"It's yours, then," Morgan promised. "All I ask is that when you're feeling up to it you write me a report on what the hell happened down there. I'll have my assistant, Marie Parker, have the job ready for you when you walk out of this place." Morgan reached down and gripped Wolf's large, callused hand, which bore many recent pink scars. "Just get well, Wolf. Take the time you need. Perseus needs your talents, your abilities. *I* need you."

Chapter One

Oh, no! Sarah sucked in a sharp breath as the Douglas fir she was working under gave a sharp, splintering crack. Scrambling, she tried to throw herself upward, out of the cavernous hole beneath its twisted roots.

A gasp broke from her as she was slammed back onto the dusty white earth and its carpet of dried fir needles. The sixty-foot tree had arched to one side, missing her head and torso, but pinning her ankles and feet beneath the massive roots. Trapped! She was trapped! And then pain shot up her legs. Groaning, Sarah lay still a moment, reorienting herself, before she struggled to a sitting position. She was in the shallow depression she had dug beneath the fir as she searched for the sapphire gravel concentrate that collected beneath the roots.

"How could I?" she whispered disgustedly, her fingers trembling as she frantically dug in and around the roots, trying to locate her ankles. "This is an amateur's mistake, Sarah Thatcher.'' And then she grimaced and stiffened. The agony was real.

Pushing strands of damp blond hair away from her furrowed brow, Sarah clawed at the loose soil, trying to remove enough from under her legs to free her trapped feet. The sapphire gravel—the gemstones in their natural state, as small, round pebbles—were piled around her with the rest of the debris.

Gasping, Sarah arched back suddenly, her fingers clutching her jean-clad thigh. The pain had increased tenfold. Had she broken one or both of her ankles? Anger at her stupidity warred with her fear of the situation. Glancing up through the fir trees, Sarah could see the clouds building. It was late August, and here in the Rocky Mountains near her tiny hometown of Philipsburg, Montana, it was common for afternoon thunderstorms to pop up, sending furious torrents of rain at a moment's notice.

Her fingers lacerated and bruised, Sarah renewed her digging efforts. Then her eyes widened: The roots of the tree were lodged against a huge black boulder. Her anger gave way to disgust—then real alarm. What if she couldn't escape? What if she really couldn't free herself? Of course, Summers would thank his lucky stars if she was found dead up on her Blue Mountain sapphire claim, Sarah thought bitterly. Gerald Summers, the local land developer, certainly hadn't wasted any time mourning her father's sudden death. But then, Summers had thought she would sell out, and he'd have been too happy to take over her family's claim.

"No way..." she muttered through gritted teeth, stretching as far as her five-foot-three-inch frame would allow. Her prospector's hammer lay mere inches from her outstretched hand. She never traveled without her rifle, a canteen of water, and her mining tools. Her fingers dusty, her nails almost nonexistent from the demands of her livelihood, Sarah groaned as she reached farther—and managed to secure the hammer. Its long, sickle-shaped point was specially designed for digging into rock or dirt.

Sarah kept her blond hair twisted between her shoulder blades in one long, frayed braid so that it was out of the way when she worked, mining the sapphire gravel that lay approximately a foot beneath the thick groves of firs on the slopes of Blue Mountain. Although it was necessary to dig holes around and between the tree roots to find the gravel, any miner knew to dig uphill, away from the tree, so that if the fir fell, it would drop away from where the miner was working.

"Stupid, so stupid, Sarah. Where was your brain this morning?" she chastised herself as she began to chip and strike at the boulder that held her captive. The hard granite gave little beneath her relentless hammering, sparks and tiny chips of the stubborn stone flying from beneath the steel tool's onslaught—not unlike the pressure she endured from Summers. He just kept chipping away at her. First, he'd murdered her father—though the county sheriff, Noonan, had called it an accident. Then her fifty-year-old mother had suffered a stroke upon hearing how her husband had died. The mine was still in her parents' names and Sarah knew Summers would love to get her out of the way. Her mother, Beth Thatcher, was semilucid these days and likely to sign over the sapphire mine to anyone without question, such was the damage the stroke had done to her memory.

"No way," Sarah whispered again, her voice cracking. But this was a stupid mistake on her part, not Summers's work. Frantically Sarah increased the power and strokes of the hammer. Very little of the granite boulder budged.

The sky was darkening, and Sarah glanced at her watch. An hour had passed since she'd gotten herself trapped. Both her legs were now numb from the knees down. *Had* she broken her ankles? Oh, God, it couldn't be! The mortgage payment on the mine was due in two weeks, as was the weighty bill from the nursing home where her mother lived. No, she had to be able to work every day, mining from sunrise until sunset. If she didn't, she'd lose everything. Biting down on her full lower lip, Sarah wiped the sweat from her dusty brow and continued to hammer at the boulder.

After another hour of nonstop pounding, her fingers and lower arms ached with fatigue. She was damp with sweat, and her loose chambray shirt was clinging to her body. Her jeans were filthy with the white, dusty soil.

Sarah eyed her trapped feet beneath the gnarled brown fir roots. No one would miss her. Her isolated cabin was five miles up the road. She couldn't count on her mother. Although Sarah visited her at the nursing home in town nearly every evening, her mother frequently didn't know the time of day, what month it was, or when she had last seen Sarah; time had become meaningless to her since the stroke.

Flopping back on the earth, Sarah closed her eyes, sucking in huge drafts of air, exhausted. Who *would* miss her? Maybe Jean Riva, owner of the small nursing home. But occasionally Sarah missed a visit to her mother in order to facet sapphires for a customer. Pepper Sinclair, a woman smoke jumper with the forest service, was stationed in town. But she rarely saw Pepper—only for an occasional meal. Opening her eyes, Sarah stared up at the turbulent gunmetal-gray sky that boiled above her. Flaring her nostrils, she drank in a huge breath of air, testing it. Yes, she could smell rain in the air. If it rained, her trap would turn into a quagmire. And even though it was nearly September, a thunderstorm could lower the temperature to barely above freezing for hours after the storm had spent itself.

Sarah knew better than to hope it wouldn't rain. She'd lived in Montana all her life, prospecting with her father and helping him mine the sapphire. Groaning, she sat back up. A thought struck her. She took the hammer and started chopping at the thick, long roots, instead of the rock. Why hadn't she thought of this hours before?

"Sarah, you're strung out. You're not thinking straight." The task seemed impossible; the abundant roots directly beneath the fir were the ones that held her captive. And she'd have to hack through the tap root, the main root that the tree sent straight down to find water, in order to free herself. But that wasn't all. Eyeing the massive trunk of the fir, Sarah realized that the roots actually suspended the main bulk of the trunk off her legs. If she succeeded in removing the roots, the tree would smash down, breaking both her legs.

Thunder rumbled, and Sarah shivered in response. Looking around, Sarah stretched out again, got a hold of her rifle and began to use the barrel to pull larger rocks toward her. Perhaps she could build a protective wall of rocks next to where her ankles were trapped to take the weight of the tree once she hammered through the tap root.

Without warning, the rain poured from the torn belly of the sky. Sarah winced as the hard, cold drops struck her sweaty body. The soil would turn slick and sucking if she didn't hurry to get the rocks in place. Her breath coming in uneven gulps, she quickly built her safety net. The hammer's wet handle was slippery in her clenched hand. Gripping it firmly, Sarah tried to ignore the downpour. Rain struck her head, rolling down her face and beneath the collar of her shirt.

The wind increased, bending the tops of the hundreds of firs that surrounded Sarah. Biting, wintry cold clawed at her, and she began to shiver in earnest beneath the sheets of rain. Her muscles trembling with the strain, Sarah worked on. Her hair fell in flat wet strands across her face, blinding her. With the back of her muddy hand, she shoved the strands away from her eyes enough to see what she was doing.

Half an hour later, the storm ceased, as suddenly as it had started, leaving Sarah stranded in a pool of muddy water. She cut a channel away from her through the mud with the butt of her rifle, allowing most of the water to drain away. Then her teeth chattering, she wrapped her arms around her drawn-up knees. Cold. She was so cold.

The wind died down, the forest around her becoming quiet and serene once more. Sarah rubbed her arms, longing for warm, dry clothes. Mud squished around her when she moved. At least half the roots had been destroyed, but she had a good three or four hours of work ahead of her.

Suddenly a sound registered, growing louder. A car? At first, Sarah thought she was hallucinating because of shock and hypothermia. She rarely saw anyone on this back road bordering forest-service land. Tilting her head, she listened. Yes! She could definitely hear the faint growl of a truck making its way up the now-muddy dirt road leading to her cabin. *Impossible!*

Grabbing her rifle, she waited impatiently for the truck to draw nearer. A sudden paroxysm of fear grabbed her heart. What if it was one of Summers's henchmen come to check up on her? Once they'd dressed as forest rangers to fool her. The ruse had worked. Sarah had been caught without her 30.06 rifle nearby, and they had wrecked her mining camp. She'd managed to knock one of her assailants unconscious with her hammer, though, and the other had run, caught off guard by a ''helpless'' woman fighting back. Although she'd pressed charges, neither man had served time in the county jail. Sheriff Noonan was on Summers's side, and he'd refused to take her charges seriously.

Her heart pounded in triple time as the truck drew close, and Sarah gripped the rifle tighter. She *had* to take the chance! So few people knew about this back road. Closing her eyes, trying to control her shivering, Sarah fired the rifle once, twice, three times. She heard the truck stop and the engine cut off. Sarah opened her eyes and could barely make out an olive-green vehicle through the trees and brush below. Who was it? She bit down hard on her lower lip. She was growing desperate. No matter who it was, she'd hold the gun on them and force them to help her get her legs free.

Wolf Harding was sure he'd heard the rifle shots. So had his half-red-wolf, half-malamute companion, Skeet. The dog barked once, his tail wagging furiously as he stuck his head out the window of the truck. Ahead and to the right, pulled off the road, Wolf saw a battered white pickup—probably ten years old. The rusty vehicle was covered with a multitude of dents and scratches. Putting his truck in park, Wolf got out, his well-worn cowboy boots sinking into the mud. He took the rifle off the gun rack on the back seat and placed a round in the chamber.

Wolf concentrated, focusing on the sixth sense that had saved his life many times before. His gaze ranged across the fir-covered hill, and he breathed in the damp, fragrant air. Suddenly he spotted movement, halfway up the steep slope. Skeet whined.

Walking around the pickup, Wolf opened the door and released the dog.

"Stay," he ordered, quietly.

Skeet was shivering with anticipation, his eyes and ears riveted to the hill. Probably a hunter shooting out of season, Wolf thought. Well, the unsuspecting poacher was going to get a surprise today. Taking out his notepad, he wrote down the license number of the white pickup, then tucked the pad back into his olive-green gabardine jacket.

"Come."

Skeet leaped and whined, but remained at Wolf's side as he quietly worked his way in zigzag pattern up the steep slope. A ground squirrel spotted Skeet, shrieked, and jumped back into the safety of his hole. A blue jay above sounded his warning cry, the call absorbed quickly by the surrounding forest. Wolf's breath came in white wisps in the chilly aftermath of the thunderstorm. A far cry from the jungles of South America, he thought suddenly. The unbidden memory evoked a powerful chill that worked its way up his back and into his shoulders, where an old bullet wound twinged in response. Some things were hard to forget.

Shaking off that all-too-recent memory, Wolf forced himself to concentrate. Hunters frequently shot deer out of season around here, he had been warned by his superior. And more than one forest ranger had been shot *at* because he'd been caught in the same area, as a warning to mind his own business. Wolf's predecessor in the job had taken a bullet in the leg doing the very same thing: stalking poachers in the national forest. Up here in Montana, Wolf thought, these people think they're a law unto themselves. And he was used to teamwork, not working alone. But a lot of things were changing rapidly and drastically in his life. Two months ago, he'd been released from his unhappy three-week hospital stay. Now, with eight weeks of forest ranger training under his belt, he was traipsing through the woods of Montana. Well, he'd wanted to get away....

Skeet growled, the hackles on his red-and-gray coat rising. Wolf froze, his eyes moving to where Skeet was looking. Up ahead he could see a huge mound of recently dug earth. Frowning, he signaled Skeet to remain at his side. He wasn't going to lose his dog to some trigger-happy poacher. His heart started a slow pounding, and he could feel the adrenaline pumping through his system, the familiar friend that heightened his senses and reflexes—perhaps to save his life, as it had before. Wolf didn't want a shoot-out with a poacher his first day on the job.

Sarah gasped as a giant of a man walked into her camp. She hadn't even heard his approach. Out of instinct, she swung her rifle into firing position.

"Hold it!" she ordered. "Don't move or I'll shoot!" He'd crouched into a combat stance.

Frightened and confused, Sarah tried to control her chattering teeth. "Who are you?" she croaked, and she saw his intent gaze soften. Her heart pounded beneath his cursory inspection. The hard line of his mouth relaxed slightly.

"Ranger Harding, U.S. Forest Service," Wolf answered the shivering woman. "You can put the gun down." He set his own beside a tree to show his peaceful intent. She seemed to be trapped beneath a tree, Wolf saw. She certainly posed no threat to him. She was covered with mud, and exhaustion was evident in her strained features. Still, she stood out like a yellow buttercup, he thought, her blond hair contrasting brightly with the lush green of the surrounding trees.

"Ranger?" Sarah said challengingly. "You'd better prove it, mister, or I'll blow your head off before you come a step closer."

Wolf was nonplussed by her angry response. She appeared to be serious. He looked down at his olive-green gabardine uniform. "I've got a badge underneath this," he offered, slowly moving his hand to open his jacket and show it to her.

"Don't move!" Sarah stiffened, and the gun's barrel wavered. Black dots swam in front of her eyes. Did that mean she was going to faint? She couldn't—not yet!

Wolf scowled. "How am I going to prove to you who I am, then?" How could something so tiny and bedraggled be so completely distrusting? But very real fear showed in her huge blue eyes, forcing Wolf to respect her anxiety, whatever its cause.

"You could have a gun under that jacket," Sarah hissed.

One corner of Wolf's mouth quirked into a bare semblance of a smile. "Lady, where I come from we hide our guns in a lot of places, under the jacket's a little too obvious."

Sarah stared at him hard. Maybe it was the faint curve at one corner of his mouth that made her want to believe him. She eyed the dog beside him—just as huge and intimidating as his master. How could she trust this man? Sarah had learned the hard way that she couldn't afford to trust anyone—even the people she loved most had abandoned her in one way or another. No, she could depend only on herself. She had no choice.

"Move slowly, mister. Show me your badge—real slowly. I'm a crack shot."

Wolf suspected that she was in a lot of pain—and possibly in shock. She was extremely pale. Wolf's protective nature reacted strongly. On the team in South America, he'd been the leader and paramedic, and now his caring instincts were aroused, in spite of this unnecessary game she was playing with him. "I'll bet you are," he said, slowly pulling the jacket aside to reveal the silver badge above his left breast pocket.

"Your credentials," the woman bit out. "A badge means nothing. I could go to Anaconda and buy one at a surplus store if I wanted."

Hollow showed beneath her delicate cheekbones, and Wolf could see darkness stalking her eyes. He was certain now that she was in shock, and going deeper by the minute. How long had she been trapped here? And what the hell had she been doing digging into tree roots? He bit back the questions and, lowering his voice, spoke as he would to calm a wounded comrade in battle. "Look, you're in no shape to be playing this silly game. From the looks of things, you're hurt."

Sarah struggled to ignore the soothing tone of his voice. She blinked her eyes several times and tried to shake off the faintness now rimming her vision. "I've got the gun. You're the one in trouble, mister. Now get your ID out and toss it over here. And don't try to pull any funny stuff."

Wolf almost wanted to laugh as he reached into his back pocket. She was so small to have such a large backbone. Carefully he tossed his ID case toward her.

"How long you been trapped?"

"I'll ask the questions!" Her hand shaking badly, Sarah fumbled for the case, then laid it in the mud to flip it open. Her gaze flicked between the ID and the man: Wolf Harding, U.S. Forest Ranger, Philipsburg. *Wolf*. The name fit him well. His features were sharp and accentuated, and there was an alertness to his eyes that she'd never seen in another man. But Philipsburg? Sarah tried for a tone of self-confident disgust. "You're a liar, mister. I've lived in Philipsburg all my life, and I haven't heard of you." Her hands tightened around the rifle.

"This is my first day on the job," he offered easily.

"Where are you staying?"

"I just rented a house over on Broadway."

Sarah wavered. His hair was black as a raven's ebony wing, and cut military-short. And his eyes . . . She took in a chattering breath. "How do I know I can trust you?"

Wolf shrugged. "Because you don't have a choice. But why should you distrust me?"

The rifle was getting heavy, and her arms were beginning to feel like ten-ton weights. Sarah knew she was getting dizzy from lack of food or water over the past six hours. "Do you know Gerald Summers?"

"No. Should I?"

Sarah probed his gaze, trying to ferret out whether he was telling her the truth. His mouth was now fully relaxed, she noted, the lower lip full and flat. "Summers is a murdering bastard. He hires people to kill for him," she said, her voice quavering. She was so chilled that she was having muscle spasms, and she nearly dropped the rifle. The ranger didn't move. His dog had lain down at his side.

Wolf shrugged. "Look, you're in trouble. You're trapped. I don't know this guy Summers."

"How long you been in Philipsburg?"

"A week."

"Where'd you come from?"

"South America," Wolf ground out, suddenly losing patience. It was a place he wanted to forget. Forever. Just saying the words brought back too many raw, unhealed memories.

Sarah blinked. Harding wasn't a Hispanic, but his skin was brown enough that he could have passed for one. If he weren't so hard-looking, some part of her paranoid brain might have believed him. Instead, to her surprise, it was her heart that shouted strongly for her to trust him.

Licking her lower lip, she whispered, "I—I was mining this morning for sapphires when the tree fell over on me."

"Sapphires?" Wolf shrugged. "Look, you can tell me how it happened later. Let me get you out of there first."

The rifle wavered badly in Sarah's hands. She took in a ragged sigh. "You could kill me. I'm so tired, and my legs are numb. I can't get myself free," she muttered, more to herself than to him. Yet he hadn't moved a muscle. His gaze suddenly warmed with a penetrating care—directed at her?

"I'm not going to hurt you," Wolf told her soothingly. What was she talking about? Who would want to kill her? "Put the rifle down," he urged, "and I'll come over and help you."

"I'll put it down, but not out of my reach, Harding." So much of her wanted to give in, to rest.... Sarah ached to believe what she thought she saw in the man's eyes. Was he really a ranger, or was this just another one of Summers's men playing a trick on her? She had no choice. She had to let him help her. Reluctantly she put the rifle down in the mud beside her.

It was so natural, Wolf thought as he quickly shrugged out of his gabardine jacket and came forward to where she lay shivering in the mud. Now he was a paramedic again. It was something that came easily to him, the one positive thing left out of the living hell he'd endured in the jungle. Bending down, he brought the jacket around her small, tense shoulders and felt her wince.

"Easy, honey, I'm not going to hurt you. It's all right. Everything's going to be fine," he murmured as he pulled the fabric snugly around her. His long, calloused fingers barely grazed her collarbone as he secured the jacket.

The woman jerked back, her eyes wide, her hand darting out for the rifle.

Instantly Wolf's hand clamped over hers. "Take it easy!" he rasped. Her blue eyes were filled with terror. He'd seen both those reactions too often in South America. Gently he loosened his fingers over her muddy ones. "I'm your friend, not your enemy. You've got to believe me if we're going to get you out of here and to a hospital."

Forcing back tears at the suddenly soft expression on his unforgiving features, she pulled her hand from beneath his. "I—I thought you were going to hit me," she muttered.

What the hell had happened to her? Wolf sat crouched for a long minute, digesting her trembling admission and watching her terror parallel her defiance of him. Trying to ease the tension between them, he rasped, "I would never hurt you," and watched with relief as some of the fear on her face subsided. "What's your name?" He eased himself up out of his crouching position. He'd have to treat her like a wild animal, moving very slowly so as not to frighten her again.

"Sarah Thatcher." She watched uneasily as he moved around her to inspect the tree and the roots that trapped her legs.

"Sarah's a pretty name. Soft, but with some backbone to it." Wolf purposely kept up the verbal patter, trying to gain her trust. "Old-fashioned sounding." He got down on his hands and knees to assess the damage to her legs. "Are you?"

She watched him guardedly. "*Old-fashioned* means *double standard,* and I don't buy that crock," Sarah said bitterly. "My mother may have, but I don't." Just his gentle touch on her jean-clad leg made her relax some of her wariness. It was a kind, professional touch, and the sound of his voice was dark and intimate. The man could charm a snake into trusting him, Sarah thought groggily as she pulled the jacket tighter around her.

Wolf turned to face her, his hand remaining on her leg. "Any lady named Sarah is bound to have an old-fashioned side," he teased. Some of the distrust had fled from her taut features. Wolf began to wonder what she would look like if she smiled. Her lips were exquisitely shaped; it was the kind of mouth a man could capture and lose himself in forever. Giving himself an inner shake, he forced himself to take on a more professional demeanor.

"Tell me about your legs. Any pain?"

"No, they're numb."

"Any broken bones?"

"I can still move my toes, so I don't think anything's broken."

Wolf nodded and gazed at the muddied boots caught beneath the roots. "Probably a lot of tissue damage. You're numb because your legs are swelling from being so bruised."

Tilting her head, her teeth chattering, Sarah stared at him. "What are you? A doctor?"

Wolf grinned self-consciously. "I was a paramedic for many years."

"Thank God," Sarah whispered.

"You believe me, then?"

She eyed him. "You're a stranger," she insisted stubbornly. "For all I know, Summers has paid you to pretend to be a ranger and a paramedic."

With a shake of his head, Wolf rose to his full six feet five inches. Skeet had crept closer, and was now lying right next to Sarah. Wolf felt an unexpected—and unwanted—surge of warmth and tenderness toward Sarah. She was vulnerable, just as— Instantly Wolf slammed the door closed on the memories surging forward. In a way, he felt jealous of his dog's ability to show his feelings openly. As he stood there staring down at Sarah, he fought to suppress the tendrils of longing laced with hope seeping forth from his shattered past. What was it about this Sarah that aroused those dangerous emotions? She was mud from head to toe, and her once-blond hair was caked with fine gray dirt.

"I guess the only way I'm going to prove myself is to get you out of this predicament," he said, struggling to keep his tone light and teasing. Moving to the tree, he retrieved a huge broken limb and shoved it at an angle beneath the trunk. Looking over his shoulder, he told her, "When I push up, I want you to pull yourself out from under there. Understand?"

Sarah gulped. "That tree's huge."

"I know it is. We don't have a choice. Get ready to move."

Turning on her side, Sarah stretched her arms outward. "Do it. Now."

Wolf's olive-green shirt stretched across his powerful back and his broad shoulders as he strained against the makeshift lever. Sarah blinked as the muscles bunched beneath the lightweight fabric. The man was like the Rocky Mountains she loved so much—hard, craggy, and powerful.

The tree began to move. Wolf grunted, digging his boots into the mud and pushing harder. Every muscle in his body screamed for relief as he forced the trunk slowly upward, inches at a time.

"Can you get out?" he rasped.

"Not yet! It's moving, though." Sarah saw the muscles in his face tighten, saw sweat pop out on his brow, giving a sheen to his darkly tanned skin. Suddenly the roots gave way, releasing her. *Now!* To Sarah's dismay she couldn't move her legs. Desperately, she lunged forward, gripping the muddy bank and hauling herself out from beneath the twisted tree, dragging her numb body.

"I'm out!" she gasped.

Wolf didn't dare risk a look over his shoulder. "Sure?" he gasped. If she wasn't completely clear when he let the trunk go, she could be pinned again. And the sudden weight could break her legs.

Struggling to get farther from the trunk, Sarah cried, "Let it go! I'm free!"

Chapter Two

Wolf leaped away as he released his powerful hold on the lever. The fir crashed into the earth, splattering mud in all directions. In one smooth motion, he turned on his heel. Sarah lay on her belly in the mud, her brow resting against her crossed arms. Skeet was nearby, wagging his tail and looking at her anxiously. Wolf felt that way, too, as he made his way to her side.

Leaning down, he closed his fingers over her small shoulders. How tiny she was in comparison to him. Delicate, like a small bird.

"Don't move," he told her gruffly. "I'm going to check you for broken bones."

Sarah lay in a haze of pain. The circulation had returned to her legs with a vengeance. Part of her wanted to remain on guard toward Wolf Harding, but the gentle way he explored her legs for injuries shattered her resolve. Despite his size—one of his hands must have equaled two of her own!—he was amazingly careful. If he *was* one of Summers's men, he could have snapped her neck by now.

Closing her eyes, Sarah groaned as Wolf's hands closed around the hiking boot on her left leg. When he carefully moved her foot, Sarah bit back a cry.

"Hurt?"

"Yes..."

"Not broken, though. That's good." He checked her right foot. Both of the sturdy leather shoes were badly cut and scarred. "You're lucky you didn't break both your ankles," he said when his inspection was complete.

"Can I turn over?" Sarah chattered. Even his warm coat was becoming damp in the mud.

"Let me help you," Wolf said, coming to her side. "My guess is that you have torn muscles or damaged ligaments. Either way, too much movement on your own will worsen your injuries."

Sarah jerked up her head as Wolf slid one hand beneath her left shoulder. "Easy," he crooned, and with one smooth motion he brought her onto her back and into his arms. Then he helped her sit up.

Though she felt his intent gaze on her, Sarah evaded his glittering gray eyes. They were like shards of clear, transparent sapphire, hard and probing. He'd lifted her into his arms as if she were a baby, cradled her for just a moment and then settled her on the drier ground. A deluge of emotions broke loose within Sarah, and she bowed her head, allowing her straggly curtain of dirty-blond hair to hide her expression from Wolf.

"Listen," he told her after a moment, resting a hand lightly on her shoulder. "I need to get you to the hospital in Philipsburg. If I take off those hiking boots, your feet will swell like balloons. You need to have your feet packed in ice—"

"No!" Sarah lifted her chin. "I'm not going to the hospital!"

Wolf studied her intently. The jut of her lower lip confirmed something he'd sensed all along about Sarah Thatcher: She was stubborn as hell. "You'd better have one good reason why—"

"I don't have to have a reason, mister. It's what I *want,*" Sarah retorted. "Just take me to my cabin. It's five miles down this road. I'll take care of myself once I get home."

He eyed her. The silence was brittle between them. "Look, you've got serious injuries, Sarah," he said, trying to keep the exasperation out of his tone. "You need professional attention. The doc will probably put you on crutches for several weeks to let you heal up."

Frustration mingled with an inexplicable desire to simply throw herself into Wolf's arms and be held. Sarah was stunned by her reaction. Wolf Harding was an utter stranger to her. Combating her heart's idiotic yearnings, she gritted out, "Please, just take me home. I'll do everything else."

Grimly Wolf watched as her face paled even more. Shock was probably the cause of her poor decision. "I'm taking you to the hospital," he said firmly.

"No!" The cry was animal-like.

Wolf's head snapped up, and his eyes narrowed.

"You don't understand!" Sarah cried, tears spilling down her cheeks. "Summers! If he knew I was hurt, if he knew I was in the hospital, he'd jump my claim. I can't stay away from it. If he knows I'm hurt, he'll steal it from me. I can't risk it! I *can't!*" Sarah threw herself over onto

her hands and knees. Making a supreme effort, she awkwardly flung herself upright.

A cry ripped from her as excruciating pain shot up
through her legs. Her knees buckled, and blackness engulfed her as she felt herself falling, falling . . .

Wolf caught her as she crumpled into a heap. With a
curse, he scooped her up. Her small form was diminu-
tive against him. Her head lolled against his chest, and
her lips parted, telling him she was unconscious.

"Little fool," he whispered, starting down the slope
toward his pickup. Wolf debated with himself. Should he
take her to the hospital as good sense dictated, or take her
back to her cabin? Skeet leaped to Wolf's side as he ne-
gotiated the slippery slope covered with pine needles.

Wolf knew a lot about injuries. Torn muscles and ligaments were not unusual in traversing the mountains and
jungles. And judging from the black-and-purple bruises
showing on Sarah's thin ankles above her hiking boots,
her injuries were extensive.

Settling Sarah on the plastic-covered seat of the forest-service truck, Wolf ordered Skeet into the rear of the
vehicle. He always carried a wool blanket for emergen-
cies, and now he covered Sarah with it. Hurrying back up
the slope of the mountain, Wolf retrieved both rifles and
slid back down to the muddy, little-used road.

Hospital or cabin? Wolf's hands tightened on the
steering wheel as he turned the vehicle and headed back
out. The forest blocked out the stormy sky. The trees reminded him of soldiers standing stiffly at attention.
Thunder rolled ominously, and it began to rain again.
The already muddy road became worse. The truck didn't
have four-wheel drive—and that was exactly what he'd
need to make it the eight miles to the main highway.

"Dammit," he whispered, glancing down at Sarah. Her hair, the color of sunlight, despite the mud, lay limply around her face, her thick braid curving across her shoulders. Once again he was stuck making do with little help. It seemed that every time one of his friends got wounded, there wasn't a prayer of a helicopter rescue or a nearby hospital. And this was no exception. The road was turning ugly, and Wolf knew he couldn't make it many more miles without getting stuck. It looked like Sarah would get her wish. At this point they'd be lucky to make it to her cabin—a hell of a welcome for his first day on the job. He reached for the radio that would link him with headquarters in Philipsburg. Maybe he could get someone out to rescue them. To his dismay, the radio didn't work. Apparently the unit had shorted out.

Wolf slammed his palm against the steering wheel in disgust, then gingerly began turning the truck to head for Sarah's cabin.

Sarah resisted pulling awake until a combination of pain and the crash of thunder forced her to open her eyes. The bare hardwood beams on the ceiling of her cabin met her gaze. Slowly, heeding her stiff, sore body's complaints, she moved one arm from beneath the blanket covering her. Frowning, she realized she was dressed in one of her long cotton nightgowns.

"The thunder wake you?" Wolf asked, rising from the hand-hewn oak rocker nearby. He watched Sarah's drowsy state turn to terror and then subside into a guardedness when she recognized him. Why was she so fearful? What was going on?

"You!"

Wolf nodded and halted by her bed, which occupied a corner of the cabin. He placed his hands on his hips. "Why not me?"

Sarah refused to meet Wolf's cool, steady eyes. "How did I get here?" she demanded, her voice scratchy. Then she realized that not only was she in her nightgown, but she'd been cleaned up, as well. Her hair was wrapped in a towel that smelled like mud. Her alarm growing, she met Wolf's unreadable gray gaze. "And who cleaned me up? And how did I get into my nightgown?"

"Guilty on all counts." Wolf crouched next to her and carefully removed the blanket covering her feet. "You were out like a light, so I did the best I could to clean you up. Your hair still needs to be washed." He noticed that the swelling had gotten worse since he'd removed her boots two hours earlier.

"I don't care about my feet!" Sarah struggled to sit up in bed, her every movement excruciating. "You *undressed* me!"

"I didn't have a choice," Wolf said in a quiet tone, holding her blazing blue gaze. "You were going hypothermic on me. I had to get you out of those clothes and into something warm. But first I had to clean you up."

"You had no right!"

"I had every right, dammit. Why don't you say thank you for saving your neck instead of chewing me out? In case you don't know it, that line of thunderstorms across the mountains is still hanging around. You could've frozen to death out there tonight."

Chastened, Sarah picked nervously at the quilt covering her. Her mother had made it for her long ago. "You didn't have to undress me completely." Even her lingerie had been removed.

Exhaling tiredly, Wolf got to his feet after covering her legs back up. "Women all look the same. Hell, I've helped deliver babies, so don't pretend I've done something wrong."

Sarah watched him stalk out of the room. Looking to her right out the nearest window, she realized it was dusk. Another thunderstorm was lashing the cabin, and above the firs she could see lightning dancing across the gray, turbulent sky. Pulling her covers aside, Sarah examined her feet, which were tightly bandaged. Her mouth dropped open. He'd torn up one of her bed sheets to wrap them! She only had two sets to her name.

The aggravating pain increased as Sarah lifted her legs and swung them across the bed. Her feet barely touching the shining hardwood floor, she groaned.

"What do you think you're doing?" Wolf demanded, appearing at the doorway.

Sarah glared at him. He was carrying a bowl of soup and a cup in his hands. "Getting up. What's it look like?"

"Get back into bed. You try and stand up again and you'll faint again. Is that what you want?" Wolf walked toward Sarah, glowering. He didn't want to growl at her. Why couldn't she be civil?

"No," Sarah muttered belligerently, her fingers digging into the sides of the mattress. "I don't want to faint again. Not ever."

"Well," he drawled, setting the bowl and the cup on her pine dresser, "then I suggest you stay put. You've probably got a few torn muscles in both legs. If you're smart, you'll stick to bed rest and take the help offered."

Giving him a rebellious stare, Sarah whispered, "Help? You're a stranger. You did me a good turn. Thank you. Now why don't you leave?"

With a shake of his head, Wolf looked around the small room. The cabin had been built the old-fashioned way—with mortar and logs. The floor, of reddish-gold cedar, was a masterpiece—a credit to the builder. "You need help, that's why."

Sarah held his hooded look, but couldn't think of a response.

Wolf offered her the cup he'd brought. "It's comfrey tea. I found the herb out in one of your cupboards. My grandmother taught me about herbs when I was a kid, and I know this one's good for muscle and bone injuries. Why don't you drink it?"

Thirsty beyond belief, Sarah took the proffered cup. "Thanks..."

Wolf smiled tentatively, watching her drink the warm liquid down in several gulps. Sarah was becoming civil by degrees. His Cherokee heritage, the wellspring of his patience, would just have to endure her outrageous behavior until he could find out why she behaved so rudely. When she'd finished the tea, she held the cup out to him.

"Want more?"

"No."

But he could see that she did and was too proud to admit it. "I'll get you some."

"I'll get it myself," Sarah said.

"You want to fall flat on your face?"

Glaring up at him, at the rugged features shadowed in the light, Sarah grimaced. Gingerly she tested her left foot, putting a bit of weight on it. The pain was immediate.

"You always learn the hard way?" Wolf demanded, taking the cup out of her hand.

Sarah ignored him and hung her head. When he came back a few minutes later, she took the cup. "Thank you."

"You're welcome." Wolf made himself at home in the rocker at the end of the bed. Facing Sarah, he noticed the way the light accentuated her soft oval face. With her hair wrapped up in the towel, she looked elegant. Her cheekbones were well shaped, and there was width between her huge blue eyes. Without trying, Wolf's gaze fell to her glistening lips as she unconsciously licked them free of the last of the comfrey tea.

"This cabin belong to you?" he asked.

"Yes. Actually, my father built it. Well, we all did."

"It's a nice place. Had a hell of a time finding it in the middle of a thunderstorm, though."

The soothing quality of his baritone voice lulled Sarah, making her feel cared for—protected. Quickly she snapped herself out of that mode. She didn't know this man. Still, he was being kind. "Dad was always a loner. He wanted a cabin in the woods away from everyone and everything," she explained.

"Was he antisocial?"

Sarah shrugged. The tea was making her feel drowsy, although hot pain throbbed in her legs. "I don't think so," she mumbled.

Wolf smiled. Sarah had a lot of her father in her, he suspected. "What's a young woman like you doing up here in the middle of nowhere? I'd expect to see someone like you living in a city."

"Don't judge a person by their looks, Harding."

"Call me Wolf."

"No."

It was his turn to shrug. "How are your legs feeling?" Wolf asked, realizing how reluctant Sarah was to talk about herself.

"They hurt like hell."

"Come tomorrow morning, the road ought to be good enough that I can get us out of here. They'll take better care of you at the hospital."

"I told you, I'm not going to any hospital. My feet feel fine! They just hurt a little."

"Probably feel like they're on fire."

"How could you know?" Sarah probed his darkened face in the dim dusk light that filtered through the window.

"I've had a few pulled and torn muscles myself."

Silence stretched between them, and Sarah chewed on her lip. It was a nervous habit she'd never been able to get rid of. "What did you mean, 'tomorrow morning'?"

"After you fainted, the storm broke. I was able to drive within a quarter of a mile of your cabin. My truck's down by the creek. When I tried to radio for help, the radio was broken. Then, when we made it here, I found that you had a phone—but it's not working, either." Wolf grinned. "By now my new boss probably thinks I've either left the country or am dead."

His smile sent a sheet of warmth through Sarah. Her gaze was riveted on his mobile mouth, which was curved with faint irony. How incredibly his entire face changed when he smiled. He must not do it often, she thought, noting how few laugh lines surrounded his mouth and eyes. Realizing her privilege in seeing him smile made Sarah feel better for no obvious reason.

"You need a four-wheel drive for this road," she agreed. "Still, I'm not going to the hospital tomorrow morning with you."

"How do you think you're going to get around, then?"

The softly asked question was underlined with amazement. "I'll hobble." She shot him a disparaging look. "You act as if a woman can't take care of herself. I've lived up here all my life, and I've weathered some pretty bad things alone." She motioned toward her blanketed feet. "I'll get by, don't worry."

Wolf sat back in the chair, digesting the hurt in her lowered voice. He saw real sadness and pain in her eyes. Perhaps Sarah was trusting him enough to show her true feelings. He was surprised at the feeling of elation that soared through him at the thought.

"Yeah, I know what you mean about being alone and having to handle things," Wolf agreed. With a sigh, he sat up and folded his hands between his legs. "You're going to need crutches, Sarah."

"So pick me up some if you want to help so badly. I'll pay you for them. Anyone in town will accept my checks."

She was right: He did want to help her, Wolf thought. "I can do that, but..."

Sarah saw a scowl work its way across his brow. "Never mind. Folks back in these mountains don't ask for help. We just get alóng without. I didn't mean to—"

"Whoa." Wolf held up both his hands. "You really jump to conclusions, don't you?"

Sarah frowned.

"Forget I said that. I'll bring you the crutches. I was hesitating because you need medical care, Sarah. I don't think you understand the extent of your injuries. You're going to be laid up for weeks."

"Weeks!" Sarah's voice cracked. "That's impossible! It can't happen! I've got bills that need to be paid. My jewelry distributors are waiting for the sapphires I mine...."

The urge to go over and simply fold his arms around Sarah was almost tangible. Wolf sat there digesting that feeling. She was bringing out a weakness in him that he didn't dare indulge. He looked over and saw tears of frustration glittering in her eyes. He grimaced, forcing back his own rising swell of emotion.

"Just what the hell are you doing, living up here by yourself? What mine are you talking about?" he growled.

Sarah gulped back her tears, dismayed by the sudden change in him. Wolf's face had gone hard again, his eyes hooded.

"Blue Mountain is made up of what's known as sapphire gravel," she explained. "The gravel sits about a foot below the soil. The sapphires in their raw state are brownish-white pebbles anywhere from the size of a pinhead to much larger. I dig the gravel out from beneath the fir roots with my prospector's hammer, then put it through three screen boxes to separate the gem from the dirt." She sighed. "I've got some rough sapphires in a tin can on the drainboard out in the kitchen if you want to look at them. It's mostly small stuff—quarter carat to half carat, maybe. Not very big."

"Sapphires?" Wolf shook his head. "I had it in my mind that you had to dig tunnels in the ground and go after that gem with a pick and a sledgehammer."

"Most places around the world you do. But here on Blue Mountain, it's easy to dig them by hand." Sarah shook her head, "Summers's land parallels ours. He owns three-quarters of Blue Mountain. I own the last quarter. His bulldozers and backhoes take tons of the dirt and gravel every day. He makes millions."

Wolf saw the anger and disgust in Sarah's eyes. "Are you making millions?" he asked, looking around the spare, clean cabin.

"No. But then, my quarter of the mountain has fewer sapphires per square foot than anywhere else on the mountain. And one person can only dig and facet so much material. Summers has fifteen men in his employ and ten faceters."

Sarah shook her head, and Wolf watched the emotions play across her features. "What's Summers done to you to make you this gun-shy?" he asked quietly.

Tears stung Sarah's eyes, and she looked toward the darkened wall. "Six months ago, he murdered my father."

Wolf sat very still. "Murdered?"

"Yes. The sheriff says it was an accident, but I know better." Blinking, Sarah turned her head and met Wolf's gaze. "My father bought this mine thirty years ago. He was an explosives expert in construction before that, for a silver mine up near Anaconda. Six months ago my dad was driving a small load of dynamite and caps to our mine when his truck blew up." Her voice grew scratchy. "There wasn't a thing left of him, and not much of the truck. Dad never carried 'hot' explosives. He never wired detonator caps to the dynamite until he was ready to use them at the mine site. The sheriff said he'd wired them before he drove the truck. He said a bump on the road must have caused the dynamite to go off."

Wolf saw Sarah's small hands clench into fists in her lap. "Is Summers the local land baron?"

Clearing her throat, Sarah nodded. "Yes. He's a greedy bastard who wants it all. He owns a silver smelter in Anaconda, and all of Blue Mountain's sapphires except for our small claim. He's already rich beyond anyone's dreams. Why does he have to have our little piece of land?''

The tragedy was clearly mirrored in Sarah's pale features. Wolf got up, resting his hands on his hips. ''You're looking tired, Sarah. Why don't you get some sleep? I'll get a blanket and use the couch in the other room, if you don't mind.''

Wolf paused in the darkness near the doorway, and Sarah thought he looked forbidding. His face was set and impassive again, his mouth a thin line holding back whatever feelings he might be experiencing. Skeet remained on a braided rug next to her bed.

''Good night, Sarah. If you need anything, call. I won't come in otherwise.''

Silence filtered into the growing darkness. Sarah stayed sitting up in bed for a long time afterward. When she was sure Wolf was bedded down on the creaky old couch in the next room, she finally lay down. She fell asleep immediately, her exhausted body finally overriding her overactive brain.

Chapter Three

Sarah struggled awake. Someone was knocking at her bedroom door. Who—? Suddenly her eyes flew open as the memories flooded back: the tree, the storm, the man who'd rescued her. *Wolf.* Light streamed through the window, and she glanced at the clock. Six a.m.

"Come in...." she called, her voice still hoarse with sleep.

Wolf opened the bedroom door, and Sarah's heart slammed against her ribs—but not out of fear. Wolf stood in the doorway, bathed in sunlight, his green cotton shirt open to show a white T-shirt underneath. His feet were bare beneath his muddy green gabardine trousers.

There was something endearing, even vulnerable, about him this morning, Sarah thought. Perhaps it was his tousled black hair, with short strands falling across his now-smooth brow, or his open, peaceful expression. As her gaze traveled to his mouth, she read an earthiness in his flat lower lip that sent an unexpected wave of heat flowing through her—an unbidden sensual awareness that caught her off guard.

Swallowing against a dry throat as Wolf slipped silently through the door, she met his drowsy gray eyes. Although her legs throbbed with pain, Sarah responded to the warmth smoldering in his gaze and momentarily forgot her discomfort. Taken aback by her heart's response to Wolf, Sarah reminded herself that she didn't have a whole lot of experience with men. Working her father's mine claim and caring for her mother had long overshadowed more personal needs. Was she wrong to think she read an answering longing in his eyes?

Wolf ran his fingers through his hair, pushing the strands aside. Sarah looked like the kind of ethereal spirit that his mind used to conjure up in the jungle after a cool night: Fog would rise in steamy, twisting columns, sometimes taking on human or animal shapes in his imagination.

"Morning..." he mumbled.

How could she have not trusted Wolf? No longer was his face hard and unreadable. Sarah felt his presence powerfully, and her lips parted as he made his way to her bedside.

Wolf longed to reach out and graze Sarah's upturned face. This morning she looked fragile and beautiful, even though her hair was in dried, uncombed strands about her face. The wariness he'd been learning to expect in her huge blue eyes was missing, and inwardly he breathed a sigh of relief. He halted near the bed.

"How do you feel?"

Sarah averted her eyes from his burning, intense ones. The man should have been named Hawk, not Wolf, she thought uncomfortably. Retreating within herself, she attemped to block out the oddly heated emotions buffeting her heart. "Okay, I guess," she offered, struggling to keep her tone impersonal.

Wolf froze internally as he saw Sarah suddenly close down and become distant. A good reminder, he thought, disgusted with himself—he had no need for confusing emotions. "Let me take a look at your ankles and feet," he said, his voice brusque as he leaned over to pull back the sheet and blanket. Sarah tucked her arms against her nightgowned chest at his action, and Wolf winced. She still didn't trust him—but why did it matter? Unwillingly Wolf admitted to himself that he knew why. A bitter taste coated the inside of his mouth as he struggled with the memories. Leaving South America should have been enough. Now this waif of a woman was reminding him of what he desperately needed to forget.

Wolf's eyes narrowed as he removed the loose bandages around her right ankle. His gaze held her hostage. "You're okay?" he ground out, disbelief in his voice.

Sarah shrugged. "I've been hurt before, Harding. Pain's something everyone experiences, don't you think?"

"I won't argue that with you," he whispered. As the bandages came off her slender feet were revealed, looking like bloated black-and-blue sausages. "Look, Sarah, you've got to go to the hospital," Wolf said, his tone nononsense. "Your feet are worse. You won't be able to walk on them this morning."

Stiffening, Sarah reached down and jerked the blankets back over her feet. "I *can't* leave!" she cried. "I told you why. If Summers finds out I'm in the hospital, he'll send his men in to start stealing my sapphires." Her voice cracked. "I can mine just enough sapphires monthly to pay my mother's nursing-home bill and the mortgage on this mine. Don't you understand? I'll lose everything if I go to the hospital! I don't have any money saved. I live month to month. My mother's depending on me. What if I can't pay her nursing-home bill? They'll throw her out. And then what will I do?''

Wolf straightened, her pain cutting through him. The despair, the fear, in Sarah's voice and eyes shook him as nothing had in years. He actually *felt* her desperation and anguish. It was disturbing to realize he was feeling deeply again since meeting Sarah.

He held out his hands. ''All right, slow down. What's this about your mother?''

Fighting back welling tears—something she hadn't done since her father's death—Sarah rasped out, ''When my dad was murdered, my mother suffered a stroke the same day. She's only fifty, but the shock of having my dad die so suddenly was too much for her to cope with. She was very dependent on him. The stroke affected her memory, so if she isn't watched closely, she'll wander off. She was in the hospital for a month, and it ate up our savings. We couldn't afford health insurance, so it took everything we'd saved.''

''When I got Mother out of the hospital, I tried to keep her at the cabin. That first night when I returned from the mine, she was gone. I found her wandering around in the woods, frightened and confused.'' Sarah took a huge, ragged breath. She would never make the same mistake her mother had—becoming dependent on someone she loved. The price of leaning on another person was just too high. ''I tried to keep her with me out at the mine, but half the time I was watching her and not working. Sapphire production fell off. I knew if I didn't do something, I wouldn't be able to make the money I needed to pay the mine mortgage.'' Her eyes hardened. "Summers is just waiting. If I default on one payment, he's going to have the bank foreclose on my mine so he can buy it.''

She rubbed her wrinkled brow. ''I didn't know what to do. Eventually I figured out that if I worked seven days a week, dawn to dusk, I could make the money it took to keep Mother in a nursing home and pay the mortgage.'' Sarah looked away, biting on her lower lip. ''I know it's not the whole answer, but it's the best I could come up with. At least she gets three square meals a day, and is taken care of...''

Wolf stared at Sarah's profile, aware of the suffering she was valiantly trying to handle by herself. How brave she was in the face of such overwhelming odds. He allowed his hands to drop to his sides. "How long has this been going on?''

''Six months.''

''And you're making ends meet?''

Sarah nodded. ''I'm a little ahead. I've got a bit of money in the bank, but I have to get more to help us make it through the winter. I can't mine during winter and early spring. The ground freezes and then turns muddy. The dirt has to be dry for me to sift the gravel.''

Wolf looked around the quiet cabin. He'd felt at home in its comfortable simplicity as soon as he'd entered it yesterday. Blue-and-white calico curtains at the windows enhanced its hominess. The handmade furniture was of the same cedar as the floors. A few framed pictures of wildflowers hung on the walls. His gaze returned to Sarah, who was watching him with open curiosity. The wariness came back into her eyes, but not as much as before.

''Why are you entrusting me with all this information?'' he asked. His tone was gentle.

Sarah shrugged. "I don't know." She sighed. "Maybe you don't look as threatening to me this morning as you did last night." She gestured to his bare feet.

For the first time, Wolf genuinely smiled. The people of South America had always regarded him as a giant and stood in awe of him. He was sure he looked far more human this morning, barefoot and out of uniform.

"Big feet," he noted ruefully.

"They sure are. What size do you wear?"

His smile widened, and an ache seized him. Sarah's mouth was pulled tentatively into a smile. It was the first time he'd seen her lips in something softer than a tight line or frown. "Thirteen," he admitted. "I have to have my shoes specially made."

"I'll bet."

"They keep me upright, though."

Sarah leaned back against the brass headboard and studied Wolf. The smile had eased the harshness from his darkly tanned features, and she felt her heart opening to him. She didn't know this man, she tried to remind herself. A huge part of Sarah, the inexperienced woman, longed to know Wolf better, to find out why that haunted look remained deep in his eyes. But she'd already learned the hard way the folly of putting her trust in anyone but herself, and she tamped down her unruly heart's yearnings.

"Now you see why I can't go to the hospital," she said quietly.

"As bad as your feet are, Sarah, you can't afford not to be in the hospital for a couple of days."

"I can't afford it."

"I can."

She snapped a look up at him.

"I've got money, so don't worry about it."

Her mouth flattened. "I don't take money from anyone. Especially strangers."

Wolf reined in his impatience. "It'll be a loan, until you can get on your feet again, so to speak."

Sarah ignored his pun. "The bottom line is, if I leave the mine unattended, Summers will send his men to steal everything I own."

"No, he won't," Wolf said smoothly, "because I'll check up on it. Most of my duties involve patrolling the forest area, the creeks, and checking for licenses. It will be easy to run by your cabin a couple times a day."

Her eyes grew huge. "What?"

"You heard me. I'll be your guard dog while you're recuperating." Wolf felt a tightening in his chest at his own confident words. Him, a guard dog. *Sure.* He'd failed miserably at that once before. So why was he reaching out to protect Sarah? Caught in his own damning trap, Wolf wrestled with his conflicting emotions.

The offer sounded too good to be true. Sarah hedged. "I don't want your money."

"Fine. Use your own, then."

"If Summers finds out I'm hospitalized, he will send his men up here, Harding."

"I'll deal with it," Wolf said with a shrug. Moving over to her dresser, he rummaged through the drawers until he found a tank top, lingerie and a pair of jeans for her. He brought them over to the bed. "Get dressed, and I'll take you in."

Sarah held on to the clean clothes in her lap. "I made a promise never to trust anyone again," she flung back heatedly.

Wolf turned at the door and studied her grimly. He was sure Sarah sensed that he was incapable of protecting her, but somehow he had to try. "You don't have a choice."

There was a sadness in his voice that he wished he could have disguised. "You're caught between a rock and a hard place."

With a shake of her head, Sarah muttered, "I don't want your help!"

"Too bad. You're getting it."

Sarah sat there, tense and frustrated. She wasn't willing to listen to her instincts, which were whispering that Wolf was trustworthy. Not after all that had happened in the past six months of her life. How many times had she dreamed of someone coming to help her defend what was rightfully hers, rightfully her family's? But no one had come.

Angrily she said, "Knights on white horses don't exist. They never did! Didn't you know that?"

A gutting pain shattered through Wolf. "Yeah," he whispered rawly. "No one knows that better than me." He turned and left the room as quietly as he'd come.

The silence wrapped around Sarah as she sat digesting the awful sound of his words, the horror that had been banked in his eyes. Then she slowly began to dress, her mind ranging from her own predicament to Wolf's admission. The anguish in his gray eyes had touched her even more than her own dire situation. Who was he? What was he doing here? And what terrible secrets weighted down those magnificent shoulders of his? And, more importantly, why did she care?

By the time they reached Philipsburg Hospital, it was 9:00 a.m. Sarah sat on the passenger side of the truck, with Skeet as a barrier between her and Wolf. She had to give Wolf credit: He knew how to drive the truck through the muddy mire of the road. Was there anything he didn't do well? Didn't know about? She stole a look at him. His

profile could have been chiseled from the rugged Rockies
of Glacier National Park. But somehow the unforgiving
set of his mouth made her heart ache for him. Sarah kept
replaying his last words, about not being a knight in
shining armor. What had happened in his past to make
him believe that? *Because, like it or not, Sarah, right
now, he rescued you,* her conscience taunted.

With a ragged sigh, Sarah closed her eyes. For the first
time in a long time, she had put herself in someone else's
hands. It was a disturbing thought—a paralyzing one.
But what else could she do?

As they neared the hospital, the truck radio unexpectedly crackled to life, so Wolf called his boss to explain the
situation, saying he'd report in shortly. Arriving at the
emergency entrance, Wolf carried Sarah into the hospital. But as he prepared to leave, he saw fear in her eyes
that she obviously was trying to hide.

"I'll try to drop in and see you late this afternoon, before I go up to your cabin," he said, trying to sound more
cheerful than he felt. Sarah sat on a gurney in a cubicle,
her long legs dangling over the side. Her bare feet bruised
and swollen. Her hair desperately needed to be washed
and brushed, the mud from yesterday's accident still
clinging to the golden strands. Her head was bowed, and
Wolf started to reach out, to graze her pale cheek to reassure her, but he couldn't even do that. Nothing was for
sure in life. Absolutely nothing. His hand stopped in
midair.

"Thanks," Sarah whispered, unable to look up. Just
having Wolf standing beside her, she felt so much safer,
as if everything really might work out—and the knowledge that he was leaving brought her ridiculously near
tears.

The urge to hold her, to whisper that things would be okay, needled Wolf. But he, of all people, had no right to guarantee that. *To hell with it.* He gripped her hand momentarily, squeezing it gently. "You worry too much, Sarah. I'll be back later," he said with all the confidence he could muster, and he released her hand. But not before her head snapped up and those glorious blue eyes of hers flared with disbelief and some other tangible but indecipherable emotion. As Wolf turned away, he tried to figure out what it was that he'd seen reflected in her lovely gaze, then shook himself, putting it firmly out of his mind. Once he'd thought he could understand a woman, but experience had taught him differently. He knew he didn't dare trust his sense of the situation with Sarah—as much as his heart bid him to do just that.

Wolf glanced at his watch. It was nearly four o'clock, the day still bright with sunshine after last night's storms. The hospital, a small two-story brick building, stood out against the side of the green mountains that surrounded the small valley town. He pulled the truck into the visitor's parking lot and left Skeet sitting obediently in the cab, his head out the window, his tongue lolling out of his mouth.

Unaccountably, Wolf's spirits lifted as he entered the hospital. All day, she'd been on his mind and lingering in his heart.

Room 205 had two beds in it, but only Sarah was there, the other bed unoccupied. Wolf halted, and his breath caught. Sarah was on crutches, looking out the west window, and sunlight bathed her form. Her once muddy hair was clean, reminding him of the golden corn silk that had tassled the green ears on his father's farm every August. It waved softly down around her shoulders like a cape. She wore a blue tank top that emphasized her small form. As Wolf's gaze moved downward, he saw to his satisfaction that Sarah's feet and ankles were snugly wrapped in elastic bandages, although they still were obviously swollen.

"Sarah?" His throat was dry, his pulse erratic, as he said her name. As she slowly turned her head, Wolf felt as if sunlight were bathing him for the first time in this last dark year of his life; a strange warmth flowed through him, easing some of the pain he carried within him twenty-four hours a day. Delicate bangs framed Sarah's gently arched eyebrows. Today she looked like a beautiful woman, not a waif. The change was heartstopping.

Sarah turned at the sound of her name—and froze beneath Wolf's unexpectedly hot, hungry gaze. Never before had she been silently caressed like this. Automatically her gaze dropped to Wolf's mouth. What would it be like to kiss him—to feel that dangerous high-voltage power that seemed to throb around him?

Shaking off the strange, heated languor that threatened to engulf her, Sarah frowned. "You!"

Taken aback by the sudden change in her, Wolf halted halfway across the room. "Me?"

"Yes, you!" Sarah watched as he took off his ranger's hat and held it in his long, callused fingers. She hobbled around, hating the crutches and especially hating the fact that she had to rely on them. "Do you know how much just one day in this place has cost me? Four hundred dollars!" She halted a foot from him and glared up into his face. "Four hundred dollars! I can't believe it! I've got to get out of here. I want you to take me home!"

Wolf gripped her gently by the arm. "Come on, sit down while we discuss this."

"There's no discussion, Wolf. I want you to take me home. You brought me here, and you can take me back. You owe me that much."

He nodded and released Sarah's arm as she crossed with some difficulty and sat on the edge of the bed. Grabbing a nearby chair, he turned it around, swung his leg over it and sat down.

"What did the doctor say about your feet?"

Wrinkling her nose, Sarah muttered, "Same thing you did. No broken bones, just a lot of smashed muscles and skin. I've got to stay on these lousy crutches a week."

Despite her belligerent tone of voice, the distraught quality in her eyes made Wolf wince. "I thought so. How do you feel now?"

"Four hundred dollars poorer."

Wolf grinned, silently applauding her spunk. "I told you—I'll help you out. A loan you can pay back with no interest."

Adamantly Sarah shook her head. "I don't accept help from strangers, Harding."

Wolf sighed. There was such turmoil and anguish in Sarah's face. And there was turmoil within him, too. He had no right to offer her help, but he couldn't seem to help himself. "You'll never be able to take care of yourself up there right now, Sarah," he warned.

Her name rolled off his lips like a whisper of wind, and it sent a warmth through her. "Yes, I can! Quit treating me like I'm some breakable piece of glass. I've survived out there all my life just fine without you!"

"But not with two injured feet."

"Stop it!" Sarah awkwardly rose to her feet again. "I'm checking myself out and leaving right now—with or without your help! If I have to walk back to my cabin, I will!''

"What's going on in here?"

Sarah jerked a look toward the door. Her doctor, Bruce Evans, stood in the doorway in his white coat, running a hand through his gray hair.

"I'm leaving, Dr. Evans."

Wolf stood up, replacing the chair against the wall. He looked at the doctor.

"I'm Ranger Harding, Doctor. I'm the one who found Sarah on Blue Mountain and brought her here. Can she make it on her own?"

Evans smiled ruefully. "About ten minutes on your feet, Sarah, and all that pain will return." He looked over at Wolf. "The answer's no. At least for a week. She needs enforced bed rest to allow those feet to heal."

"I'm sorry, Doctor, but that's not an option." Sarah made her way slowly to the door. "Now stand aside. I'm checking myself out. I can't afford the bill that comes with this rest you're talking about."

Evans's fatherly face gave Wolf a pleading look.

Grimly Wolf stalked over to where Sarah stood.

"Get her a wheelchair," he ordered Evans. "I'll take her home with me for a week."

Sarah's mouth dropped open. "What? Go home with you?" Shock made her voice come out squeaky, not at all in keeping with the confident image she was trying to project.

"That's right." Wolf's tone brooked no argument.

Sarah's eyes grew huge.

"It's me or the hospital, Sarah. Make up your mind."

Damn, but she was stubborn.

Evans smiled, placated. "Wonderful solution, Ranger Harding. I'll get the nurse to bring you a wheelchair, Sarah."

Once they were alone, Sarah whispered fiercely, "I'm not going home with you! You take me back to my cabin or else!"

In that moment, Wolf saw just how fragile Sarah really was. Instead of losing patience, he said softly, "Honey, you're in need of a little care right now." He hitched one shoulder upward, his voice turning apologetic. "I'm not the best of caretakers, but I'll do the best I can for you. I've got a small house with one bedroom. I can sleep on the couch in the living room. I'm not such a bad cook—and it's a place for you to rest and heal up." He held up his hands. "Do we understand each other? I'm a friend doing a favor for a friend. Nothing more or less."

Stunned, Sarah couldn't say anything for several moments. She just didn't have the money to stay and pay a huge hospital bill. And right now, her feet were aching as if they were being smashed all over again. The pain was nearly unbearable. But worse than that, when he'd called her "honey," a dam of feelings, both good and bad—emotions she'd held onto so long by herself—flowed through her unchecked.

Sarah realized she had no other friends. She didn't dare have friends. Still, she knew in her heart that she needed help. But her recent past caught up with her, and her voice shook with anger. "You promised to drive by my cabin a couple times a day. Why not take me there instead—you can still check in on me."

Wolf felt as much as heard Sarah's panic. She didn't want to lean on anyone for help. That much he understood, but when he caught and held her distraught gaze, he didn't really see anger, he saw vulnerability.

"The doctor said you had to stay off your feet for an entire week, Sarah. Checking on you twice a day isn't going to do it. I can see it in your eyes. You don't really believe what you're saying."

Fear struck deeply within Sarah. Wolf had seen through her anger and knew her true feelings! Grasping at straws, she snapped, "I'm not going to be your housekeeper, Harding!"

"I'll keep house for both of us."

"Then what do you want out of this?" she demanded. "Everybody always expects something."

Wolf smiled gently. "Where I come from, we were taught to offer our home, food and the roof over our heads to total strangers. This isn't out of the ordinary for me, Sarah, even if it is for you."

Warily Sarah demanded, "Where do you come from?"

"The Eastern Cherokee reservation in North Carolina. I was born and raised there. My father's a full-blooded Cherokee. He met my mother when she came to the reservation to teach. The native American way is to offer help when it's needed, Sarah." He held her mutinous blue gaze. "And you need help."

Sarah was losing the struggle to stay independent, and she knew it. No matter how much she wished her feet hadn't been injured, there was no contradicting the doctor's diagnosis. It would take at least a week for them to heal enough that she could walk again. Silently Sarah vowed never to let her guard down around Wolf Harding. She sensed that to do so could be devastating—in ways she couldn't even imagine. "Okay," she muttered defiantly.

Wolf felt Sarah's disappointment at giving in. And she had every right to be wary of him, as harsh experience had taught him in South America. Still, a strange light-heartedness flowed through him. "It's not a prison sentence, Sarah," he said, and his voice came out almost teasing.

Sarah struggled to rally, knowing Wolf didn't deserve her anger. "But my cabin...the mine..."

"I've already been up to your mine and cabin twice today. Everything's quiet. Don't worry."

"I'll need stuff from the cabin," Sarah said unhappily.

"I'll drive up there tonight and get clothes and anything else you want for your stay with me."

Sarah moved aside when the nurse brought in the wheelchair. She needed no nudging to sit down in it and take the pressure off her throbbing feet. Wolf was immediately at her side to take the crutches. Just his nearness sent an unexpected sheet of warmth through her, and for just a split second, she wavered. The absurd urge to simply open her arms and move into Wolf's arms was nearly overwhelming. Confused, Sarah sat awkwardly in the silence, unstrung by him. Her entire world was unraveling, and it was all she could do to continue to hold herself together. But, whether she liked admitting it or not, Wolf's quiet, steadying presence was shoring her up.

Skeet barked once in greeting when Sarah climbed into the truck with Wolf's help. The dog thumped his bushy tail.

Sarah rallied at Skeet's enthusiasm, offering a slight smile as she patted the dog's huge head. "I'll bet you thought you'd gotten rid of me, huh?"

Wolf climbed in the driver's side and shut the door. "He won't mind the company. In fact, he'll like it."

"Will *you?*" Sarah asked sourly as Wolf drove away from the hospital.

With a shrug, Wolf glanced over at her, feeling the tension building between them once again. "Does it matter what I think?"

Sarah set her lips and stared straight ahead. "Yes."

Wolf didn't want to lie to her, but he couldn't tell her the truth, either. It was just too painful to talk about. "It will take some getting used to," Wolf admitted, "but I'll handle it."

Inwardly Sarah sighed. Living with Wolf was going to be like living with a wild animal. He was so unpredictable. And so were her wildly fluctuating emotions whenever he was near her.

"We have some talking to do now that we're alone," Wolf said seriously after a few minutes of driving in silence.

Sarah looked at him. She was trying to hold herself apart from him—trying to pretend she didn't care what he would say. "About what?"

"I snooped around your mine this afternoon and took a closer look at that tree that fell on you yesterday."

"Yes?"

Wolf held her gaze. "The tap root and half the roots on the other side of the tree had been sawed through. Did you know that?"

His words sunk in, and Sarah gasped. "Someone deliberately sawed through those roots?"

Sarah folded her arms defensively against her breasts as Wolf nodded confirmation. "Summers," she bit out. "It was that bastard Summers! He sent some of his hired guns up there to do it." She closed her eyes, suddenly feeling very alone and afraid.

Wolf forced himself to pay attention to his driving. "Look, I'm filing a police report on this with the sheriff's office, Sarah. Something has to be done about it. Before, I figured you were blowing things with Summers out of proportion." His straight black brows dipped. "Now I know you aren't."

"Sheriff Noonan will circular-file your report, just like he did mine on my dad's murder, Wolf."

The sound of Sarah saying his name moved through Wolf like a heated wave, thawing his once-frozen emotions. "You're paranoid, but in some ways, after looking at what someone did to that tree, I don't blame you." And then, trying to lighten the darkness he saw in her fearful eyes, he said, "I kinda grow on people like moss on a rock. This week at the house won't be too bad on you." He desperately wanted Sarah to believe he could help her through this period. But could he? He didn't know. He'd failed before—and a life had been lost. But as he stared over at Sarah, painfully aware of her situation, Wolf knew he'd never wanted to protect anyone more.

Sarah sighed, fighting the emotions his gruff kindness aroused in her. "When are you going to file the report?"

"Tonight. I'll get you comfortable at the house, then drive up to your cabin. My last stop will be at the sheriff's office."

The news of the cut roots had shattered Sarah, although she fought to appear calm. She not only felt the fear, she could taste it. Summers was out to get her claim—one way or another. Never had she felt so nakedly alone. But Wolf's voice was a balm to her raw nerves. His nearness enforced a sense of safety she desperately knew she needed, even as she struggled against it. With a shake of her head, Sarah muttered, "I'd just never have believed a stranger would come into Philipsburg and help me out so much." She looked deep into his gray eyes. "Are you sure there isn't a reason why you're doing this?"

Wolf didn't want to think about reasons. Was it to atone for—to somehow try to change—what had happened in South America? Could he really help Sarah? Even as he wrestled with his own uncertainty, Wolf still saw clearly that if he didn't reach out to help her, Sarah would be in even more immediate danger. He tried to smile to reassure her. "Like I said before—I'm Cherokee, and we'll open our homes to a stranger who needs help."

Sarah stared out the window of the truck, not convinced by Wolf's explanation. She sensed that there was more that he hadn't said. She saw the turmoil in his eyes, and felt the sudden tension around him. Wolf was an enigma, hiding behind something she couldn't identify—yet.

Frustrated, Sarah forced her focus to the town they were driving through. Philipsburg was a small, hundred-year-old silver-mining town that had gone bust. The streets were narrow but paved. Most of the buildings were of wood-frame construction, not more than two stories tall. Many needed a coat of paint from weathering the harsh Montana winters where the wind swept down off the rugged Rockies and through the small valley.

On Broadway, at the edge of the town, they pulled up in front of a yellow one-story house. Red geraniums lined the walk, but the grass was predominantly brown, in dire need of water because of the scorching summer heat. Wooden stairs led up to a wide, screened porch with a swing. Wolf turned off the truck engine and motioned to the house.

"We're home."

The words sounded so good that Sarah's throat tightened. Once she'd had a home. And two parents. Now she lived in an empty cabin. The loneliness of the past six months cut through her. Sarah's imagination caught fire, and she wondered what it would be like to wait for Wolf to come home every night.

"Yes," she whispered, her voice cracking. "We're home."

Chapter Four

"Ranger Harding, I think you're making a mountain out of a molehill." Sheriff Kerwin Noonan eased back in the creaking leather chair and held Wolf's opaque stare.

"Aren't you interested in who sabotaged Sarah Thatcher's mining claim? You know, if I hadn't taken a wrong turn and gone down that road, she could have died out there." Wolf was quickly getting the impression that Noonan abused his power. He had a cockiness, a know-it-all attitude, that automatically rubbed Wolf the wrong way. He had to struggle to keep his voice neutral and hide his mounting anger.

Noonan stroked his steel-gray mustache. "Sarah's always been a precocious thing, Harding. I watched her grow up from a skinny kid who was always in trouble and fighting with someone at school into a young woman who still had axes to grind. She ain't got the sense God gave a goose, jumpin' at shadows and accusin' Mr. Summers." With a shrug, Noonan added, "She's always been a troublemaker. If you're smart, you won't get mixed up with her."

Wolf dropped his written report on Noonan's cluttered desk. The jail was quiet, with only a lone drunk in one of the two cells. "I don't think," Wolf said softly, "that Ms. Thatcher's personality has anything to do with the fact that someone sawed through those roots. She certainly didn't do it to herself."

Eyeing the report, Noonan sighed. "All right, Ranger, I'll look into it. But I can tell you right now—ain't nothin' gonna come from my investigation. She pulled the same stunt when her daddy blew himself up with that box of dynamite in the back of his pickup. That girl came loose at the hinges, a wild banshee swearin' up and down that Mr. Summers had murdered him. Well, wasn't no such thing. Thatcher blew himself to smithereens all by himself. Pure and simple."

"I'm interested in anything you find, Sheriff," Wolf said, settling his hat back on his head.

"How's the girl doin'?"

It was obvious to Wolf that Noonan didn't respect women. Nor, plainly, did he see Sarah as the woman she had become. "She's going to be on crutches for a week."

Noonan's eyebrows rose a bit. "Too bad. I suppose she's heading back to her cabin out there in the middle of nowhere?"

Wolf shook his head. "No, I've offered her a place to stay until she can get mobile again. The doctor wants her off her feet for a while."

"Harding, the town'll talk."

"Let them."

"Your landlady, Mrs. Wilson, won't take kindly to that sort of arrangement."

Giving him a flat stare, Wolf said, "The only arrangement Ms. Thatcher has with me is that I've offered her a roof over her head and some food to eat."

With a grin, Noonan nodded his head. "Just remember, Harding—you've got a wildcat living under the same roof with you. Better watch it, or she'll turn around and bite the hell out of you. Anybody who gets mixed up with her is courtin' big trouble."

Wolf said nothing, turning on his heel and leaving the small, cramped jail facility. Sarah's paranoia about people in general—and especially strangers like himself—was becoming more understandable all the time. No wonder she feared trusting anyone but herself. What the hell had happened to her? Grimly he walked back out to the forestry pickup, where Skeet was waiting in the cab. He'd already picked up Sarah's clothes—what there was of them.

She'd also had him pick up some of her lapidary equipment. There was a large grinding machine with several wheels attached that would polish a stone to perfection. And the faceting machine, about as large as a dinner plate, with a round, movable surface, would allow her to continue working and bringing in some income while she stayed off her feet. Faceting was easy, she'd assured him.

As he'd moved through her cabin, collecting her few belongings, the financial deprivation Sarah suffered became very clear to Wolf. She hadn't embellished the reality of her situation.

Driving out of the parking lot, Wolf headed home. How good that word sounded to him. *Home.* Having Sarah there made it seem like one. Wolf couldn't hide from the fact that for many years he'd dreamed about a home and a family. But his life had veered off in another direction, one that he'd never forget, not until the day he died.

Twilight washed Philipsburg in an apricot hue as the sun dipped behind the mountains. The orange color softened the aging Victorian buildings, built during the silver and copper boomtown period so many years before. It was a town that had relied on mining to keep it alive. Now that the mining, for all intents and purposes, had been stolen from the earth and sold, Philipsburg had died. But, like many towns Wolf had seen, this one was resurrecting itself slowly, one new building at a time, because of tourism and Montana's nationwide reputation as a hunter's and fisherman's paradise.

With a grimace, Wolf thought how his own life paralleled that of the town. So much of him had died down in South America. The rebuilding had barely begun. Taking leave from Perseus had been the first step. Wolf knew instinctively that Sarah was touching the new, emerging chords within him as a man, touching his soul in some wonderful yet undefined way.

Perhaps it was the wildness Noonan had accused Sarah of that appealed to his primal nature, the part of him that, although wounded, had survived. Wolf didn't really perceive Sarah as wild. She'd merely used her instincts to survive—just as he had done.

Hope sprang in his heart, new and fragile. Sarah was untamed, and that excited him. He'd seen too many women beaten down, submissive beneath men's needs and society's expectations. Somehow, Sarah had not conformed in the way most women did.

His mouth was set in a grim line as he turned down the street that would lead him to the house. The price Sarah had paid thus far for not bowing under pressure had been heavy. Did the other townspeople feel as Noonan did about her? If so, Sarah had been an outcast all her life, and the thought tore at Wolf's emotions.

Then, at the thought of seeing her, his heart began to beat a little harder in his chest. The feeling was delicious, and he savored it like a man starved too long for emotional sustenance. How long had it been since he'd felt these gentle tendrils take root to remind him of a less harsh and demanding world? He frowned. Could he afford to let himself get close?

Sarah heard the key in the lock and sat up tensely on the overstuffed couch. Her swollen feet rested on an upholstered stool. It was 6:00 p.m.—and Wolf had said he'd be home later. Was it him, or one of Summers's henchmen? Her breath caught as the door opened and Wolf entered, his height and build making the doorway look small in comparison. The instant his gaze met hers, she saw an incredible change come over his face. The thin line of his mouth softened perceptibly. The fatigue in his gray eyes lifted, replaced by something warm that made her feel welcome in his home. Relaxation replaced harshness. She gave him a nervous half smile of welcome.

"See? I'm being a good patient," she offered. "My feet are up where you told me to keep them."

Wolf grinned as he closed the door and ambled into the small living room. The couch was a boring beige, but he'd thrown a quilt made by his grandmother across the back of it. The colors woven into it were red, blue, yellow and black, to denote the major directions as seen by the Cherokee. It made the room come alive with vibrancy.

"Why do I get the feeling that you hobbled over and put your feet up two minutes before I arrived?"

Sarah's uneasiness increased. "Are you psychic or something?" she croaked.

Wolf placed his keys on the cherrywood desk and dropped his hat on top of them. "I've been accused of being that from time to time."

"You're downright scary."

"So I'm right?" he asked, coming over and halting beside her. Sarah's hair was plaited in two long braids, and the style suited her. Her cheeks, once waxen, were flushed, and she fiddled nervously with her fingers in her lap. Disappointment flowed through Wolf. Sarah still didn't trust him.

"I can't lie," she said softly. "Yes, I was hobbling around here a couple of minutes before you pulled up."

"So why bother to look like you'd been following my orders?" he teased, starting to grin.

His melting smile seemed to embrace Sarah, and she suddenly felt beautiful beneath his searching, hooded gaze. Wolf was making her hotly aware for the first time in her life, that she was a woman. She saw the interest in his eyes—and the discovery as exciting as it was scary. Sarah had no experience with a man like Wolf. "I guess I didn't want to disappoint you." And then, disgusted by the admission, she muttered defensively, "I don't know."

"Well," Wolf told her, "I appreciate it. I was worrying all day you'd be resting and bored out of your mind."

"I wasn't *that* good."

Wolf lifted his chin and looked around. He noticed that small things, such as the vase full of wildflowers, had been moved slightly. "You dusted."

Sarah wrinkled her nose. "I can't stand a dirty house." Then she quickly amended herself. "I just picked up here and there, tried a little vacuuming, that was all. Your house really isn't dirty."

"Just messy," Wolf agreed. He tilted his head when he saw the wariness come back in her eyes. "What's that look for?"

"Aren't you going to chew me out for doing all that walking around?"

"Why should I? I'm not your keeper. Everyone's responsible for themselves."

"You mean that?" Sarah's gaze probed his laughter-filled gray eyes.

"Sometimes. The Cherokee part of me believes it thoroughly. My white side doesn't."

"I hate men who treat me like a half-wit," Sarah agreed. "Just because I have blond hair doesn't mean I'm dumb or helpless."

"I'd never make the mistake of thinking that," Wolf said wryly. "Hungry?"

"Starved." Sarah was suddenly eager to share the evening with Wolf. There was so much she didn't know about him, and so much she wanted to know. She'd had time alone to feel her way through her reactions to Wolf. All her life she'd been wearing male clothes, and she worked in a male occupation. No one had ever really looked at her as a woman until she'd seen that awareness in Wolf's eyes. He seemed to delve beyond the clothes she wore and the way she made a living to truly see the woman she was. That realization aroused something in Sarah, and she wanted to explore Wolf further, curiosity driving her as never before.

"How about a steak, a baked potato and a salad?" Wolf asked over his shoulder as he headed for the kitchen.

Sarah grabbed her crutches. "Fine with me. I'll eat anything."

Wolf turned. "Why don't you sit and rest?" He noticed at the entrance to the kitchen that not only had Sarah done his three days' worth of dishes, but the counter was shining, and the table was neat and clean.

"I don't sit or rest very well." Sarah placed the crutches beneath her arms and followed him out to the kitchen. Wolf's bulk seemed to fill the room. She sat down at the table, resting the crutches against the wall. There was something pleasant in just watching him move about the kitchen. Despite his size, he had a catlike grace, never bumping into things the way she did.

"I called over to the nursing home and checked in with the supervisor," Sarah told him. "They know I'm going to be laid up and won't expect me to visit Mom this week."

Wolf glanced over his shoulder as he placed two huge potatoes in the microwave. "Did they tell your mother what happened to you?"

"No," Sarah whispered. "She won't even miss me not being there."

The pain, her pain, stabbed at him. Wolf closed the microwave door and took two steaks from the refrigerator. "Doesn't she recognize you even a little bit?"

"No. Usually when I visit her she reacts to me as if I'm a stranger."

"That must be hard on you." Wolf turned, seeing the hurt in her huge blue eyes.

"Yes . . . it is. . . ."

Placing the steaks in an iron skillet, Wolf turned up the gas flame on the stove. "My mother died of a heart attack. I guess in some ways we were lucky. She died instantly." Wolf caught himself. He never spoke about his past or his family. Perplexed, fighting an inner battle to remain detached from Sarah, Wolf castigated himself.

Just one look at her and all his intentions melted like ice beneath sunlight.

"How old were you?" she asked softly.

Uncomfortable, he muttered, "Twelve."

"Oh, dear." Her heart twinged with pain—his pain. Wolf knew loss. That was why he could understand her. Her determination never to trust anyone softened even more as she watched him working over the stove.

Wolf turned when he heard the tone of her voice. Sarah looked so unhappy that the urge to sweep her into his arms and hold her tightly against him was nearly overwhelming. "That was a long time ago," he told her gruffly. "Save your feelings for someone who counts."

Sarah scowled as he quickly turned away again, busying himself with kitchen duties. "As if you don't count," she muttered. "Who rescued me from under that tree? And took me in for a week because I couldn't afford the hospital? You count a lot in my book."

The fervency in her voice broke through another painful barrier in Wolf. He turned and mercilessly met her soft blue gaze. "Honey," he growled, anger vibrating in his voice, anger aimed at himself, "I'm not worth caring about. I'm no one's ideal."

Sarah winced at the cold blade of anger in his voice. Why was Wolf so down on himself? Hurt by his unexplained harshness, Sarah sourly reminded herself that they weren't friends. Friends could confide in one another. Still, curiosity ate at her, and she choked out, "You're a man with a lot of secrets, aren't you?"

Wolf's scowl deepened. Panic surged through him. Sarah unerringly sensed that he was hiding a great deal from her. Well, wasn't he? Hell, he was desperately trying to hide it from himself. His voice was clipped with warning as he retorted, "You've got the curiosity of a cat."

"And that isn't going to stop me from finding out why you think so little of yourself," she answered steadily.

Wolf's gut tightened, and he tasted fear. "If you're doing it for curiosity's sake, don't try and unlock me." Wolf stared at her, the challenge in his gaze backed up by the growl in his voice. "I don't play those kinds of games with anyone."

Sarah gave him a tight smile, feeling shaky and euphoric at the same time. The potential thrill of knowing Wolf on a more intimate level was exciting, despite her fear. Sarah felt as if she were walking on a high wire, far above the ground. One small misstep with Wolf and she'd fall to her death—only it wasn't a physical death, but an emotional one. Her curiosity warred with the knowledge of potential danger. Despite her head's warning, her heart demanded to know his terrible secret. "Haven't you noticed yet? I don't play games, either."

"No," Wolf admitted in a rasp, "you don't." He stood at the counter, afraid. Afraid that Sarah was going to gut him of his past.

Sarah felt a bristling kind of power throbbing around Wolf, and decided to back off—for now. "Speaking of games, which one did Sheriff Noonan try to play with you?"

Wolf felt incredibly vulnerable in Sarah's presence. He sensed her tenacity, her determination to reach the very heart of his dark soul. He sighed silently to himself, grateful that she had switched to a more benign topic. Returning his attention to the stove, he checked the steaks.

"Noonan didn't take my report seriously."

Sarah nodded, feeling a palpable release of the tension that had been building between them, but still wondering why Wolf had gotten so tense and angry. "I figured as much. He never does," she muttered.

"Why?"

"He's on Summers's payroll, that's why. Noonan's a banty rooster, full of himself, strutting around because he's got police power behind him. The folks around here won't buck him." She added grimly, "But I have and will."

Going to the refrigerator, Wolf pulled out salad makings. He divided his time between cutting up vegetables and watching Sarah's darkened face. "What's going on here, Sarah? The sheriff accused you in so many words of being a troublemaker since the day you were born."

"As far as he's concerned, I have been. Wolf, you don't appreciate what I keep telling you—Summers runs this town. Those that are against him are too scared to challenge him."

"Except for you?" Wolf guessed, pleased at the way his name rolled off her lips, low and husky.

"There were others," Sarah admitted unhappily, "but they've moved away. They got tired of butting heads with the bastard."

"And you stayed? Why?"

Sarah idly watched Wolf cut up the carrots. Despite the large size of his hands, he was incredibly skillful, handling the knife with ease. "I'm a fourth-generation Thatcher, that's why. All my family is buried up on the hill behind town. Four generations of my family have given their lives to this life, Wolf. I love this place." Her voice grew low with emotion. "I love the mountains and the mining. My dad switched from silver to sapphire mining when things went bust around here. Montana is one of the few places in North America where you can find gem-quality sapphires that rival the best in the world."

Wolf set the table, placing the bowls of salad on it. "I never knew anything about sapphire mining."

With a shrug, Sarah leaned over and picked up a small leaf of lettuce and munched on it. "Montana sapphires have the same cornflower-blue color as the ones in Sri Lanka do." When she saw he didn't understand, she added, "Sapphires come in a lot of colors—bright orange, pink, red, green, blue, white and yellow. The ones worth the most money are the dark cornflower-blue ones. The red stones are known as rubies. Corundum is the material they're both made from."

"I didn't realize sapphires came in that many colors."

"Most people don't, because the jewelry industry has pushed blue ones on the public for the last fifty years."

"What do you do with the other colors?" Wolf pulled the baked potatoes out of the microwave and deftly set them on the two plates. Sarah sat at the table, nibbling at her salad and looking as if she belonged there. The sudden thought was heated, filled with promise, but quickly, Wolf pushed the longing away. He wasn't worthy of someone like Sarah.

"You saw all my lapidary equipment when you picked up my faceting machine?"

"Yes."

"My dad taught me how to facet when I was a kid. I facet all the sapphires I find, then sell them to a national gem distributor. He takes the colored sapphires, too. They become background gemstones in individual pieces of jewelry."

"Sounds like you could make a lot of money." Wolf brought the skillet over and transferred the steaks onto their plates. After setting the skillet in the sink and filling it with water, he joined Sarah at the table.

Sarah hungrily dug into the succulent steak, which Wolf had cooked perfectly. "That's the rub. The miner gets very little money. It's the middleman, the distributor, who really makes a killing on the sapphires. You have to remember, most of the gemstones aren't of the highest quality. A lot of them have inclusions or fractures, that lower their value. To make good money, I'd have to find a ten- or fifteen-carat sapphire with very few inclusions." She smiled across the table at her. "That hasn't happened yet."

"It will," Wolf promised her. He was starving. Starving for Sarah's bright, spontaneous company. Her enthusiasm was a new side of herself that she was allowing him to see. There was no wariness in her lovely blue eyes now, and for a moment Wolf allowed himself to wonder what Sarah would be like if she let that passionate intensity she held for sapphires to translate into emotions she could share with him.

Chortling, Sarah said, "You're psychic, so I'll believe you."

"But you're able to mine enough gems to pay your bills?"

"That's right. But I have to keep at it, Wolf." She frowned. "Being off my feet for seven days is really going to hurt me. The money I had saved went for that damned hospital bill."

Wolf said nothing, his conscience smarting. "Why has Noonan got it in for you?"

Sarah poured Italian dressing on her salad. "When I was in high school, I got Rickey Noonan, his only son, in big trouble. Rickey was pushing drugs, Wolf. The sheriff's son. Can you believe it?"

"Honey, there isn't much in this world I haven't seen in twenty-eight years of living. I believe you."

Every time Wolf used the endearment, a giddy sensation flowed through Sarah. She forced herself not to stare at him. What kind of magic did Wolf have over her? She struggled constantly to resist his powerful, quiet charisma. Dismayed at her inability to control her responses to him, she frowned and said, "Rickey was a bully in high school because of his father's power. He talked my best friend, Jody Collins, into taking drugs. Jody tried to commit suicide and I found her just in time. After that, I was so cotton-picking mad that I swore I'd get all drug pushers out of our school. I called the FBI and told them what was going on."

Wolf's eyes widened. "You went to the FBI?"

Indignantly, Sarah said, "Sure! Wouldn't you, if you knew the whole town's legal system was rotten to the core?" Sarah saw his mouth twitch with amusement. "Wolf, it wasn't funny at the time. I was seventeen and scared to death. I didn't even tell my parents what I was doing because I was afraid Noonan would get even. The FBI came and caught Rickey and his gang dead to rights. But when it was all over and done with, my name accidentally got dragged in to it. From that moment on, Noonan had it in for me."

"Did he hassle your parents?" Wolf watched her lick her buttery fingers after wrestling with the baked potato. There was something beautifully sensual and basic about Sarah, and the thought sent an ache surging through him.

"Noonan went after me first. I'd just gotten my driver's license, and his deputies pulled me over so many times for supposedly speeding that I just quit driving."

"What did he do to your dad?"

Sarah sighed and pushed her plate away. She'd lost her appetite. "Noonan conspired with Summers, and they went into cahoots," she said grimly. "Summers wanted our claim because the majority of our sapphires are the cornflower blue variety. You can take a clear or very light-colored sapphire and heat-treat it to turn it cornflower blue."

"Heat-treat it?"

"Yes, there's a special thermal oven. You put the rough, unfaceted stones in and literally bake them, like a cake, at a certain temperature for a certain length of time to improve and deepen their color."

Wolf shook his head. "Obviously there's a lot to gemstones that I didn't know."

Sarah nodded. "I grew up with it, so I take it for granted. I'm sure if the public knew how many gemstones were heat-treated, they'd be shocked."

"What does heat-treating do to them beside make them a darker blue?"

She gave him a smile. "You ask the right questions."

"In my line of work, my life depended on it," he murmured. Now where did that come from, Wolf wondered. Sarah's mere presence had him revealing pieces of himself. He saw her eyes widen—saw that curiosity burning in them. Before she could ask, he added, "So what does baking do to the sapphires?"

Sarah desperately wanted to pursue his statement. What line of work? But she saw the warning in his eyes and swallowed her curiosity. "It makes them far more brittle than their untreated cousins. For instance, if a woman accidentally banged her sapphire ring on something, it could crack or possibly shatter."

"So an untreated sapphire is tougher? Less likely to crack?"

"Exactly," Sarah said, pleased with Wolf's quick grasp of her business. "If a gem distributor doesn't have high principles, he'll often pass on heat-treated sapphires along with untreated ones and not tell the jeweler."

She opened her hands. "There's a lot of difference between jewelers, based on their gem knowledge and experience. They're only as good as their training, Wolf. I've taken courses with the Gemological Institute of America over the years and caught up with what the unscrupulous gem dealers do to gemstones. A lot of jewelers can't afford to get that kind of schooling. It takes money and time to educate and keep up with the guys who would sell you red glass and make you think it was a ruby. Some jewelers can afford the expensive equipment it takes to examine each stone—if you look at it under a microscope, you can see whether a stone's been heat-treated."

"Fascinating," Wolf murmured.

With a mirthful laugh, Sarah nodded. "If only people who bought gemstones realized some of the things that went on, they'd be a lot more inclined to educate themselves before they bought a stone, believe me. That and question their jeweler about his or her experience and training."

"So your mine produces more of the industry-standard color, and that's why Summers wants it?"

"Exactly. For some reason, our land had the right chemistry conditions when the sapphires were forming, millions of years ago, and so they tended to clump on that side of the mountain in that deep blue color. Summers is smart enough to know that he can't pass heat-treated stones on to his distributors without telling them."

"So he's looking at your mine as a source of the higher-paying sapphires?"

"Yes. I get more money per point on the facets of my stones than he does. Heat-treated sapphires are worth less—at least from miner to distributor. Once they hit the retail market, unsuspecting customers could be charged the same amount of money, regardless. Although a good jeweler will use heat-treated stones in a setting like a brooch, pendant or necklace, instead of in a ring, where it's likely to get struck or hit, and will charge less, accordingly."

"Fascinating." Wolf saw her worrying the flesh of her lower lip. "So when did Summers start wanting your land?"

"About ten years ago. He had some of his hired guns come over and break up our mining equipment. When Dad refused to sell or back down, they beat him up—and again a couple of times after that."

Wolf saw the fear lurking in Sarah's eyes. "What else happened?" he probed softly.

Nervously Sarah muttered, "They ran my dad off the road, trying to make him wreck. When that didn't work, they broke into our cabin and scared the hell out of my mom. She's a real gentle soul, Wolf, nothing like me. I have my dad's genes. I'm a fighter, and I don't back down when trouble's staring me in the face. Over the years, Summers continued to hassle us. Once he had his men steal all our lapidary equipment. It cost thousands of dollars, money we didn't have, to replace it."

Wolf set his plate aside. "What did Summers do to you?"

Squirming in her chair, Sarah whispered, "After Dad died, six months ago, they started putting real pressure on me. A couple of his men showed up dressed up like forest rangers. They knew I carried a rifle with me everywhere I went. I've been known to fire over their heads if

I catch them around our property. They disguised themselves so I'd trust them.''

Grimly Wolf folded his hands against his chin. "That's why you were so leery of me."

"No kidding. I didn't recognize you, and Summers hires men from out of state to do his dirty work. I'd fallen for the forest-ranger trick once, and wasn't about to fall for it again."

Wolf's throat tightened with barely held emotions. "What happened?"

Refusing to look over at him, Sarah said, "I'm ashamed to talk about it. I mean, I was so stupid, so naive, when they walked into camp. Rangers are around fairly often, since the mine sits in the national forest. I didn't think anything of them coming for a visit. . . ."

Without thinking, Wolf reached over and gripped her clasped hands on the table. He saw the shame in her eyes, and he couldn't stand aside and not try to ease her discomfort. No one should suffer alone. Her head snapped up and he saw the devastation in her features. "Sarah," he told her quietly, "you can tell me."

His hand was rough and callused on hers. Sarah was wildly aware of Wolf's warmth and strength. It drove tears into her eyes, and she quickly bowed her head. "I'm still angry about it. I believed those two, and let them in my camp. Anyway, they got close enough to haul me out from beneath the roots of this fir I was working under by the scruff of my neck. My blouse ripped . . ." Sarah shut her eyes. Her voice was low and off-key. She couldn't stand to know what Wolf thought of the next admission. Forcing herself, she whispered, "I—I fought them. They pinned me down."

Automatically his hand tightened around her small ones. Fury, cold and biting, wound through Wolf. Sarah's voice was wobbling, and her skin had gone damp. His mouth grew dry. Terrible scenes from his past blipped in front of him as he held Sarah's wide, frightened eyes. "Did they . . . rape you?"

Sarah shook her head, still refusing to look up at Wolf. "No. I made a grab for my prospector's hammer and swung it as hard as I could at the guy who had pinned me. It knocked him out for a second. When he let go, I scrambled up. Once I was on my feet, the second guy took off running. By the time I got to my rifle, they'd both hightailed it out of the area."

"When did this happen?"

"Three months ago."

Wolf released a shaky breath, feeling perspiration collect on his brow. He consciously forced himself to relax. "No wonder you didn't trust me."

Sarah lifted her lashes just enough to risk looking at his features. There was harsh anger in his thundercloud-gray eyes, and the fury was translated into the gravelly snarl in his voice. "I survived," she said quietly. "That's what counted."

The urge to gather Sarah into his arms and protect her nearly undid Wolf. He gently squeezed her fingers, then reluctantly released them. A flashback overcame him: He was walking into the village, seeing the dead and dying, hearing the screams of unprotected children and the cries of women. He squeezed his eyes shut. "No," he managed to say hoarsely. He shook his head, forcing the memory away. "There's more than just surviving something like that, Sarah. A hell of a lot more."

The rawness of Wolf's voice forced Sarah to make eye contact with him. Something tragic, something terrible, had happened to him. His face was twisted with pain, and his eyes were filled with such anguish and understanding that tears leaked out of hers.

"Then, I don't know what it is," she whispered, self-consciously wiping the tears off her cheeks. "I survived. I'm alive."

Wolf sat back, wrestling with an array of unexpected emotions from the past that were now coupled to the present. "Women and children who've been victimized wear the scars for the rest of their lives, Sarah, unless something's done to help them undo the trauma."

Tilting her head, she held his gray gaze, which was still dark with tortured secrets. "Ever since it happened, I've been really jumpy," she admitted.

"I'm sure. Do you get nightmares?"

Sarah hesitated, the need to share her worst fears with Wolf outdistancing her usual shell of self-defense. "Yes...sometimes.... Usually, I can't get to sleep." She gave a small shrug and looked away. "It's stupid. I see their shadows on the walls in my bedroom. I'll just be falling asleep, and I'll see them moving toward me."

Wolf nodded. He knew the litany all too well. "Insomnia, nightmares, and a special kind of wariness."

"I call it animal awareness. My hearing's sharper now—my senses are alive like never before since it happened," Sarah said. She rubbed her arms, suddenly chilled.

Wolf frowned and slowly got to his feet. "Let's get those feet of yours soaked in warm water and ice-pack them before you go to bed," he said gruffly. He didn't want to talk any more about violence. He walked toward the counter, a terrible sinking feeling stalking him as he realized that he hadn't been able to escape what had happened in South America. It was here, all over again, right in front of him. The place was different—and the names—but the situation was all too familiar.

Wolf rested his hands against the counter and bowed his head, feeling torn apart inside. Sarah, so small and spunky, had more backbone, more guts, than he did. She hadn't run. He had. A wrenching sigh tore from him. What was he going to do? Run again? Leave Sarah to fight her battle alone?

"Wolf? What's wrong?"

He shook his head. "Nothing."

Sarah slowly got to her feet with the help of the crutches. She swung herself to the counter, a few feet from him. Although she could see only his harsh, unforgiving profile, the set of his mouth shouted of some inner pain he was carrying within him like a living thing. "Look, my troubles and problems are my own. You don't have to take them on—or even get involved. I really appreciate you giving me a place to heal for a week, but you don't owe me anything." With a little laugh, Sarah added, "I owe you, if the truth be known. You saved my life and gave me care when no one else would."

Something old and hurting snapped within Wolf. He turned to her, his breathing harsh. "This time," he gritted out, "I'm not running. Sorry, Sarah, but you're stuck with me. We're going to push Summers and Noonan until they get the message to leave you and your mine alone."

Sarah's lips parted beneath the vehemence in his voice, the agony and anger in his eyes. "But...why? I'm nothing to you."

"You don't understand. I don't expect you to. Once, a woman gave me a place to heal, and I paid her back by failing her." Sarah's eyes grew huge, and he held up his hand. "I don't want to talk about it, Sarah. I can't ever go back and change the past, but I can change the present for the future. I'm being given a second chance, and I'll be damned if I'm going to fail this time. No, you're stuck with me for the duration, whether you like me or not. We'll find out who did this to you, and we'll bring them to justice."

Sarah stared up at him. The vibrating emotion coming out of Wolf made her want to cry—not for herself, but for him. She was right: Something awful and terrifying had happened to him, to those he cared for. Swallowing, she gave a jerky nod of her head. "Okay, I can use the help. I can't pay you..."

Wolf managed a twisted smile that didn't reach his eyes. "Honey, you don't owe me a thing, and never will. By Cherokee tradition, this situation is seen as a test. I failed the first time. Now the Grandparents are giving me a second chance." Softly he added, "And I'm not going to blow it this time, not this time...."

Chapter Five

Shaken by the intensity of their conversation, Sarah placed the crutches aside and awkwardly moved to the kitchen sink. She saw Wolf frown, his gray eyes turning molten with concern, and it unstrung her badly.

"What do you think you're going to do?" he demanded.

"Wash dishes before I soak my feet."

"No way. You can't stay on your feet that long." Wolf grabbed her arm before he could think what he was doing. Sarah's skin felt firm and velvety beneath his grasp, and he froze.

With a gasp, Sarah stared up at him. His hand seemed to brand her where it touched her arm. Never had she been more vividly aware of herself as a woman. Her heart beating erratically, she felt the burning heat of his stormy gaze upon her. The longing she felt was so intense that it took her breath away, and she was drowning, mesmerized by the changing color of his eyes, with all her being, Sarah felt Wolf's need of her.

The discovery was molten. Unconsciously she swayed forward, and at the same moment, excruciating pain shot up both her legs. With a little cry, she tried to grab something, anything, to take the pressure off her injured feet and ankles. Instantly Wolf's arms went around her and she felt the shock of his strong, unyielding body meeting the softer curves of her own. Her eyes shuttered closed as the pain swept upward, making her light-headed. Sarah allowed herself, for the first time in a long time, to lean against a man. Only Wolf wasn't just any man. She knew that as surely as she could feel her heart pounding in her breast.

Her cheek pressed against the fabric of his shirt, Sarah heard the drumlike beating of Wolf's heart. The smell of him, a man who worked in the fragrant pine forest she loved so much, was Sarah's undoing. Absorbing his male strength, the care of his arms as they swept around her, she surrendered to him in every way—if only for a brief moment. As he held her snugly against him, a small sigh escaped her lips. How long had she gone without any support? Just this once, her heart pleaded with her, let someone else help. Let someone else care.

Wolf released a groan as Sarah collapsed against him. Instantly he realized what had happened. His surprise at her surrender was followed by a massive desire to protect her that tunneled up through him as she sagged against him. She was so small—small and strong at the same time. He felt her capitulation to him, stunned by it, euphoric over it.

For just that moment spun out of time and reality, Wolf allowed Sarah to rest against him. Knowing her past, knowing how strong she'd had to be for so long, he understood her need to lean on him. But it was more than that, as he savored her lithe form. He could feel the birdlike beating of her heart, wildly aware of her small breasts pressed to his chest, of her slender arms moving around his waist.

He inhaled her womanly scent, deeply, raggedly. The memory of a woman seared him, and, fighting himself, he leaned down and pressed his lips to Sarah's sunlight-colored hair. The strands were thin and fine, like her. He could smell the fragrance of her shampoo, the fragrance of her as a woman, and it shattered his efforts to remain detached.

"Sarah . . . no . . ." he growled, and gripped her arms. Gently he pushed her away from him and reached for her crutches. It was the last thing in the world he wanted to do. He saw her head snap up, saw her pain-filled eyes widen with shock, then hurt. He knew she wouldn't understand why he was breaking their embrace.

"No . . ." he said, trying to soften the growl in his voice as he helped her place the crutches beneath her arms. Helplessly he watched as a flush stained Sarah's features. A huge part of him wanted to tell her the truth, the awful, sordid truth. But what would that do? Only make her see him as he saw himself. Bitterness coated his mouth, and he lifted his hands.

Humiliated, Sarah realized she should never have tried to walk without the aid of her crutches. Pain throbbed through her feet, and she felt stupid. "I'm sorry . . ."

"Don't be," he rasped.

Sarah touched her brow, dizzied at having unexpectedly found herself in Wolf's arms then abruptly pushed away. In his eyes she saw anger, mixed with the fire of longing, and she became confused. If only she had more experience with men, maybe she could understand what was going on between them. She'd seen the need for her in his eyes. She was sure of it! So why had he shooed her away?

Sarah gripped the crutches more tightly, unable to look up at Wolf, mortified by her own weakness. She had reached out to him trustingly....

"I'm going to go watch some television," she muttered as she moved past him. More than anything, she didn't want Wolf to apologize. It was humiliating enough to be rejected. She didn't want him adding to her shame by mouthing some inane reason for not wanting to hold her.

Scowling, Wolf watched Sarah hobble out of the kitchen. Her head was down, the golden sheet of her hair hiding her expression, but he'd heard the pain in her voice, and it made him feel worse than ever. Closing his fists, he railed at himself for his mistake. His protective side was working overtime with Sarah.

Sarah was far from helpless, he realized harshly. Because of the past, he was overreacting. There was a big difference between Sarah and Maria. But the situation, the danger, was the same. Glumly Wolf moved to the table. He'd told Sarah she wasn't a housekeeper, and he'd meant it.

His conscience smarting, Wolf cleared the table and began to wash the dishes. He could hear the television in the next room—the national news was on—but his heart centered on Sarah. He shouldn't have pushed her away so quickly. He'd hurt her, sending her the wrong message. The past was looming over the present, and Wolf didn't know how to handle the turmoil of emotions raging within him. He was projecting onto Sarah all the pain and failure of his past. It wasn't her problem, he reminded himself tersely. She had enough problems of her own.

With a shake of his head, Wolf concentrated on the dishes. Somehow, the drudgery of the duty soothed some of his fluctuating emotions. Still, he wondered how Sarah was feeling. He tried to block from his memory the awful expression of loss on her face when he'd forced her from his embrace. His mouth tightened. If only he'd been more guarded, more alert.

Closing his eyes, his hands in the warm, soapy water, Wolf realized for the first time that Sarah liked him. Why else would she have willingly fallen into his embrace instead of reaching for the counter or her crutches when her legs gave way? Then his mind—that cold blade of reality—reminded him that maybe Sarah was just feeling emotionally torn apart from sharing her traumatic past. Maybe she'd merely needed a haven, a set of arms to hide in for just a moment, and it had had nothing to do with liking him in a personal or intimate sense.

As he stood there feeling his way through the situation, his heart gently informed him that Sarah liked him a lot more than either he or she honestly realized. Wolf had always had good sense about people—until recently. Now he no longer dared trust the instincts that had always kept him in harmony with himself and the world around him. Peru had proven that his senses, his understanding, were faulty. People had died—*he'd* nearly died—because he'd believed he knew what to do and blindly acted on it.

Sarah had just as blindly acted upon her need to be held, and he'd denied her that safe harbor. Wolf silently chastised himself. Sarah deserved someone a hell of a lot better than him. Why had he been placed in her life? Swallowing hard, Wolf forced himself to finish the dishes. Somehow he had to apologize to Sarah, to make her understand it wasn't her he was rejecting—it was himself.

In an effort to break the tension strung between them, Sarah asked Wolf to set her faceting machine up out on the porch. They worked out on the porch for nearly an hour after the dishes were done. Sarah sat at the small wooden table where her faceting machine had been placed and plugged in. She was nervous in Wolf's presence. The message he'd given her was that she wasn't worthy of him—as a woman—and it left a very real hurt in her heart. Yet he had been so solicitous after coming out of the kitchen.

They'd taken special precautions not to accidentally bump or touch each other as they worked. Gradually, as all the equipment was put into place, some of the tension drained away, and for that Sarah was profoundly grateful. She looked up at Wolf, glad to see that the heavy scowl across his brow had relaxed.

"Tomorrow morning I'll start faceting these." She took a small plastic container and opened it. At least a hundred rough sapphires spilled out into the palm of her hand. Placing them beneath a lamp that Wolf had moved from the living room to her workbench, she motioned for him to look at them.

"See? Their colors are all different."

Wolf came close and leaned over Sarah's shoulder. He should have been looking at the rough sapphires she'd mined. Instead, he was studying her long, graceful fingers. Their nails practically nonexistent from digging in the dirt and sapphire gravel. He noted a number of small scars on her fingers and hand, too, but nonetheless she had an artist's hands, he thought.

"Nice," he grunted.

Sarah twisted a look up at him, wildly aware of his closeness. There was such sadness in Wolf's eyes now. Something within her reached out to him, and she was helpless to stop it. "Wolf, what's wrong?"

Abruptly he straightened. "Nothing."

Stung, Sarah felt heat rushing into her face. She was blushing—again. No man, not even Philip, who had captured her heart years earlier, when she was young and trusting, had made her blush so often. Casting around for a safe topic as the tension leaped violently to life between them again, she said, "I'm really tired. I think I'll go to bed."

Wolf nodded and moved to the entrance. "Take my bed."

Sarah's head snapped up. "What?"

He saw her cheeks flame a dark red. Shoving his hands in his pockets, he muttered, "I said, take my bed. I'll sleep out here on the living room couch."

Wolf's bed. Panic broke in Sarah. She stood up, nearly tipping the chair over. Catching it, she rattled, "I couldn't possibly take your bed, Wolf. I'll sleep on the couch." The memory of him pressing her to his strong, unyielding body, his arms going around her, the male scent of him, was permanently lodged in her heart. Sarah couldn't sleep on Wolf's bed. It would bring all those wonderful sensations back to the surface.

She forced a light smile as she got her crutches. "It's no problem. That couch is fine, Wolf. Really, I've created enough problems for you already by being here. I don't want to cause more. Keep your bedroom. I'll just sleep out here." She motioned toward the living room.

Frowning heavily, Wolf searched Sarah's features. She was forcing herself to placate him because he'd hurt her.

Dammit, anyway! Moving aside as she hobbled toward him, Wolf desperately sought to let her know that he hadn't rejected her. "Look," he grumbled, running his fingers through his hair, "you need a good night's sleep. This couch is lumpy and short. You need to stretch out and give those feet all the room they want."

She brushed by him and went into the living room. It was almost painful to be that close to him. Her heart was beating so hard in her chest that she took a long, ragged breath. She stopped in the center of the room, desperate. "Wolf, I want the couch, okay? No argument."

Turning, he held her guileless blue gaze, which broadcast her anxiety all too well. Wolf felt miserable. If only he could explain... He jammed that thought deep down inside him. "You're right," he snapped. "There isn't going to be an argument on this, Sarah." Pointing toward the hallway and the connecting bedroom, he said, "That is your room while you're here. Understand? And don't give me grief about it. Your feet need to heal, and—" he jabbed his finger at the old, worn couch "—they sure as hell won't do that on this thing."

Sarah moved restlessly around in the queen-size bed. She was used to her small bed, not this rambling expanse of mattress. Wolf's emotional reaction had jarred her. Opening her eyes, she stared sightlessly up at the darkened ceiling of the quiet bedroom. *Wolf's bedroom.* He slept in this bed. Unconsciously she smoothed her hand out across the cool cotton sheet and tried to imagine what it would be like for him to be lying next to her.

The thought stunned Sarah. She just hadn't been drawn to that many men in her life. There was Philip, but that had ended badly. Sitting up, the sheet falling away to expose her thin cotton nightgown printed with tiny violets, she frowned. The clock on the dresser opposite the bed read 2:00 a.m. Her feet were throbbing, but that wasn't why she was restless and unable to sleep.

Wolf's words, the look in his eyes—as if some part of him were dying inside—kept her awake. Kept her thinking. Grasping her crutches, which leaned against the wall next to the bed, Sarah slowly got to her feet. Perhaps a cup of tea would help her sleep.

The light from the street filtered in through the dark orange drapes and the sheers as Sarah made her way slowly down the carpeted hall. At the entrance to the living room, she suddenly realized that Wolf was sleeping on the couch, which was located opposite where she stood.

Leaning on her crutches, Sarah's heart started a slow, heavy pounding in her breast. Wolf was far too long for the short couch. It was very warm in the house, the summer heat lingering without a cooling breeze to push it outside, where it belonged. The white sheet he wore across his naked body had slid down and pooled around Wolf's waist, the outline revealing his narrow hips and long, powerful legs. Both his feet were exposed, as he'd kicked the sheet aside. Her gaze moved appreciatively upward to his slab-hard torso and his dark-haired chest.

A small gasp escaped Sarah as her eyes adjusted to the gloom. Was she seeing things? Was it her overactive imagination? Narrowing her eyes, her heart pounded painfully. Wolf's chest bore a crisscross pattern of puckered pink-and-white scars, as if someone had taken a bullwhip to him. No, that was impossible. Sarah closed her eyes and shook her head. What was happening to her? What craziness descended on her when she was in Wolf's quiet, powerful presence?

She reopened her eyes and studied his chest again. Yes, there were scars there. Too many to count. How on earth had he gotten them? Her gaze moved to his face, and the pain she'd felt for him disappeared. In sleep, his face was tranquil. She gripped the handles of her crutches as he stirred and muttered something in his sleep, turning onto his side. One of his arms hung over the edge of the couch, his curved fingers resting against the carpeted floor. He was bathed in sweat, and the sheen emphasized the muscles across his shoulder and upper back.

There was such a powerful beauty to Wolf. Sarah wavered. Should she go back to the bedroom or try to quietly reach the kitchen for the cup of tea? The tea was terribly tempting; it was the only thing that settled her nerves and imagination enough that she could get to sleep. Moving slowly and quietly forward, Sarah opted for the tea.

Wolf slept lightly, as was his custom. A vague noise awakened him instantly, and he jerked into a sitting position, his fists cocked. Disoriented for a second, he saw Sarah, in a knee-length nightgown, freeze in the center of the room.

"Oh, dear. I'm sorry, Wolf. I thought I was being quiet." Sarah stood there uncertainly. Wolf's eyes were softened by sleep. Black strands of hair hung across his brow.

"Sarah?" he croaked, frowning. "What's wrong? Are you all right?" He rose to his feet without thinking, wrapping the sheet around his waist.

Sarah's eyes widened, and she sucked in a quick breath as Wolf approached, casting a giant shadow in the gloom of the room. "I'm fine ... fine ..." He moved with such fluid ease. As Wolf drew near, Sarah could easily see the terrible series of scars on his chest, and the sight made her want to cry. What kind of pain had this man endured?

Wolf halted inches from her. The fine, thin blond hair about her face and shoulders was like a wraith's. He searched her eyes for the real answer, knowing that what she said might cover what she was really feeling. "Bad dreams?" he asked gently.

Sarah hesitated. "No...yes...in a way.... I slept for just a little while and then woke up." She managed a sad smile. "I got to thinking about what you said in the kitchen last night...."

"Oh."

The word came out hard and flat. Sarah knew Wolf didn't want to talk about it. "When I get like this, a cup of tea always helps me sleep. I was trying to cross the living room without waking you to get to the kitchen." Unhappily she added, "It didn't work."

Relieved that nothing was seriously wrong, Wolf relaxed. He bunched the sheet around him more securely where it had parted to reveal the length of his hairy thigh. Sarah had a high flush to her cheeks, and he read in her face a mixture of awe, fear and longing that made him acutely sensitive to how he affected her as a man.

"Could you stand some company?" Wolf asked. He wanted to join her but knew better than to push himself on her. Let her decide, he thought. He saw the indecision in her eyes turn to surprise.

"Sure, if you want."

He forced a sleepy smile. "Let me get more decent and I'll join you."

Nodding, Sarah suddenly remembered her own thin cotton nightgown. It wasn't sheer, but she felt vulnerable in it and wished for her robe. "I'll be right back. I want to get my robe."

"I'll get it for you," he said easily. "My pants are in the bedroom."

"Okay, I'll make the tea," Sarah said, aware of an oddly breathless quality in her voice.

Wolf padded down the hall to his bedroom, allowing the sheet to drop to the floor once he'd entered. With a scowl, he looked at his bed. The blankets were on the floor, the sheet twisted like a rag. Sarah was more than just a restless sleeper. Aching to hold her, but knowing that wasn't the answer Sarah needed, Wolf crossed to the dresser and put on a pair of jeans. He pulled a clean white T-shirt over his head. Maria had been deathly afraid of him without clothes. His uncovered chest had made her shrink back in terror.

Wolf slammed the door on the flow of memories. But since being around Sarah, he couldn't seem to force his feelings and memories away as easily as he once had. "Damn," he whispered, padding out of the room in his bare feet, Sarah's robe in his hand.

They sat at the darkened table, each holding a cup of steaming-hot tea. Sarah was delighted when Wolf found a lemon in the refrigerator and placed a few slices on a small saucer between them. And instead of sugar he'd offered her sweet clover honey.

"When I was a little girl, my mom would fix me tea with lemon and honey when I was sick," Sarah said in a quiet voice. "I loved it. She always said the lemon had lots of vitamins."

Wolf nodded, his arm resting on the table, his large hand curved around his china cup. "Tea won't fix what happened to you, though, Sarah."

"I suppose not," she responded sadly.

"Tell me something. After those two jerks jumped you, did you go get help?"

"What kind of help? I reported it to Sheriff Noonan—but that's like spitting in the wind."

"An abuse or crisis center of some kind?"

She smiled wryly. "Here in Backwater, U.S.A.?"

"Did you talk to anyone about the assault?"

With a shake of her head, Sarah said, "No, but what good would that do, anyway?"

"Talk's part of the healing process to anyone who's been traumatized."

"I wasn't hurt much. I had a black eye for a week, was all."

"You were a victim," Wolf said. "It makes you start behaving unconsciously to protect yourself from another possible similar situation."

"Oh, my jumpiness and paranoia?"

He smiled. "I like your honesty, Sarah Thatcher. It's one of many good traits you have. Yes, your hyperalert state is what I'm talking about."

She turned the teacup around in her hands. "There's nothing wrong with me."

"Oh?"

Sarah eyeballed him.

"Then why did I see fear in your eyes when I got up off the couch and walked toward you a little while ago?"

"Well…" Sarah stumbled over her words. "You came out of the shadows. I told you before, at night, shadows look like those two men coming to attack me again. I wasn't reacting to you."

Wolf held her serious gaze. Did he dare hope that was the truth? He had failed miserably before—failed in a way that had cost the person he loved, first her peace of mind, then her life. He couldn't bear to face the pain of the rejection he'd suffered. But, even more, he didn't dare face the possibly life-threatening consequences for

Sarah if he ran. Gruffly he probed Sarah's fear. "Are you very sure of that?"

"Of course I am."

"I don't scare you?"

"No."

He smiled slightly. "Your heart doesn't start pounding when I approach you?"

Sarah lowered her lashes. That was exactly what her heart did, but it certainly wasn't out of fear. It was out of some forbidden, sweet excitement he created within her. "You don't scare me," she assured him.

Wolf couldn't believe the relief he felt at Sarah's admission. Her soft blue gaze made him want to reach out and embrace the hell out of her. "I'm glad," he muttered darkly. "I'm no prize, but maybe I can help make a difference in the situation for you. I hope I can...."

Sarah heard the raw pain in Wolf's tone and noted that he refused to meet her gaze. "You're a prize in my eyes," she admitted unsteadily, her emotions overwhelming her. "I don't know what you see in me, and I guess it doesn't really matter. I'm just grateful you're standing between me and Summers and his men. I've lived with horrible daily fear this last six months." She managed a painful smile as he raised his head. "You're a shield to me, Wolf."

Wolf turned his cup slowly on its saucer. If he told Sarah the truth, how much she touched him, how she made him feel alive again, she might run. Worse, if Sarah knew the truth of his past, she'd probably want him to leave. Clearing his throat, he said, "I've always had a place in my heart for underdogs." That should be nonthreatening enough. Her young face was so young and serious.

"I can use all the help I can get," Sarah admitted, a catch in her voice. "If you want to be my guard dog, I'm all for it."

The light, the hope, shining in Sarah's eyes was so endearing, he kept his doubts to himself. Anyway, he wasn't about to make the same mistake with Sarah that he had with Maria—was he? "I'll do anything I can to help you, Sarah," he vowed. "All you have to do is tell me what you want. Communication is the key." This time things just had to be different.

Sarah thrust her hand across the table. "You've got a deal, Ranger Harding. And you've got my thanks. I don't know how I'll ever repay you."

Wolf gripped her hand gently, amazed all over again at how small, yet how strong, Sarah was. "The native Americans have a saying that you need to take to heart."

"What's that?"

"Expect nothing, receive everything."

"Meaning?"

"Don't set expectations. When you do, you set your own limitations and can't move beyond them. When you expect nothing, you become open to more than you ever thought or dreamed possible. It also means, receive help in whatever form it comes to you. There's no need to pay it back."

His callused grip was strong without hurting. Sarah wanted to continue to hold Wolf's hand, but didn't dare. He was far too vulnerable, and she was far too fragile emotionally. She mustn't read anything into their unexpected agreement. "No matter what anyone says, Wolf, in my eyes, you're a knight in shining armor," she whispered.

He released her slim fingers. "Honey, I'm a failure in so many ways, I can't even begin to tell you."

Stubbornly Sarah shook her head. "In my heart, you're a winner." She slowly got up, placing the hated crutches beneath her arms. The look in Wolf's eyes was a blend of relief and hope and denial. But that was all right. *By the time this is all over,* Sarah promised him silently, *I'm going to get you to realize just how wonderful a person you really are—faults and all.*

Chapter Six

The tantalizing odor of bacon frying slowly woke Sarah the next morning. She had shoved both pillows off the bed during her slumber, and the blankets were tangled hopelessly around her legs and body. With a groan, her feet throbbing, she pushed her blond hair out of her face. Lifting her chin, she squinted at the clock on the dresser. It was 7:00 a.m. Wolf had to be to work at eight.

Sitting up, Sarah rubbed her face sleepily, her legs hanging over the side of the bed. The sensation of knowing Wolf was nearby, and the odor of frying bacon, aroused a homesickness within her. How much she missed her father and mother! She assimilated those feelings as she sat there. Yet, with Wolf having unexpectedly entered her life, she'd never felt safer or stronger. He gave her strength, she realized as she slowly tested her weight on her feet.

"Oww..." She grimaced. Well, pain or no pain, she had to get to the bathroom. Maybe a nice hot bath and a soak for her poor injured feet would help. Reaching for her robe, Sarah shrugged it across her shoulders. She hated being forced to use these crutches. They were symbolic to her, too, and as she gripped them and stood she understood why. All her life she'd been independent— confident that she could stand alone to handle anything that came along.

As she hobbled to the master bathroom, across from the bed, Sarah realized that some of her shock over the past six months had to do with the fact that she'd come up against something she couldn't deal with successfully on her own. She leaned the crutches next to the door and closed it. The pain made her compress her lips as she leaned down to start the bathwater running.

Later, as she allowed herself the luxury of a long, hot bath, Sarah realized that Wolf was symbolic to her, too. But how far could she trust him? She'd trusted her father to be there for her, and he had been ripped from her life. She'd turned to her mother, and she, too, had abandoned her—in a different way. Wiping the perspiration off her brow, Sarah sat up and scrubbed her pink skin with the lilac-scented soap. Whether she wanted to admit it or not, she did trust Wolf. Did she have any choice? She frowned as she stood up and pulled the plug. Did she want a choice? After toweling dry, Sarah brushed her teeth, combed her hair and pulled on a pair of well-worn denims and a pink tank top. She tried to ignore the horribly swollen and bruised feet sticking out from beneath her jeans. Because Wolf was a paramedic, the doctor had told her to let him wrap her feet morning and night.

Her heart began beating more strongly as she hobbled down the hall on her crutches, Ace bandages sticking out of her back pockets. Skeet met her halfway, his large yellow eyes shining, his huge, brushy tail waving back and forth in greeting. Sarah smiled and stopped to pet him.

"You're looking happy this morning," Sarah told the dog as she continued into the living room. Ahead, she saw Wolf's broad back as he worked in the kitchen. Her stomach growled. She was starving! How long had it been since she was this hungry? A long time, she realized.

Her pulse was doing funny things as she hobbled to the entrance of the kitchen. Wolf was busy working at the counter, cracking eggs as the bacon sputtered in a skillet on the stove. The table was set for two. He glanced over his shoulder, and her heart skittered violently as his gray eyes narrowed on her.

"Morning," Wolf said. "Come and sit down. I've got breakfast almost ready." Wolf tried to keep his voice unruffled. Sarah had never looked prettier. The pink tank top brought out the natural flush in her cheeks. He was glad to see that she looked rested. He hadn't slept at all well last night after their midnight tea, because he'd kept rehashing their conversation in his mind.

Sarah gave him a slight smile of welcome and moved slowly into the kitchen. Wolf's hair was recently washed and combed, the kitchen light bringing out the blue highlights in the shiny strands. His skin was scraped free of the beard that had darkened his face since around 5:00 p.m. yesterday. He looked less forbidding without it, Sarah decided as Wolf pulled out a chair for her to sit on.

"Thanks," she whispered, meaning it. Philip had never been this thoughtful, but then, Sarah reminded herself, Philip hadn't been as old or mature as Wolf, either. She sat down carefully, placing the two huge Ace bandage rolls on the table. She wished her heart would settle down.

"How are the feet this morning?" Wolf asked as he poured the scrambled eggs into the skillet. Glancing at Sarah, he saw her poor feet stuck out in front of her, black-and-blue and swollen.

"Better."

His mouth twisted, and he turned his attention to scrambling the eggs. "Really?"

Sarah heard the irony in his voice. "Well..."

"You can tell me the truth, you know."

She stared hard at his back, which was covered now by his dark green work shirt.

"They hurt," she admitted.

"How much?" Wolf lifted the skillet off the stove and divided the scrambled eggs between the two plates on the table. He saw the darkness in Sarah's eyes. "A lot of pain?"

She nodded.

"After breakfast I'll wrap your feet so you won't be in as much pain," he said soothingly. Placing the skillet in the sink's soapy dishwater, Wolf brought over the plate of fried bacon, as well as some toast. He set them down and pulled up a chair opposite Sarah.

"Dig in," he invited. Suddenly an unexpected rush of happiness filled him, and he marveled at how glad he was that she was here to grace this old kitchen. She had a healthy appetite, and he was glad to see her eat. Skeet sat nearby, thumping his tail, looking for a handout.

"Don't give him anything," Wolf warned.

Sarah grinned over at the dog who sat a foot away from her. "He's got such a wistful look on his face, Wolf. How could you not feed him?"

"Harden your heart and tell him no. He's already been fed this morning." A grudging smile came to Wolf's mouth as he buttered a piece of toast then slathered red raspberry jam across it. He envied Skeet's ability to make Sarah smile. What could he do to make her smile—or maybe even laugh? Hell, ever since they'd met, it had been one crisis after another. Not much room for laughter or play. As Wolf munched on the toast, he realized that in the past year of his life he'd become so accustomed to living in crisis mode that he hadn't even noticed until this moment what he was missing.

With Sarah present, Wolf felt lighter, happier, than he could remember being in a long time. Maybe he was finally ready to come out of that long tunnel of grief. When Sarah looked up at him, laughter dancing in her dark blue eyes, Wolf felt his heart explode with joy.

"Harden my heart? Really, Wolf. I never could get tough with kids or animals." She wrinkled her nose and chuckled as she picked up the jar of jam. "I guess I should include insects, too. I never could smash an ant or get hyper about a spider crawling around, either."

"Good Indian traits," Wolf said, forcing himself to chew his toast. A winsome smile touched Sarah's mouth, and he felt himself drowning in the blueness of her sunlit eyes, and absorbed the moment like a greedy thief. The need to be liked ate away at Wolf. Sarah wasn't afraid of him, didn't look at him with terror in her eyes, as Maria had after... With a sigh, Wolf forced the memories away.

"What are good Indian traits?" Sarah teased. She couldn't help but enjoy Wolf's company. The cabin had been so lonely for the past six months—she'd been starved for the chance to share with another person. The corners of Wolf's mouth drew into a slight smile at her question, and a sheet of warmth flowed through her.

"Most Indians see the world as connected," Wolf explained. "The Cherokees have a saying—All my relations. It means we honor the connection between the bird that flies in the air and the fish that swims in the water and the beetle that makes her home in the ground. Medicine people say they can see a river of light flowing in and around everything, and for them, that proves this connection theory."

"I like that viewpoint," Sarah said thoughtfully. "I worry about digging sapphires because it exposes the tree roots." She shrugged and sipped the fragrant black coffee. "At least I put the dirt back to save the trees. Summers uses backhoes and bulldozers to rip the trees out to get at the sapphire gravel. He's left a path of destruction all across Blue Mountain."

"I noticed that the other day," Wolf said. "Sure you aren't part Indian?"

She laughed and picked up a strand of her hair. "With this hair, and blue eyes? Give me a break!"

Sarah's laughter touched Wolf's heart like a healing balm. It was a low, husky laugh filled with delight, and Wolf smiled fully in response.

"Where did your folks come from?" he asked as he pushed his empty breakfast plate aside in favor of his coffee cup. Suddenly he was eager to learn every detail about Sarah.

"My dad is a mixture of English and Scottish. My mom is mostly Dutch." She smiled fondly. "I've got Mom's hair and Dad's eyes."

"You have beautiful skin, too," Wolf offered. Sarah's fair complexion was the color of thick cream.

Sarah flushed and raised a hand to her flaming cheek. "Thanks," she said softly. Wolf's eyes burned with a desire that sent a ribbon of heat through her. So why had he pushed her away from him yesterday? Allowing her hand to drop, she pretended to be interested in clearing the plates away.

Wolf felt Sarah's discomfort. Was it because she wasn't used to being complimented? Or was it him that made her uncomfortable? Uncertain, Wolf said, "Time's getting late. I want to wrap your feet before I leave."

"Sure," Sarah muttered, and she pushed her chair away from the table. She watched Wolf unwind from his chair, thinking how stalwart he was. He was a man of incredible strength, not only in the physical sense, but emotionally, too. As she handed him the first Ace bandage, his fingers touched hers. A delightful sensation skittered along her hand, and she swallowed convulsively.

Wolf knelt and gently lifted Sarah's foot. Her ankle was so delicate, yet her calf was firmly developed from her hard physical work. "You're in good shape," he said as he rested the heel of her foot on his thigh.

Shaken by his touch, Sarah struggled to gather her strewn thoughts. "Thanks..." She watched, mesmerized, as Wolf's callused hand flowed carefully across her foot, examining it intently.

"They look a little better this morning," Wolf commented, feeling like a thief as he ran his hand in a practiced manner across her swollen extremity. He began to wrap her injured foot with the sureness born of much experience.

"You said you were a paramedic," Sarah said.

"Yeah."

Wolf's single-syllable response was cold, but somehow Sarah didn't mind the rebuff. Wolf was obvious about letting her know when she asked the wrong question, but she sensed it wasn't a bluff. "Where were you one?" she persisted.

Wolf glanced up at her, frowning. He returned to wrapping her foot, and the moments dragged by. Finally he sighed and said, "The Marine Corps."

"You're a marine?"

He saw the surprise and pride in her eyes. "Was."

"For how long?"

Wolf felt his gut tighten. "Eight years."

"Did you like it?"

"Yes."

Frustrated, Sarah eyed him. "Wolf, you're about as open as a locked safe, do you know that?"

He had the good grace to blush under her fervent observation. "It just comes naturally, honey. I can't help it," he said, trying to lighten his tone.

"Why not?" Sarah tried to ignore the endearment, although it tugged at her heart.

Wolf realized Sarah wasn't going to back off this time. He finished wrapping her foot, pleased with his handiwork. Then he lifted her other foot and began to work on it. "I was a recon marine, and they specialize in certain areas. I liked the medical area, so I took paramedic school a long time ago," he said quietly, keeping his eyes on her foot.

"Why did you like the Marine Corps?"

His mouth pulled into an unwilling grin. "Are you always this nosy?"

Sarah matched Wolf's grin with one of her own, drowning in his light gray gaze. She could read so much in his eyes: fear, joy, desire—and that haunted expression. "When it's important, I am," she flung back archly.

"I'm not important," Wolf growled, getting serious.

"To me you are."

Wolf shook his head. "You're young and full of idealism, Sarah."

"And you aren't?"

"I feel a hundred years old, and no, I don't have any idealism left in me. It got kicked out of me a long time ago."

"By the marines?"

"By life, honey."

Sarah enjoyed Wolf's tender touch, feeling the ache in her feet lessen as he deftly bandaged her feet. "Are you implying that because I live in isolation here in a very unpopulated area of America that I'm naive?" she retorted.

Wolf finished his task and rested his hands on his thighs as he held her challenging blue gaze. The fire in her eyes, the stubborn set of her mouth, touched him. "I see you as naive, yes."

"I don't know whether that's a compliment or an insult, Wolf."

Wolf slowly straightened, rising to his feet. The pleasure of talking with Sarah was going to make him late for work. He retrieved a sack lunch he'd packed earlier. "It just is what it is," he told her softly.

"You think I'm like a child. Is that it?" Was that why he'd pushed her away? Did he see her as immature?

Wolf groaned and held up his hand. "No, I don't see you as a child." Far from it. If Sarah could look inside his heart, she'd find out how badly he wanted to know her better. "You're a beautiful young woman. And in some ways, because of where you live, you are—" he groped for the right word "—untouched by the world at large."

"Untouched?" Sarah demanded, frowning. Wolf saw her as protected from real life? Oh, come on!

Glancing at his watch, Wolf gave her an apologetic look. "Sarah, I'm going to be late if I don't get going. Let's continue this conversation tonight, all right?"

Her lips compressed, Sarah watched as he quickly slid the breakfast dishes into the soapy water. "You're getting off lucky, Harding," she said, half serious, half teasing.

The urge to walk over to Sarah, lean down and plant a very long kiss on her petulantly set lips was almost Wolf's undoing. The fire in her eyes, he knew, reflected her sensitive roller-coaster emotions. Sarah's world was one of strong, passionate feelings—a world Wolf desperately wanted to explore. A world he knew he must forbid himself.

"I've got to go. Do you want me to leave Skeet at home with you today?" Worry gnawed at Wolf. He'd left Maria undefended, and— Swallowing, he added, "Skeet's a good guard dog."

Home. The word struck Sarah hard. Yes, this was a home. The discovery was bittersweet. "No, I'll be fine. Nothing will happen to me here." She saw the concern in his darkening gray eyes. That haunted look was back. Why? Sarah gave him a confident smile and waved. "Get going or you'll be late for work, Wolf."

"I've got a roast pulled out of the freezer, thawing. Will you—"

"I'll take care of it. Although I'm overly protected, young and naive, I think I can handle putting a roast in the oven so we have something to eat for dinner, Wolf."

His mouth worked into an unwilling grin. "Anyone ever accuse you of having a dry wit, Ms. Thatcher?"

"Only naive men like you, Mr. Harding."

With a laugh, Wolf waved goodbye to her, Skeet at his heels. As he walked onto the back porch and out into the morning sunlight, Wolf thought he had never felt happier. Sarah was far from naive, and they both knew it. As Wolf opened the door so that Skeet could bound into the cab, he smiled. He didn't deserve Sarah. He didn't deserve the feelings of joy coursing through him, but he couldn't help himself. After nearly a year of darkness and despair, Sarah's smile, her feisty courage, were helping him to heal.

As he backed the pickup out of the driveway, Wolf worried about Sarah's safety. He tried to tell himself that she would be safe at his home. Sarah wasn't Maria. Sarah knew how to fight back, how to survive. Still, as he'd put the truck in drive and headed down Broadway, his gut was tight with foreboding.

Sarah decided to leave the damnable crutches in the corner of the porch as she hobbled to the faceting machine. She'd rather endure the pain. Morning sunlight flowed strongly through the screened-in area, and robins sang in the trees surrounding the small, green lawn.

Faceting was second nature to her. She fitted the jeweler's loupe over her eye and inspected each stone minutely. Many of the rough sapphires had too many inclusions. No matter how carefully they were polished and faceted, those stones would always have a dull look to them.

The time sped by as Sarah found fifteen rough sapphires worthy of being faceted. She became lost in the process itself, unaware of the hours passing. The radio was playing in the living room, the music softening the grinding noise that the faceting machine made as the hard surface of the sapphire was polished away.

Sarah's stomach growled ominously. Glancing at her watch, she smiled. Noon exactly. Hobbling without the aid of the crutches, Sarah made it to the kitchen and peeked into the refrigerator.

As she made herself a tuna sandwich, she realized with a start that she felt incredibly happy. Ever since her father's death, she'd felt as if she were in a cocoon of grief.

Sarah sat down at the table, a glass of iced tea in hand, the sandwich on a plate. She frowned. It was as if she could still feel Wolf's presence in the small kitchen. Despite his height and size, he moved deftly around the area, never knocking into anything. As she began slowly chewing the sandwich, Sarah's heart centered on Wolf.

Why had he been so worried about leaving her alone? She knew Summers well enough to know that the bastard would never openly attack her and risk eyewitnesses. No, Summers was careful, waiting until she had her guard down.

Suddenly Sarah wished Skeet had stayed with her. It would at least give her someone to talk to—even if he couldn't answer her back. The wish that her mother was more aware of her made Sarah sigh. Right now she wanted to talk to her about all these crazy feelings alive within her, clamoring for attention. Philip had never made her feel like this. But then, she reminded herself grimly, Philip hadn't really loved her.

Deciding she had more questions than answers, Sarah cleaned up the kitchen and went back to work. As she hobbled through the living room, the phone rang. She hesitated, wondering if she should answer. After all, this was Wolf's home, not hers. But what if it was Wolf calling to see how she was? If she didn't answer, he'd panic and come back to check on her. Or would he?

Sarah muttered under her breath. Her imagination was getting the best of her. She meant nothing to Wolf. Moving toward the ringing phone, Sarah reached out and picked it up.

"Ranger Harding's residence."

"You're dead."

Sarah froze. Her fingers automatically tightened around the phone, and she gasped. Then anger followed quickly on the heels of her shock.

"Who is this?" she demanded.

No answer.

Sarah's breathing became erratic. She knew that whoever was on the other end hadn't hung up. "You bastard! Who do you think you are threatening me? Go to hell!" She slammed the phone down.

Shaking, Sarah stood with her arms wrapped around herself. Her heart pounding, she looked anxiously around the small house. The dainty white lace curtains moved slowly as a summer breeze stirred through the living room.

You're dead.

It had to be Summers! He'd hired someone to call her. To threaten her! Anger and fear warred within Sarah as she stood on her throbbing feet, rooted to the spot, unsure of what to do. Her first instinct was to call the ranger station and tell Wolf. No. She couldn't begin leaning on him. She had to handle this herself.

Gnawing on her lower lip, Sarah shivered involuntarily. This was the first time she'd ever received a threatening phone call. There was no point in calling Sheriff Noonan to report it. Her stomach was tight with terror.

Forcing herself to move, Sarah went back to faceting, far more alert, far warier, than before. What should she do? What *could* she do? Every particle of her being cried

out to tell Wolf. Her hands shaking badly, Sarah reposi-
tioned the stone on the machine for the next facet.

"No!" she whispered forcefully as she gently set the
stone on the grit-layered wheel. Turning the machine
back on, she watched it for a long moment. Summers was
just like that grit—he was wearing her down a little at a
time. Sarah raised her head, tears stinging her eyes.
Everything was closing in on her. The only good thing in
her life was Wolf. Her father was dead, and her mother
was, too, in a sense. Sarah squeezed her eyes shut, tears
running hotly down her cheeks. She couldn't stand if
Wolf was hurt or killed defending her. No, she just
couldn't put him in that kind of jeopardy.

Wolf noticed that Sarah was jumpier than usual when
he got home that evening. During their dinner of pot
roast, baked potatoes, gravy and carrots, the phone rang.
Sarah jumped, her eyes huge. Wolf answered the call—
from the ranger station telling him about a change in his
assignment the next day. When he sat down again, he
noticed how pale Sarah had become.

"Are you all right?" he demanded, slicing into the
thick, juicy pot roast.

"Yes, I'm fine. Fine."

"You're as jumpy as I would be if I found myself in the
middle of a minefield," he noted dryly.

Sarah forced herself to begin eating again, her heart
banging away in her throat. "Are you always this alert?"
she muttered.

"It saves lives," he answered darkly, and shoved a
piece of potato into the gravy.

Lives. Her life. Maybe Wolf's. Sarah choked down a
small piece of beef, not tasting it. The very thought of

Wolf being hurt because of her put a knot in her stomach.

"Aren't you hungry?"

Sarah shook her head, afraid to look up. Wolf read her eyes and face too easily.

"Are your feet bothering you?"

"Yes." It was a white lie, Sarah told herself as she pushed the plate away. If she didn't get out of the kitchen, she was going to tell Wolf about the call. Desperation fueling her, she got up and moved around the table, careful not to engage Wolf's gaze.

"Sarah?"

"I'm okay!" she flared, and left the kitchen.

Scowling, Wolf looked toward the living room. Finally, he returned his attention to the food on his plate. He'd had a long day out in the field, walking along the many local trout streams, and he was more tired than usual. Part of it was due to lack of sleep last night, but the bigger part was from worrying about Sarah's safety all day. He saw Sarah limping down the hall toward her bedroom. She was probably going to soak her feet. He'd wrap them later, before she went to bed.

"Dammit," he growled. Sarah had made a wonderful dinner, but his emotions were in tatters. Just being around Sarah made him achingly aware of how much he wanted her—on all levels. Wolf had given the situation with Sarah a hard, realistic look today.

Pushing his plate away, Wolf got up. The chair scraped back, further testing his already taut nerves. Maybe kitchen duty would help take the edge off him. In some ways, he thought, this was going to be the longest week of his life; in other ways, he had never felt as content. There was no explanation for it. He'd never before looked forward to such small, seemingly meaningless things in his life. But now, the thought of Sarah eating, pushing her spun-gold hair behind her ear, sharing her winsome smile with Skeet or just moving with unconscious grace, made him appreciate living as never before.

All evening Sarah worried that the phone might ring again. She took an early bath, pulled on her cotton nightgown and robe and hobbled back out to the living room. Wolf was sitting on the couch watching television when she came and sat down next to him.

"I'm kind of tired. Would you mind wrapping my feet? I think I'm going to bed early." She handed him two Ace bandages.

Wolf nodded and eased out of his sprawled position on the couch. He could see that Sarah was tired from the darkness beneath her blue eyes. As he knelt down at her feet, he looked up at her. "You never said how your day was."

She shrugged and leaned against the couch, her arms around herself. "I got some stones faceted. That was good." At least that wasn't a lie. Her skin tingled as he gently grazed the skin of her foot.

"They look a lot better tonight."

"I threw the crutches away," she muttered.

Wolf grinned as he placed the heel of her foot across his thigh. "Maybe walking on them increased the circulation and helped reduce the swelling."

Sarah watched, fascinated, as Wolf's large, scarred hands carefully wrapped her feet. She never felt pain when he touched her—only a simmering heat that taunted her like the threat of a thunderstorm on a hot summer day. "You mean you aren't going to chew me out for not using those crutches?"

"Am I your keeper?"

She shrugged and made a wiry face. "No woman should be kept."

"I agree."

"You're really different from the guys I've known," Sarah said. "Why is that?"

The pleasure of touching Sarah was humbling to Wolf. Her feet were delicate, despite their swollen condition. "Must be my Cherokee heritage," he teased. "Women are treated as equals in my tribe."

"Will miracles never cease? At least there's somewhere on this earth where we're not maligned or mistreated."

"Now, don't waste your anger on me. I'm treating you like an equal." Wolf tried not to smile, but he saw the laughter dancing in Sarah's eyes. He liked making her happy.

"You're too smart for your own good, Harding."

"Yeah, I know. But my mother taught me when I was knee-high to a cricket that women were just as strong, bright and resourceful as any man." He captured her other foot and inspected it closely. What would it be like to simply run his hand the length of her slender leg? Instantly he blocked the molten thought and began wrapping her foot.

"I think I'm lucky," Sarah admitted. "Dad showed me how to change tires and put oil in the old pickup, and taught me mechanical things. Mom taught me how to sew, cook and clean."

"There's no reason a woman shouldn't be taught those things."

"Well," she said unhappily, "there are plenty of men who think we're nothing but housekeepers."

Wolf's laughter boomed through the living room. He sat back, his hands on his thighs, and held her mutinous gaze. His breath jammed in his chest as she began to laugh with him, her husky voice as refreshing as clear, clean water. With a shake of his head, he studied her.

"Were you always this rebellious?" he teased.

Sarah felt heat rushing to her face and knew she was blushing—again. "I don't see it as being rebellious. I see life as one of justice for everyone."

"Yet you willingly made dinner for us tonight."

"That's because you asked," she said pointedly. "You didn't expect it of me."

"I think," he said lightly, "what you're really telling me is that you don't want to be taken advantage of."

Sarah's eyes widened as she held his warm gray gaze. "You understand."

Wolf smiled a little. "I like your courage, Sarah Thatcher. You've got brains and a backbone. You keep fighting for what's rightfully yours. Every step you take opens up doors for other women who might not have your strength, conviction or courage. You're doing a good thing."

"Yeah, and it could get me killed," she muttered, more to herself than him.

A pang went through Wolf's heart and rattled his conscience. "I guess," he began in a low tone, "that the Great Spirit puts tests in front of us to make us stronger."

Sarah wrinkled her nose. "Right now I don't feel very strong." *Just scared. Scared to death.* She ached to confide in Wolf, to tell him about the phone call. But why? To involve him and, perhaps, make him a target, too? No, he was too fine a man, a man who reveled in her independent nature.

Without thinking, Sarah reached out, covering Wolf's hand with hers. "You're so very special, Wolf. I just hope you know that." Reluctantly she removed her hand as she saw the startled look on Wolf's face, and the stormy quality of his eyes. "Good night," she whispered sadly. "I'll see you in the morning...."

Chapter Seven

You're dead.

Sarah jerked awake, screaming. Breathing hard, she hunched over in the bed and buried her face in her hands. She was shaking badly, and the cry was still echoing in her brain. Perspiration dampened her gown, which clung to her.

"Sarah?" Wolf hesitated fractionally at the door.

The darkness was relieved only by the streetlight outside the curtained window. Sarah gasped at the sound of Wolf's thick, sleep-ridden voice. Before she could raise her head, she felt his callused hand slide across her shoulders in a protective gesture.

"Honey, what is it?" Wolf's heart was pounding unrelentingly in his chest. His mercenary instincts had taken over when Sarah's scream had jolted him out of his sleep. His eyes slitted, adrenaline pumping into his bloodstream, all his senses screamingly alert, he checked out the room, the window, the door to the master bath-room. Nothing. He glanced down at Sarah. It had been a nightmare....

Without thinking, Wolf sat down on the bed next to her, and pulled her into his arms. She was trembling badly, and she pressed her face to his chest, sobbing for breath.

"It's okay...." He tunneled his fingers through her mussed hair. "You're safe, Sarah. You're safe...." Wolf shut his eyes, feeling her begin to cry, although she made no sound. It hurt to think that she couldn't even give voice to whatever nightmare had been stalking her.

Leaning down, blindly following instinct, Wolf grazed her temple with a kiss, gently massaging her neck and her tensed shoulders with his hand. "Go ahead and cry, honey," he whispered raggedly.

Sarah's hands curled into small fists, and she let her-self sob, the sound echoing in the room. Just the touch of Wolf's hand, soothing her, allowed the trauma to be given a life of its own in strangled, hiccuping sounds that came from deep within her. She was safe. Safe for the first time in a long time. Wolf was holding her, rocking her, and she felt more like a hurt child than a woman. He was her protector, keeping her safe when the nightmare had stripped her of her defenses, leaving her nakedly vulnerable to the world that wanted her dead.

Dead.

Wolf whispered words of support near her ear, and Sarah surrendered completely to him. To his arms. To his voice. To the warm strength of his body that surrounded her. Her world dissolved in a rush of hot, blinding tears, of animal sounds jagging up through her and making her throat raw, releasing so much that she'd tried to suppress for so long. Only Wolf's voice and the tender touch of his hands upon her existed.

Gradually, with each stroke of Wolf's hand across her hair and down her back, Sarah's inner focus began to lessen. Her peripheral awareness began to return, and as the last sob rattled through her, she unclenched her hand and spread her fingers against the soft, thick hair sprinkled across Wolf's chest. Somewhere in her muddled senses, Sarah felt his muscles tense beneath her tentative exploration, and she felt his arms draw her even more tightly against him.

Wolf leaned down, seeing Sarah's cheeks shining with spent tears in the grayish light. Her glistening lips were parted, pulled into a tortured line of anguish. He smoothed the tangle of blond hair away from her cheek and tamed it behind her delicate ear. With his fingers, he began to dry her cheeks and brush the tears from her lower lip. She sniffed and pressed her face against his chest.

A tender smile pulled at Wolf's mouth. He wanted nothing more than this moment. He was vibrantly aware of Sarah's body, meeting his, fitting against his. Her skin was warm and damp from her weeping, and her fingers now tangled in the hair on his chest. The minutes fled by, and Wolf agonized, not wanting the embrace ever to end. He could smell the fragrance of her recently washed hair, the scent of lilacs filling his nostrils.

More than anything, Wolf was aware of the aching contact wherever their bodies touched. Sarah's knee-length cotton gown was a thin barrier between them. Luckily, he'd found a pair of pajama bottoms and started wearing them since she'd been staying with him. Wolf smiled a little when Sarah licked her lower lip, then raised a hand to wipe away the beads of tears still clinging to her lashes.

He cleared his throat. "Better?" His voice was thick and unsteady, betraying how much her tears affected him. Wolf was no stranger to tears. He'd shed more than he would ever have thought possible. And he'd once watched the woman he'd loved cry even as she rejected his embrace. With a sigh, Wolf realized that Sarah had allowed him the privilege of holding her while she wept. Whether or not she would ever realize it, the act was a healing one for him.

Sarah nodded, not trusting her voice yet. She was wildly aware of Wolf's massive body, his powerful arms encasing her, his hand gently moving up and down the length of her arm, soothing away any last vestige of pain. His voice was shaky, and so was she. Wolf's male scent entered her awareness, and she inhaled deeply.

Realizing that she'd trusted—completely surrendered to—Wolf, Sarah lay in his arms, confused. Her head was screaming at her to move away from him. But her heart, which had held so much fear and grief alone for so long, begged her to remain within his embrace. As Sarah slowly opened her eyes, she remembered their previous embrace, and how Wolf had pushed her away.

Not this time, her heart whispered. But her head won the struggle, and she started to move.

"Stay," he rasped, his arms tightening momentarily. Wolf held his breath. He knew he had no right to ask such a thing of Sarah. He hadn't earned this privilege, but he couldn't help himself. Sarah somehow flowed around all his rational reasons, leaving him helpless to deny her anything.

Sarah capitulated, still raw from weeping, in need of human care and love. Her eyes opened. *Love?* Where had that word come from? And just as swiftly as the thought had come, Sarah rejected it. Love meant trust, offering her heart to be trampled and destroyed. She sniffed and pressed her hand to her eyes, feeling a fresh flow of tears welling.

Wolf reached over to the bedside table and pulled several tissues from the box there. "Here," he said, placing them in her hand.

"Thanks..." Sarah said brokenly.

"Bad dream?"

Sniffing, she nodded and bunched up the damp tissues, loath to leave Wolf's embrace. "I—" she bit back the truth about the phone call. "I-it was a violent one..."

Wolf nodded and stilled his hand against her arm, content just to hold Sarah. "Yeah, they're all too familiar to me."

"You?"

"Pretty frequently." His voice grew wry. "I almost think I'd miss them if they suddenly went away some night."

Twisting a look up at his deeply shadowed, harsh features, Sarah blinked belatedly remembering the terrible scars she'd seen on his chest and back. "You never told me...."

Bare inches separated their faces, their lips. Wolf placed a steel grip on his desire. Sarah was wide open and vulnerable. It was wrong to take advantage of her. Completely wrong. He held her wounded-looking gaze. Her eyes were dark with fear. "I don't usually admit to having them," he told her huskily.

Sarah became lost in the turbulence of his gray eyes, at a loss about whatever terror-filled past still remained alive in him. She was too raw herself to deal with whatever Wolf carried, anyway. "They're awful," she managed.

"Yeah, but eventually they lose some of their punch," he said, and captured a stray strand of her hair, moving it away from her face. "It's nightly therapy," Wolf joked. "Cheap and free." It was a lousy joke, and he knew it. The anguish on Sarah's face made him grimace. He didn't want her worrying about him; she needed to focus on her own needs.

"The best therapy," he said, clearing his throat, "is talking."

"Interesting theory, coming from you," Sarah noted in a scratchy voice.

"The shoe's on the other foot, honey. It's your turn. What was the nightmare all about?"

Honey. Sarah melted every time the endearment crossed his lips. It touched her heart, tugged at her lonely soul. She lowered her lashes, unable to hold his burning gaze. He seemed to see right through her. Relaxing in his arms, she sighed and whispered, "Ever since my dad was killed in that explosion—I've never cried."

Wolf's brows moved upward. "Never?" His arms tightened briefly around Sarah. Wolf, too, had hidden his tears, pretended they weren't there or that he was tough enough to take it. But there had been unbidden times when the tears had refused to be held back—and, exploding with rage and helplessness, Wolf had cried alone.

"N-no. I had to be strong for Mom." *For myself.* Sarah sniffed and wiped her nose. "It was such a shock," she went on in a hoarse tone, "my dad dying and all. H-he always dreamed of finding that one huge cornflower-blue sapphire that would haul us out of poverty and make us millionaires." Sarah closed her eyes and absorbed the feel of Wolf's hand briefly grazing her cheek, where fresh tears flowed. "Dad loved us very much. He was my idol. He was an honest man. He worked sixteen hours a day during the summer to make enough money to tide us over during the winter.''

''He sounds a little like my father,'' Wolf said, thinking fondly of his own dad.

''My dad gave me my work ethic, Wolf.'' Sarah opened her eyes and lifted her head to meet and hold his warm gray gaze. ''He taught me to go after what I wanted.'' Swallowing hard, Sarah dropped her gaze. ''After he was murdered, my whole world fell apart. I—I didn't realize how much my mother depended on my dad until she had that stroke. I just didn't realize...'' Another sob escaped her.

Wolf nodded and pressed a kiss to her hair, wishing he could take away the fresh pain that had surfaced. ''Maybe you weren't aware of the love they had for each other when you weren't around.''

Sarah gave a small, helpless laugh. ''I guess you're right, Wolf—I'm naive. After Mom had the stroke and I put her in the nursing home, I had to clean out a bunch of drawers at the cabin to take her clothes to her.'' She picked at the damp tissue still wadded in her hand. ''In one drawer I found a whole box of letters my dad had written to her when he was serving in Vietnam.''

Wolf felt Sarah tremble and realized intuitively how much she needed to share this with someone—even him. ''Tell me about it,'' he urged gently, stroking her hair with his hand.

The touch of Wolf's hand upon her hair broke the dam that had held back Sarah's grief. ''Th-they were love letters—'' She choked softly and pressed the tissue to her eyes. ''There must have been a hundred of them. When I first discovered them, I didn't know what they were. I opened one and read it. What my Dad wrote was beautiful. When I realized it was from the sixteen months he'd spent in the army, I sat down on the floor and read every one of them.'' She sniffed. ''That was when I realized just how much they loved each other.''

''That must have been healing for you,'' Wolf murmured, looking down at her flushed features, her bright, tear-filled eyes.

''It was and it wasn't. I just didn't know, Wolf! I never saw them kissing or stuff like that. I never saw my dad come up and put his arm around my mom, or reach over and hold her hand. Nothing...''

''They came from a generation that believed in showing their love behind a closed bedroom door,'' Wolf reminded her quietly.

''I don't ever want that! I want my kids to know I love my husband. I want them to see us kissing, touching and holding. I want them to be hugged, to be touched and held—'' Sarah broke off, realizing what she'd said. Sniffing, she muttered, ''I'm not getting married, anyway. It's not worth it, Wolf.''

''Why not?''

''Marriage is too risky.''

''You mean, loving someone?''

With a quirk of her mouth, Sarah gazed up at him. In that moment, he appeared so wise and understanding. He seemed to see beneath her painful words. ''Yes...I guess so.''

''Why?''

''Because—because if you give your love, it's taken away.'' Sarah realized how lame that sounded.

Wolf nodded. ''Your love for your dad was ripped from you?''

''Yes.''

''And then, in a way, your mom abandoned you, too. Right?''

Wolf's insight was startling. Sarah eased out of his arms. She stood up and moved a few feet from the bed. Sarah tried to smooth the wrinkled cotton gown. The silence deepened in the room. Sarah knew she couldn't evade Wolf. He didn't deserve that from her. Finally she clasped her hands in front of her and looked over at him.

"I know she didn't do it on purpose," she admitted in a broken whisper. "But—Mom's gone. All that's left is her body. She rarely ever recognizes me anymore. I'm—" she choked "—a stranger to her."

Rising, Wolf slowly approached Sarah. He placed his hands on her slumped shoulders, hoping in some small way to absorb her anguish. "Love is risky," he admitted thickly. "No guarantees, Sarah. Not ever."

She touched her heart with her hand, feeling the pain. "I-I just don't have any more to give, Wolf."

"I understand better than you think," he rasped. His hands tightened on her shoulders. "Feel like trying to go back to sleep? It's 3:00 a.m."

Sarah heard that awful anguish in his voice again and looked up, seeing clearly the haunted look in his gray eyes. Someday she'd get him to share that pain as he'd convinced her to share hers.... Suddenly, exhaustion descended upon her like a heavy blanket. Her eyes, burning from her many tears, felt heavy-lidded. She nodded, realizing she had to sleep. When Wolf removed his hands, she felt alone as never before. Searching his harsh, unreadable features, she asked, "Will it come back?"

"The nightmare?"

"Yes."

"Probably not." He gave her a slight smile meant to buoy her. "But if it does, just scream and I'll be here for you. Deal?"

She smiled a little, remembering the deal she'd had with earlier him, and their handshake. Her lower lip trembling, she whispered, "Deal."

Sarah awoke the next morning. It was nearly 10:00 a.m.! With a start, she sat up in bed, her head aching from all the crying she'd done the night before. With a groan, she touched her brow. Slowly her conversation with Wolf floated back to her and, more importantly, his tenderness toward her. Taking in a ragged breath, she tried to push away the feelings he'd aroused. She had to keep her distance—it was a matter of survival!

After washing and dressing in a pair of jeans and a short-sleeved yellow blouse, Sarah hobbled—without the crutches—to the living room. The house was quiet. How she missed Wolf's larger-than-life presence. Skeet was gone, too.

In the kitchen, she found a note near the automatic coffeemaker.

Sarah—
I'm going to drop by at noon and check on you. I didn't want to wake you up this morning to wrap your feet. Just take it easy today, honey. You've been through a lot. Wolf.

Sarah's hand trembled. Her gaze caught on the word *honey*. With a small sound, she dropped the note into the wastebasket. Trusting Wolf meant giving him something in return—her heart. Pressing her hands against her eyes, Sarah stood, feeling torn apart.

The phone rang.

With a gasp, Sarah jerked a look toward the living room. *No!* The phone rang again. And again. Her heart pounding, Sarah stood, unsure whether to answer. It could be Wolf calling to check on her. Or it could be—

Pressing her hands against her ears, Sarah tried to blot out the harsh sound. After fifteen rings, it finally stopped. Her mouth was dry, and her heart was pounding raggedly in her breast. What if it was yesterday's caller? What would he say to her?

"Oh, God..." Sarah whispered, and sat down hard on the chair, her knees buckling with fear. Wildly she looked around the kitchen. Wolf's kitchen. He was in danger, too. She'd placed him in danger. But what if it had been Wolf calling her? Sarah knew her mind was running rampant with dread.

Trying to calm herself, she realized that when Wolf came home at noon, she could ask if he'd called. If he had, it would clear her conscience. But what if he hadn't? Shouldn't she tell Wolf about the threat? Maybe it was meaningless—another of Summers's mind games. Maybe.

Sarah knew she had to get busy. That was the way to drive the fear away. She hobbled to the porch and looked around carefully before stepping through the door. Then, warily, she peered out at the surrounding yard. Finally satisfied, she began faceting her sapphires. But no matter how hard she tried to hold her concentration on what she was doing, she longed for Wolf's return.

When Wolf returned to the house, around noon, Skeet stayed outside, content to sniff the boundaries of the wire fence that enclosed the backyard. Entering the house, Wolf took off his hat and placed it on the desk, calling, "Anyone home?"

"I'm in here," Sarah said from the kitchen.

Wolf smiled uncertainly as he entered the kitchen. Sarah stood at the counter, making sandwiches. She looked feminine in a puff-sleeved yellow blouse. Her hair hung in two pigtails. "You look like a little girl ready to go jump rope," he teased. His heart beat erratically in his chest as memories of holding Sarah flooded him. Hell, he'd thought of nothing else all morning. At the office, his considerable paperwork had stared back at him as he reran the entire sequence from last night.

"Oh, the pigtails," Sarah said belatedly. She looked up at Wolf, and her heart melted. He looked so strong and capable, and she felt none of those things. "Sit down. I made us tuna sandwiches." Nervously, she brought over a jar of sweet pickles and placed a bag of potato chips on the table between them.

"You didn't have to go to the trouble," Wolf murmured, appreciative of her efforts. He sat down and smiled at Sarah. Her face was pale, the flesh drawn around her eyes and mouth, but he wrote it off as the result of the emotional storm she'd weathered last night.

Sitting down, Sarah managed a small smile. "That's what I like about you—you don't take me for granted," she said. She picked at a potato chip, her stomach knotted. Somehow she had to find out if Wolf had called her. "How did you manage to get away? Weren't you out patrolling in the woods?"

"Today was paper-crunch day," Wolf told her, munching on his sandwich. "One day of the week is stay-at-the-office day. Well," he hedged, "sort of."

"What do you mean?"

"Early this morning I took a run by your cabin, just to check on it, before I headed to the office."

"How is it?" Sarah asked quickly, thinking of the threat.

"Quiet. I went in and had a look around. Nothing's been disturbed."

"And the mining area?"

"Fine."

"No evidence of anyone digging?"

"No, everything's quiet." Wolf wondered why Sarah was so nervous.

"D-did you call me this morning. Around ten?" Sarah held her breath.

Wolf shook his head. "No. Why?"

Sarah shrugged. "No reason..." The urge to blurt out the truth nearly overcame her. Maybe it had been one of Wolf's friends calling. But he'd never mentioned anyone. Panic ate at her.

"Maybe the word's got out to Summers that I'm checking your place two or three times a day."

She grimaced. "Knowing Summers, he's just waiting for the right opportunity." Giving Wolf a pleading look, she whispered, "Please be careful out there. I don't trust him, Wolf. He could jump you the way he jumped me."

Wolf saw the terror in her eyes, heard it in her voice. Reaching over, he captured her hand and squeezed it. "I'll be okay, honey. Stop worrying."

Just Wolf's touch momentarily staved off her panic. Trying to gather her strewn feelings, Sarah asked, "Have you heard from Sheriff Noonan?"

"I called him this morning. I can't say he was real happy to talk to me." Wolf scowled. "He doesn't have any suspects. I don't think he's done a damn thing, if you want my gut impression."

Sarah swallowed hard, feeling a lump of fear form in her throat. "Maybe you ought to back off, Wolf."

"Why?" He saw the worry in Sarah's eyes.

"Well...because.... I've pushed Noonan before, and that's when the goons jumped me."

"They won't jump me."

Moving restlessly around in her chair, Sarah whispered, "I just worry about you, Wolf."

Her admission hit Wolf as a pleasant surprise. "You do?"

"Yes," she muttered with a frown. Wrestling with her feelings, she added, "I'd worry about any friend who was tangling with Noonan, that's all." She stole a look at Wolf. "Not that I have friends..."

"Because having friends means reaching out and trusting someone?"

She shrugged painfully. "It sounds stupid when you say it."

"It's not stupid," Wolf murmured. Sarah wasn't eating. She was just sitting there, tense, her hands in her lap. "When you've been hurt repeatedly, it's tough to reach out again." The corners of his mouth curved gently. "I'd like you to think of me as your friend—if you want."

Sarah bit on her lower lip and forced herself to hold his gaze. "You have been a friend to me from the beginning," she admitted hollowly. "I-I've just been afraid to admit it to myself, Wolf."

"Because with the admission come the feelings."

"Exactly."

He stopped eating, his own heart opening to her vulnerability, her honesty. "It's better to have someone to turn to when you're feeling alone," he offered gently. "I know having you here has helped me—in ways you could never know."

Perplexed, Sarah stared at him. "There's so much I don't know about you, Wolf!"

Wolf knew he had to steer her away from his problems; she had enough of her own to handle without becoming entangled in his miserable life.

"How are your feet feeling?" he asked, changing the subject. He took another bite of his sandwich.

"Better, but not good enough." Although Sarah could have sworn that Wolf's magic touch was speeding up the healing of her feet. She removed the Ace bandages and stuck her feet out so that he could see them.

"They don't look as bruised," Wolf said, pleased.

"Thanks to you," she said, with a warm look in his direction.

"Healing comes in many forms."

"Who taught you about healing?"

"My grandmother. Her name was Bear Woman. People with bear medicines have great healing abilities, and she passed a lot of her knowledge on to me when I was a kid."

"Tell me about your life on the reservation," Sarah asked hopefully. So far, he'd gently parried all her attempts to know more about him.

Putting his plate aside, Wolf drew the cup of coffee into his hands. "My grandmother was a medicine woman for our tribe. Besides teaching me healing skills, she taught me a lot about how to survive."

"Oh?" Sarah saw the darkness come back into his eyes, as it did each time she touched on some distant unhealed memory. Instinctively she knew he, too, had to talk if he was to heal.

"When I was twelve, I went on a vision quest. For three days, I fasted and prayed with a pipe my grandmother had given me. On the third day, I had a vision. I walked back to her cabin—in the Smoky Mountains of North Carolina—and told her about it." Wolf smiled softly. "She was such a wise old woman. I can't tell you about the vision—to do so is to break the power of it. But, in general, she spoke to me about being a warrior, someone who would do battle of one sort or another all my life."

"And so you went into the Marine Corps?"

Wolf hedged, then softened. To hell with it. It was too hard withholding information from Sarah. "I spent eight years in the Marine Corps after I got out of high school, Sarah," he explained.

"But you're a forest ranger now. Did you get out of the marines and come here?"

Frowning, Wolf knew he couldn't lie to Sarah. Inhaling deeply, he took in the hope and interest shining in her blue eyes. Finally he said, "No. I got an invitation to join Perseus, so I did."

"What's Perseus?"

"It's a private security company run by Morgan Trayhern—a man I trust with my life. We work as troubleshooters sent all over the world, and we interface with the U.S. government. I've spent a lot of time in Colombia, Venezuela and Peru."

Sarah was thrilled that Wolf was finally opening up to her. And then she realized humbly that it was because she had offered her friendship to him. She had finally trusted him; now he was beginning to entrust her with his past. "Then you're like a soldier?"

"A mercenary," he said flatly.

"Did you . . . did you kill people?"

"My job was to train the police or military of each country. I was an advisor, Sarah."

"I'm glad," she whispered.

He held her gaze. "I have killed."

"In defense of yourself?"

"Myself or others." Wolf shook his head. "I tried to defend—help—others. I failed sometimes. . . ." Just the admission sheared painfully through Wolf, but he knew it was necessary to give it voice.

"I hope I never have to kill another human being." Sarah shivered at the thought. "You don't have the eyes of a killer. Summers does, and so do his hired guns."

"I didn't say I enjoyed killing, Sarah. I've got a conscience." Wolf grimaced. "And it never lets me forget the faces or the situations when it happened."

"And so you quit because you didn't want to kill?" Sarah probed, still not understanding why Wolf was here in Montana. She sensed that something terrible had happened to him, and that was the reason he was here, instead of some more exotic place.

Wolf looked away from Sarah's gaze. The truth tasted bitter in his mouth. The awful need to confide in her was almost overwhelming. But he couldn't tell her—not yet. Sarah was still too vulnerable. He didn't want to dump his problems on her. They had time, and he'd pick and choose when it was right to reveal his past. A terrible fear gutted him. When Sarah found out what he'd done, wouldn't she distrust him? She'd withdraw her friendship—and the hope he saw blazing so strongly in her eyes would disappear.

"I'd had enough killing. Enough fighting. I got wounded in Peru, so I came home to heal. In a sense, a huge part of me died down in Peru."

"When I first met you, Wolf, I could see such darkness in your eyes sometimes, as if you were lost in a black pit."

"You're not far off the mark," he agreed quietly, staring down at his empty coffee mug. "I wanted a quieter life, a life that hinged on helping living things, not fighting drug lords. I told Morgan that I wanted a job as a forester, and he used his influence to get me into the ranger program. They sent me here after training.''

"You wanted to be alone," Sarah murmured. "To heal."

Her insight stunned him. Just the way Sarah whispered the words made his heart lurch with awareness of her, of her beauty as a woman with an incredibly understanding soul. "Yes."

For a long time, Sarah didn't speak. "Isn't it funny how we met each other? You came to Montana to get away from everything that had hurt you. I was fighting a battle that I knew I was losing an inch at a time." She shook her head. "Wolf, you're walking right back into the fire by helping me. You know that, don't you?"

He smiled at her candor. "In the Cherokee way, honey, walking through the fire is a part of life. Yeah, I know I'm repeating a cycle I've been through before. But you don't deserve to be abandoned." He stretched his arms out before him. "I'm going to try to help you. I've failed before, Sarah. Badly. But if you'll take a chance on me, I'll try to be there for you." *Please,* Wolf prayed, *this time, I must not fail.*

"How did you fail?" Sarah asked, seeing the haunted look return to his eyes. "You've said that before."

Wolf shook his head. "I don't want to talk about it yet, Sarah."

Sarah sat back. Wolf had divulged far more than she'd thought he would. But whatever terrible secret he carried was still there, eating away at him. A huge part of her wanted to help him—and believed she could. Then Sarah realized just how much of her trust she was willing to give him in order to do it. The thought frightened her, and she retreated. "You don't know Summers," she cautioned.

"He's dangerous, and he'll kill." Rubbing her arms, suddenly feeling chilled, she added, "I've got this awful feeling, like he's lying in wait for me. I've been expecting him to raid my cabin, steal my lapidary equipment. Something . . ."

"Maybe the word's got out that you have a big guard dog," Wolf teased gently, getting to his feet. He took the cups and saucers to the sink to wash them.

Terror, shadowy and powerful, swept through Sarah. She looked up at Wolf, appreciating his strong back and shoulders. What burdens had he carried alone on those broad shoulders? He needed to be held, too, to be kept safe from a dangerous world. The desire to get up, slide her arms around him and do just that nearly overwhelmed Sarah, but she fought the urge.

Still, she couldn't shake the terror leaking through her. Should she tell Wolf about the phone call? But what could he do, anyway? Quit his job and make a bristling armory out of his house, waiting for Summers to try to kill her? It was stupid, she decided. She had to hope that the phone call was only a scare tactic.

"Let's get your feet wrapped," Wolf said as he finished his duties at the kitchen sink, "and then I've got to get back to the paperwork."

Sarah nodded and handed him the first Ace bandage. "Will you check the cabin before you come home tonight?"

Wolf knelt down and examined her foot. "I always do," he assured her. "You can expect me home around six tonight."

The moment Wolf turned into the fir-lined narrow dirt road that led to Sarah's cabin, Skeet started to whine. The sun had dropped behind Blue Mountain, but pale daylight lingered. Automatically Wolf looked for the cause of his dog's reaction, and as he turned the corner, he got his answer. Two pickups, one black and the other tan, were parked next to Sarah's cabin. The hair on Skeet's neck bristled, and he growled low and deep.

"Easy," Wolf said soothingly, quietly bringing the truck to a halt and pulling off into the trees. Wolf opened the door and got out, leaving Skeet in the cab. He didn't want the dog shot if Sarah's visitors were some of Summers's henchmen. As he walked quietly toward the cabin, Wolf put a round in the chamber of his rifle. Hearing voices inside, he moved quickly to the open door. He saw three men dressed in jeans and cowboy shirts standing inside. Before they realized he was there, Wolf had imprinted their faces on his memory.

"You men got business with Sarah Thatcher?" he demanded, moving into the doorway and blocking any possible escape.

One man, heavyset with a black beard, swung around, a startled expression on his blocky face. Almost as quickly, his two cohorts did the same.

The bearded one sneered. "What's a forest ranger doing here?"

Wolf saw that some of Sarah's lapidary equipment had been piled in several boxes on the floor. The men appeared to be ready to haul the boxes out of the cabin.

"Not the same thing you're doing here, that's for sure," Wolf snarled. He kept the rifle pointed at them. "What the hell do you think you're doing?"

"Get him!" the black-bearded one yelled.

Wolf sensed someone behind him. Too late! Bracing himself, Wolf whirled and threw out his foot, connecting solidly with another of the men, this one blond. His boot sank deep in the man's gut. From behind, Wolf heard a rush toward him. A fist hit him squarely in the right kidney. Groaning, he staggered forward, raw pain radiating through his back. The rifle dropped from his hands.

"Get the son of a bitch!" Black Beard screamed. "Beat the hell out of him! Show him he can't interfere!"

Wolf staggered and turned, parrying another blow and throwing one of his own. His fist connected solidly with the man's square jaw, the tremor jolting up Wolf's arm and into his shoulder. Out of the corner of his eye he saw Black Beard running toward him. Breathing hard, Wolf tried to keep his footing, but the two men leaped at him at the same time. He slammed to the floor, the breath knocked out of him. And then the fists started to come at his face, two, three at a time. Pain arced and exploded through his brain and mercifully, Wolf lost consciousness.

Chapter Eight

It was dark when Wolf regained consciousness. He was lying on the floor of Sarah's cabin. He vaguely heard the sound of Skeet's nonstop barking coming from the truck. Groaning, he lay very still, getting his bearings and wondering if he had any broken bones. He was thankful Sarah hadn't been here when the henchmen had come. Revulsion and disgust flowed through him as he slowly sat up, every bone and muscle in his body protesting. If Sarah had been here, they might have raped her—or killed her. Or both.

The metallic taste of blood in his mouth was overwhelming. Thirsty, Wolf lurched to his hands and knees, then woozily staggered to his feet and over to the kitchen counter. Turning on the faucet, he cupped the cold water in his hands, throwing it on his bruised and puffy face. He winced at the cold—startling and soothing at the same time. Grabbing a towel hanging on a nearby nail, he buried his face in the soft folds of the terry cloth and leaned heavily against the counter.

Taking careful steps across the room, Wolf turned on the light. It hurt his eyes, and he squinted. The two boxes filled with Sarah's lapidary equipment were still on the floor! At least the bastards hadn't managed to steal anything after all.

Looking at the watch on his wrist, Wolf took a good thirty seconds to figure out what time it was: 8:00 p.m. Sarah would be worried. Lurching to the phone on the table next to her bed, Wolf sat down. Thankfully, he'd called the telephone company to repair Sarah's phone several days ago. Grimacing, he dialed his home number. The phone rang and rang. He prayed she'd pick it up. Finally the phone was picked up, and he heaved a sigh of relief.

"Hello?"

Wolf heard the carefully concealed terror in Sarah's voice. "Sarah, it's me, Wolf.... Something's happened up here at your cabin—"

"Wolf? You sound awful! What's happened?"

"Honey, it's okay," he mumbled, discovering several loose teeth on the left side of his face. His cheek had already swollen. He must look like a chipmunk carrying nuts. "I'll be home in an hour."

"You don't sound good. Wolf, what's wrong?" she demanded.

"I'll tell you when I get home. Just have some hot water and bandages ready, Sarah."

Sarah gave a low cry, caught herself, then became more coherent. "Bandages and hot water. Okay, I'll have them waiting for you, Wolf."

He wanted to smile, but couldn't. "Sounds good, honey. See you soon." He placed the phone back on the receiver and sat there a good minute before moving. Sarah had tried to be so brave about the conversation. Rising slowly, Wolf automatically placed his hand against his back where his right kidney was located. The bastard who'd hammered him there had meant to take him out— permanently. Luckily, he was in good shape, and he'd been turning as the blow was delivered, or he might not be walking.

As he pulled the door to Sarah's cabin shut, Wolf saw that the lock had been broken, probably with a crowbar. He'd have to replace it for her. His mind was spongy, and as he slowly put one foot in front of the other his need of Sarah rose with burning intensity. As he pulled open the truck door, Skeet whined and wagged his thick, brushy tail. Giving the dog a reassuring pat on the head, Wolf hauled his tired, aching body onto the seat. Somehow, he had to drive home. Somehow.

Despite the pain in her feet, Sarah walked quickly out the rear door of the house when she saw the lights of Wolf's truck in the driveway. It was dark, and she could barely make out that it was him as the truck pulled to a stop. Her heart hammering, she jerked open the driver's side door.

"Wolf?" Her voice was high and off-key.

The instant her hand settled on his shoulder, Wolf leaned back against the seat. "It's okay, Sarah—"

She gave a little cry. Wolf's face was swollen and bloodied. She should have told him about the phone call! Shaken, Sarah whispered, "Come on, put your arm around me. I'll help you into the house. Her voice was trembling with anger and terror as he reached for her. She bit back a groan as Wolf's weight sagged against her. He was none too steady on his feet, but she managed to guide him up the concrete steps and through the door. Her own feet were screaming in pain, but she ignored them.

"Just get me to the bathroom," Wolf rasped.

Sarah did as she was ordered. He sat down on the side of the bathtub, gripping the side of it for support. Quickly she pressed a cold cloth to his face. One eye was almost swollen shut, the bluish color pronounced around it.

"Who did this?" she asked in a wobbly voice, unable to contain her fear. Gently she dabbed away the blood, which made the injury look a lot worse than it really was.

"Don't know. Three men," Wolf said, his speech slurred. He touched his jaw. "Got loose teeth on this side."

"If you're lucky, they'll tighten up in a couple of days. Hold still—this is going to hurt." Sarah applied a washcloth with a hefty dose of soap on it. Wolf never moved, never flinched, never even showed any expression. Sarah remembered his mercenary duties in Peru.

"Is this what happened to you down in Peru?" she asked, quickly rinsing away the soap with fresh, clean water.

Wolf slid a glance upward, wildly aware of each of Sarah's touches. "Yeah . . . this was a normal, daily kind of punishment. . . ."

Swallowing against the lump in her throat, Sarah continued to clean up his face. "Tell me what happened to you down there. *Please.*"

His defenses were down, and he knew it. Wolf was hurting too much, needing Sarah too much, to try and fight her request. His voice was low, off-key. "A woman I knew . . . that I loved . . . was raped," he admitted finally. "Gang-raped."

"Oh, God," Sarah whispered, "I'm sorry. For her and for you." The bleak devastation lingered in his eyes.

"Be sorry for the hell Maria went through, but don't be sorry for me," Wolf said roughly, unleashed emotion flowing like a bitter river through his heart.

Sarah sat very still, realizing the agony Wolf was experiencing. In a hushed tone, she said, "Go on."

A tremor went through Wolf. He shut his eyes. "I've never told anyone about it . . . about Maria. After it happened . . . Not even Morgan."

Sarah felt Wolf's fragility, the secret pain he carried, so evident in his roughened voice. "You told me talking about a trauma was a good thing. Why don't you apply it to yourself? You've already helped me. Maybe you don't realize it, but you have…and I'm grateful for your understanding."

Wolf glanced up at Sarah. He realized how privileged he was to see the vulnerable side of her, and the thought was like sweet, molten heat flowing through his ice-cold soul. "It's ugly," he warned her.

"What about Maria? You said you loved her?"

Wolf cleared his throat—suddenly constricted with tears. "Yeah . . . She was a beautiful Peruvian woman, your age." Wolf stared down at his bruised, swollen hands, his mind and heart going back to that time and place. "We met over a pig drowning in a pond, if you can believe it. She was up to her knees in the water, the red skirt she was wearing hiked up around her hips. The pig was thrashing around out in deep water because a jaguar had chased it into the pond to catch and drown it. Maria was there when it happened. She yelled at the cat, and he took off."

Wolf tried to smile and failed. "She was so damned angry at that pig because he was swimming farther out into the pond instead of back to the shore. I offered to go get it for her. When I brought the pig out and put it in her arms, she offered me and my men a meal at her village. A real hot meal. I took her up on it in a second. She was one hell of a cook, and I was grateful for village hospitality. But Maria was kind to everyone.''

Wolf closed his eyes and then opened them, staring at the opposite wall of the bathroom. "I was stationed near her village for over a year, and eventually, we fell in love. Because I'm part Indian, and her people were of Incan heritage, I was respectful of their laws. I courted Maria. I had plans for us—lots of plans. When my mission was completed, I was going to marry Maria and bring her back to the States with me.''

Wolf's gaze moved back to Sarah. There was such compassion and understanding in her shadowed eyes. "Maria's village was surrounded by coca plantations, and there was a lot of drug activity—the making of cocaine from the coca leaves. The head of the village, Juan Renaldo, forbade his people to get involved with the drug trafficking. Instead, they asked for protection from the Peruvian police. It was a clean village, and that's why I was assigned with my team to protect them from the drug armies. More than once, men from the village had shown us caches of cocaine and pointed out those from surrounding villages who were in the drug trade. It made for a lot of enemies and bad blood.''

"My team fell for a trap, and we left the village unprotected for the day. When we returned, the village had been burned to the ground, most of the men killed, and the women—raped." Wolf's voice fell. "It was a warning from Ramirez, the drug lord, to the survivors.''

Sarah took in a shaky breath. "My God, I'm so sorry, Wolf. Poor Maria.''

Wolf nodded dully. "The rape really messed her up in the head. My men and I, along with another U.S. team, helped rebuild the village and get the people back on their feet physically. But the emotional scars it left behind couldn't be erased." He shook his head. "The survivors were scared. They lost their joy, their natural optimism. No one smiled very much after the raid. Even though I loved Maria, she was afraid of me. I mean, really afraid of me."

"Because you were a man, and it was men who'd hurt her?" Sarah guessed.

"Yeah."

The unhappiness in his face was almost too much to bear. "What eventually happened to you and Maria? Did she decide not to marry you?"

It hurt to talk, to feel so deeply again. Wolf squeezed his eyes shut. "I tried to love her the best I knew how, to convince her I loved her. Maria couldn't stand to be touched by me. She couldn't stand being held. It reminded her too much of being pinned down by those bastards who raped her. I tried to understand. I tried..." Wolf stopped, the pain working up through his chest. More than anything, he owed Sarah the last of the story. The real truth that would show him to be the miserable failure he really was.

"Ramirez set us up again, and I fell for it. I fell for all of it," Wolf told her bitterly. "A second time, we left the village unprotected. When we were out chasing Ramirez's men, he came into the village and killed again." Wolf desperately struggled to control his wildly fluctuating emotions. "Maria was murdered by the bastard," he rasped.

Sarah gave a little cry and pressed her hands against her lips. She stared down at Wolf and saw the terrible carnage of what had happened. Suddenly she realized why he'd made all those oblique references over the past week; that he was a failure, that he couldn't protect anyone, including her. Reaching out and placing her trembling hand on his slumped shoulder, she whispered, "Did you feel like you killed her?"

"I did," he muttered harshly. "I lost it after I found Maria dead. I went crazy. Ramirez was still running around loose. I'd already seen the daily fear and agony Maria had gone through. Who knows what she suffered at the end? I was helpless. What were words? Even while she was still alive, I hadn't been able to reach her. I couldn't even comfort her, one human being to another, when she needed to feel safe. I couldn't even do that for her. I failed her. I'd left her unprotected...."

Wolf rubbed his face savagely. "I went on a rampage. I swore I'd kill those bastards who'd murdered Maria."

"Those scars on your chest," Sarah whispered. "Don't tell me—"

"I tangled with Ramirez and his army," Wolf told her. "We fought several pitched battles around his home. I got too bold—I wasn't thinking straight—and Ramirez captured me. Killian, one of my men, tried to rescue me, but they got him, too."

Sarah shook her head. "What did they do to you?"

"Tortured me," he said numbly.

"My God! How did you survive?" she cried.

"One minute at a time. One second at a time. Ramirez had me in his special torture chamber for a month until Jake, the third man on my team, along with the Peruvian police, was able to bust me out and get me to a hospital. Killian was tortured, too, but thank God, not as bad. Ramirez was paying me back for killing his men. I was the one he wanted, because I was the leader of the team."

Shakily, Sarah covered her face with her hands. "And I thought I had problems. My God, I don't. I really don't."

Wolf forced himself to sit where he was. If he moved, he'd get up, pull Sarah in his arms and hold her. Not because she might need him, but because he needed her. And that wasn't fair. He didn't deserve her comfort. "Your problems are similar. Summers isn't as overt as Ramirez, but his goals are the same, Sarah." With a sigh, Wolf added, "That's why I promised I'd help you." Holding her tear-filled gaze, he continued. "Summers sees you as a continuing threat to him, and he's going to keep going after you. He doesn't have much to fear from the judicial system here. It's the old-boy network in action. He's got his connections. That's why I'm going to walk at your side through this mess. We'll find your attackers, and we'll find out who wanted you to die trapped beneath that fir. With or without Noonan's help."

Sarah studied him for a long time in silence. "I need to tell you about the phone call I got, Wolf."

Wolf took the washcloth and pressed it to his swollen cheek. He heard guilt in Sarah's voice. "What call?"

Rubbing her brow, she rattled, "The phone rang, and I picked it up. A man on the other end said, 'You're dead.'"

Wolf scowled, and it hurt. "Sarah—"

"I know, I know. I should have told you." She reached out and touched his shoulder. "I'm sorry, Wolf. I thought it was just one more of Summers's harassment tricks to scare me off. Oh, God, if I'd thought he was going to have his men jump you at my cabin, I'd have told you—I was trying to keep you out of it!"

Wolf awkwardly patted her hand. "It's all right," he told her in a gravelly voice. "We'll get through this."

Sarah stared down at him, tears in her eyes. "Why are you doing this for me?"

He shrugged. "Maybe I'm doing it for a couple of reasons. One of them is guilt. Every night, I see the faces of those who died in Peru. There isn't anything I don't remember about the massacre at the village, Sarah." He was loath to give voice to the other reason: He cared about Sarah—one hell of a lot. He'd been given a second chance to rectify his poor choices in Peru. He found it shocking that Sarah hadn't condemned him for his failures. Instead, she seemed to take hope as never before. He knew he couldn't divulge how he felt about her.

"It must be a living hell for you."

"We all live in a hell of some sort," he muttered.

Sarah said nothing, realizing Wolf was living with one of the worst emotions she could name—guilt. "It wasn't your fault that it happened, you know," she finally said.

"What?"

"Maria's rape."

Wolf shook his head. "Sarah, I'll go to my grave being sorry about that—for being stupid enough to be tricked by Ramirez into leaving her unprotected. Hell, I left the whole village wide open for a second attack."

"Still," Sarah said softly, "with time, some of the pain will dull. At least that's what everyone tells me about Dad's death." She rubbed the area where her heart lay. "It felt pretty raw in here, until I cried in your arms last night...."

"At least you cried," Wolf whispered huskily. "That's a good sign the healing process is going on. While I was recuperating in the hospital, I started doing some investigation on rape and what it does to a person's head and emotions. I had to try and understand Maria's actions toward me. If I'd known then what I know now, I would have gotten her to a therapist in the nearest city. She needed help, and so did I.''

"But you didn't know how to help her," Sarah said, feeling deeply for Wolf. "That's not your fault."

He rallied beneath her warm blue gaze, which was sparkling with unshed tears. How easily touched Sarah was beneath that tough shell she wore to defend her own fragile, wounded emotions. "No, I didn't know," he agreed heavily. "But—" he tendered her an intense look "—I do know now, and that's why I'm treating you the way I do. You're a victim of violence, too. And you need time to heal. I was never able to help Maria. All I did was make things worse for her, and what we shared between us died."

Sarah didn't have the words to help Wolf. Gently she steered him to another topic. "You said there were a couple of reasons for helping me. What's the second one?"

Wolf wrung out the cloth and placed it back against his cheek. If he told Sarah the truth—how much she touched him, made him feel alive again—she might run. Or, worse, tell him to go away, as Maria had. Clearing his throat, he said, "I've always had a place in my heart for underdogs." Wolf glanced up to see what affect his words had on her. Her young face was so grave and serious.

"There isn't a woman alive who isn't an underdog," Sarah said. She'd finished cleaning up his face, and now she treated his scraped, bloodied hands. Her own hands shook slightly as she dressed his wounds, her mouth a tight line, as if she were trying to stop herself from crying. Her reaction moved Wolf deeply.

"Well, we'll see if I can help even out this situation. I don't know if the men who hit me at your cabin were Summers's men—"

"They're Summers's men, all right," Sarah gritted out, washing her hands off in the sink and putting the bandages away. "That's how they work. They sneak up behind you, and they always work in pairs or a trio."

Wolf's face was aching like hell. "There's some aspirin in there, Sarah," he said, indicating the medicine cabinet. "Get me a couple of tablets?"

"Sure." She glanced down at Wolf's features. They looked washed out beneath the harsh glare. It was nearly 10:00 p.m., and he was exhausted. She handed him the aspirin and a glass of water.

"You have to report this to Sheriff Noonan. Tomorrow morning."

Wolf choked down the bitter-tasting tablets and finished off the water. He handed her the glass and thanked her. "First things first. I'm going over to the hospital emergency room tomorrow morning to find out if any of those jokers went over there. I know for sure I busted one guy's nose, and I'm pretty positive I heard the jaw of a second one crack. They'll need X rays and medical help, and the hospital's the only place around here to get them. When I've got their names, I'll start an investigation on my own, before I go to Noonan."

Sarah winced. "Sounds like you gave them worse than you got," she said, pride seeping into her voice.

"We'll see," Wolf rasped. "Look, I need to lie down."

"Yes, you do. On *your* bed." Sarah gave him a hard look. "And don't argue with me, Wolf. Ever since you started sleeping on that couch, you've had circles under your eyes."

Wolf slowly rose to his full height. How beautiful and defiant Sarah looked in her cotton nightgown and robe, her silky golden hair like a cloud around her shoulders. He longed to lose himself in those wide blue eyes.

"No, Sarah, I'll be fine out on the—"

"Damn you!" Sarah grated out. "Don't you dare argue with me, Wolf Harding!" She grabbed him by the arm and used all her strength to haul him out of the bathroom and toward the bedroom.

Wolf gripped her arm and gently drew her to a halt. "Now listen..." he rasped in the darkness of the hall, wildly aware of how close she stood to him. "You sleep on the bed. No argument, Sarah. Your feet are still healing up."

"I thought I was stubborn, but you're worse than I am! I refuse to sleep in your bed tonight!" She jerked out of his grasp and spun around to head for the living room and claim the couch before he could.

His patience thinning, Wolf gripped her shoulder. "All right," he muttered, "we'll both sleep in my bed. Now come on."

Gasping, Sarah was propelled ahead of him into the bedroom. "Wolf, this is ridiculous! I—"

He shut the bedroom door with finality and stared at her through the gloom. The defiance in her eyes made him want to smile, but his face hurt too much for him to attempt it. "Relax, will you? We both need a good night's sleep. I'll be damned if you're going to sleep on that rickety old couch."

Sarah's eyes widened as Wolf stripped out of his blood-spattered green shirt, then pulled his white T-shirt over his head. Her mouth went dry, and her heart started to leap and flutter. The sight of Wolf's powerful chest made her take a step back, but when Wolf turned, she saw a huge black bruise midway down on the right side of his back and gave a low cry of alarm.

Wolf froze at the sound of Sarah's cry. Before he could turn to see what had upset her, he felt the coolness of her hands against his back.

"What happened here, Wolf? Look at this. Look at this! It's awful!"

He stood very still, a groan threatening to rip out of him. Sarah's hands fluttered like a butterfly around the injury. She placed one hand flat against his rib cage beneath his right arm. The other gently touched the bruised area.

"I got hit from behind. The bastard tried to take me out with a kidney punch."

Biting down hard on her lower lip, Sarah explored the bruise. "It's so swollen, Wolf. You ought to go to the hospital. Really, this looks bad...."

Wolf turned and gently placed his arm around her small shoulders, drawing her in front of him. The genuine concern in her eyes melted him, and he ached to cup her small face and kiss those delicate lips.

"Honey," he rasped, "I'll be all right. Just you touching me made the pain less." Without thinking, because Sarah invited his tender side, Wolf grazed her deeply flushed cheek with his lips. Her skin was as firm and soft as a ripe peach. "Look, let's get some sleep. I'm about ready to fall over." The statement was a blatant lie now that Sarah was standing so close to him. Wolf tried to separate right from wrong. She was so damned enticing, yet he saw fear lurking in the recesses of her eyes. He didn't want to hurt Sarah as he'd unthinkingly hurt Maria. He removed his arm from her shoulder.

"Come on," he coaxed huskily. "You get in bed and turn your back to me. You'll be safe, understand?"

Swallowing, Sarah nodded, her cheek tingling where his lips had brushed it. The burning fire in his hooded eyes made her ache with a longing she'd never experienced in her life. Confused she whispered, "Sure..." Turning away from him, she did exactly as he asked and took one side of the bed. She pulled the sheet up to her waist, her back to him.

Sarah lay there, hearing Wolf's clothing drop to the floor beside the bed. She swallowed again, convulsively, unable to contain her vivid imagination, raging over the image of what it would be like to be pulled into Wolf's powerful arms in passion rather than comfort. He could crush her, he was so large in comparison to her. Yet his touch was always gossamer, painfully arousing her needs as a woman.

When the bed sagged and creaked beneath his weight, Sarah stiffened momentarily. And then she relaxed as he spread his weight out across the mattress, leaving plenty of room between them.

Wolf pulled the sheet up across his hip to his waist. He couldn't lie on his right side, his normal side to sleep on, because of the bruised kidney. Instead, he had to lie on his left side, facing Sarah's back. Just the way her golden hair lay in silky abandonment made him want to reach out and thread his fingers through it. Her cotton nightgown was cut low in the back and revealed her long, deeply indented spine. Wolf ached to reach out and pull her against him. He could almost feel her small breasts against his chest, the light warmth of her breath caressing his neck, her hands wrapping around his waist...

Chapter Nine

Wolf awoke with a start, bathed in sweat. Disoriented momentarily, the sudden movement making his body ache, he opened his eyes and blinked away the perspiration. The room, his bedroom, was washed by the early-morning light. His nostrils flaring, he inhaled sharply, a new and unfamiliar scent surrounding him like the caress of a lover.

His muddled senses sharpened, became focused. The scent, delicate and sweet, drifted toward him again. He inhaled deeply, and old, painful memories stirred to life. Then Wolf realized with a start that Sarah lay curled up next to him. Her small hand was pressed against his naked chest, as was her brow. He lay very still, not daring to move, not daring to breathe.

Sometime during the night—and Wolf sure as hell didn't know when—she had left her side of the bed, turned over and curled up in almost a fetal position against him. His eyes narrowed as he surveyed the small form covered with the crinkled white nightgown that had ridden up on her thighs during the night. Her face looked peaceful, her lips parted in sleep, fine strands of blond hair lying against her cheek.

Without thinking, Wolf barely touched her soft skin as he slipped his finger beneath the silky strands and pushed them back off her face. How serene Sarah looked. An explosion of joy rocked through him as he savored the fact that she was touching him. His heart started a hard, powerful thudding. Her hand was warm against him, as was her moist, shallow breath. Unconsciously his breath seemed to be synchronized with hers as she slept trustingly beside him.

Shifting all his awakening awareness to her, Wolf could feel the cool silk of her hair against him where her brow met the wall of his chest. Her position was endearing, telling him that Sarah probably had little experience with men. Her long, coltish legs were tucked up tightly against her body, not touching him at all. Her position was that of a child seeking safety.

Still, Wolf lay there trembling inwardly, grateful that Sarah trusted him that much—even on an unconscious level. In sleep, people showed their true selves, he believed. If she didn't trust him, she wouldn't have found her way into his arms. Savoring Sarah, Wolf closed his eyes tight as tears sprang to them. His mouth moved into a tight line as he fought back the sudden and unexpected deluge of emotion throbbing through him.

A few tears leaked out from beneath Wolf's lashes, making warm tracks down the sides of his face. Sarah didn't see him as a miserable failure, even though he'd admitted the truth of his past. What kind of forgiving heart lay in her breast, that she could grant him that kind of understanding—that she hadn't judged him? He still judged himself harshly—but, at the same time, he savored Sarah's reaction to him. For the first time in a year, hope entwined his heart. Hope for a future—if he could protect Sarah. If he could keep her safe.

Slowly, because he didn't want to awaken Sarah, Wolf lifted his arm from where it rested against his body. He didn't need to open his eyes to know where Sarah lay. He carefully placed his arm across her shoulders.

A sound, like a softened groan, issued from Wolf as his arm rested around Sarah's shoulders. The moment brought exquisite pain from the past, yet simultaneously was freeing to Wolf. Sarah lay sleeping against him, and he absorbed her into him, silently promising her he'd keep her safe—even if he had to give his life to do it.

Sarah awoke slowly. Morning sounds filtered into her awakening consciousness, and she forced her eyes open. Sunlight poured through the sheers at the window, illuminating the bedroom. What time was it? Groggily she raised her head from the mattress, seeing her pillow, as always, on the floor. It was 9:00 a.m.! She'd overslept. The bed was empty, Wolf's larger-than-life presence gone.

Turning over onto her back, Sarah closed her eyes. What crazy dreams she'd had last night! Dreams of Wolf holding her so gently that she'd wanted to cry. Lifting her hand, Sarah realized with a start that her cheeks contained dried tears. Where did dreams end and reality begin? Had she really been in Wolf's arms last night?

Sarah lay there, her gaze on the plaster ceiling as she absorbed fragments of memories, dreams, from last night. Unconsciously she slid her arm across the bed to where Wolf had slept. The sheet was cool to her touch, but a slight depression still existed where he'd lain. Her heart did funny leaps as she felt her way through the possibility that Wolf had held her as she slept. A part of her was disappointed. If he'd held her, he could have gone one step further and kissed her. And then she'd have awakened, and Sarah knew, in the dreamy state between wakefulness and sleep, she would have made love with Wolf.

The thought was as startling as it was heated. With a tremulous sigh, Sarah closed her eyes. Yes, she wanted to love Wolf. The man had had so much taken away from him. So much. She knew instinctively that she could heal some part of him by loving him. Making love was a simple act that could do so much to heal—or to rend apart. Sarah knew that from bitter experience. Her disastrous relationship with Philip had taught her that she didn't have what was necessary to make a relationship work.

Wolf's love of Maria was something she could understand—that special, fierce emotion that overlapped each day's activities, that gave each hour a special meaning. Opening her eyes, Sarah rolled to her side and tucked her hands beneath her cheek. She stared at Wolf's pillow, which had been punched and shaped to cradle his head.

Worry over how Wolf was this morning after the beating made her get up. Pushing her hair off her face, she brought her legs across the mattress and rested her toes on the carpeted floor. Outside the closed bedroom door, she could hear Wolf moving around.

Concerned, she quickly got dressed and brushed her hair. She ignored the crutches in the corner. Today she would walk a lot more on her still tender feet, she decided. She could no longer afford the luxury of remaining crippled. Wolf was in as much danger as she was, and he needed to know she was strong and reliable. Besides, sapphires needed to be dug, faceted and readied for Kirt Wagner, her distributor, by the end of the month. Without the needed money, Sarah knew, she wouldn't be able to make her mother's nursing-home payment. And that just couldn't happen.

She opened the door and discovered Skeet there to greet her. She smiled and patted the dog's broad head. He turned and trotted alongside her as she moved down the hall. Sarah found Wolf in the kitchen, making breakfast. The smell of ham was heavenly. She stood at the entrance watching him cook.

"Morning," Wolf said. He'd awakened a half hour earlier. Now he turned to see Sarah standing uncertainly, her blond hair framing her face and shoulders. Today she'd dressed in well-worn jeans and a green tank top, leaving her feet bare. Her blue eyes looked warm and serene, in sharp contrast to how he felt inside this morning. Getting to hold Sarah had been a double-edged sword, Wolf thought, arousing other, more sensual feelings of longing to plague his wounded heart.

Sarah smiled sleepily and said, "Hi..." She moved slowly toward the gas stove, where Wolf stood, turning the ham in the skillet. "I overslept."

Wolf tore his gaze from hers. The sweetness of her innocent smile, the care in her azure eyes, damn near unglued him. It took everything he had to stop himself from putting down the fork, letting go of the skillet and sweeping Sarah uncompromisingly into his arms.

Scowling, he forced himself to pay attention to the frying meat. "That makes two of us."

"Yes..." Sarah looked at her watch. "It's almost nine-thirty. How are you feeling?"

Wolf tendered her a slight smile. His face was still puffy, and one corner of his mouth hurt like hell. "I've missed something by not seeing you this time of morning," he admitted huskily. When Sarah tilted her head, not understanding his comment, Wolf added, "You look pretty."

Heat suffused Sarah's face, and she quickly avoided his burning look. Had Wolf really held her last night? His voice was low and vibrating, like the earthy growl of an animal. Her heart suddenly pounding, she turned and moved to the opposite counter. His compliment had shaken her. It was as if he could look into her heart and mind and know that she wanted to kiss him, to love him.

"Thank you," she whispered, reaching for two plates from the cupboard. But to love Wolf meant to trust him, to give everything she felt to him. And Sarah couldn't do that—the danger to them was too real. What if Wolf was killed? Sarah hated herself for thinking it, for allowing herself to feel, even for a moment, the terrible pain it created in her heart. Somehow she was just going to have to deny her feelings toward Wolf. Grasping at another topic, she said, "You still didn't tell me how you're feeling."

Wolf's mouth curved again. "How do I look?" he asked dryly.

"Like hell."

"Well, that's about how I feel."

Sarah placed the plates on the table and got out the flatware. "Your face is a mass of bruises, Wolf. Shouldn't you go to the doctor? You've got to be in a lot of pain."

"I'm okay. I called in and told my boss I was taking the day off. I want to do some checking around for those three men." The pain of longing he felt for Sarah at that moment was far greater than the pain from the beating he'd received the night before. He wondered distractedly if Sarah realized how much he wanted her.

After placing two paper napkins beside their plates, Sarah went over and poured them each a cup of coffee. "Are you going to report this to Sheriff Noonan?"

"Yes, I will," Wolf assured her. He saw the fear darken her eyes. "Stop worrying."

"How can I?"

"Because I can take care of myself, that's why." Although not very well, it was obvious, Wolf thought, feeling a deep, cutting doubt that he could keep Sarah safe. He motioned for her to sit down. "How do you want your eggs?"

Eating was the last thing on Sarah's mind. Something had changed between them, something that was now translucent, like a fine blue sapphire revealing its true shimmer in sunlight after merely glowing in indoor light. Sarah stood several seconds longer than necessary, caught in the burning intensity of his gaze.

Wolf saw the look, and his mouth went dry. She was as hungry for him as he was for her. The realization was startling, lush. Never had Wolf wanted a woman more than he did Sarah. Had she known that he was holding her last night? Could that explain the subtle change in her attitude toward him? He was afraid to ask. Afraid of finding that the answer was only some silly dream of his scarred heart.

"Wh-what?"

"Eggs," he repeated gruffly. "How do you want them?"

"Uh...scrambled, please." Sarah quickly turned away, her cheeks burning like fire. Shakily she placed the plate of ham on the table and sat down. What was going on? One moment she'd glanced at him, only to find herself gently snared in his fierce dark eyes, eyes that spoke a silent language of need for her. Rubbing her face, Sarah wondered if it was her overactive imagination. It had to be! But the dream, the exquisite memory of his arm around her, drifted back to her as she sat there, her heart slowly coming back to a normal beat.

Fighting to overcome her powerful feelings toward Wolf, she croaked out, "You know Noonan won't help you. Reporting this will be a mistake."

"Maybe. Maybe not. I want the report, Sarah. When I catch those men and bring them up on charges, Noonan isn't going to be able to sweep it under the rug like he's done in the past."

Her eyes widened considerably. "You're going after them?"

"Yes." Wolf had scrambled six eggs. Sliding half onto her plate and half onto his, he set the skillet back on the stove.

She watched as he sat down and gave her a slice of toast. "You're walking on Noonan's territory. He won't take kindly to you investigating," she warned.

Wolf buttered his toast and took a forkful of scrambled eggs. "Honey, I don't care what Noonan does or doesn't like."

"Oh." Because of her worry for him, Sarah couldn't even taste the eggs or the toast. The silence in the kitchen deepened as they ate. Half the eggs still remained when Sarah finally gave up and pushed the plate away.

"Aren't you going to eat them?" Wolf asked incredulously.

"No."

"Why not? Are you full?"

With a half shrug, Sarah pulled the cup of steaming coffee toward her. "Not exactly."

"Look at me."

Sarah refused.

"Sarah?" Wolf placed his hand on her arm. "What's wrong?"

The gentleness in his voice forced the truth from her. His fingers, long and callused, seemed to brand the skin of her arm where they rested. She ached to fling her arms around him. "I . . . uh, I'm worried about you. Okay? Those three jerks who jumped you could do it again. Next time . . ." She looked away. "Next time they might kill you, Wolf."

Wolf's fingers tightened on Sarah's arm. Her forlorn expression wasn't lost on him. She cared for him. The discovery was wonderful. Exhilarating. And he wouldn't play games with her by asking her why that worried her. Instead, he said softly, "I haven't been taken out yet, Sarah. I'll be careful, I promise." When she lifted her chin and looked at him, his heart melted with such fierce love for her that it nearly smothered him. "I've got too much to live for. Do you understand that?" he said roughly.

Sarah wasn't sure what he meant by that statement. She was bathed in the shadowed look from his gray eyes, and his voice, low and soft, flowed across her as if he'd stroked her. Shaken, she could do nothing but nod, words jammed uselessly in her constricted throat.

Wolf nudged the plate in her direction. "Go on, try to finish the eggs."

Touched to the point of tears, Sarah hung her head, her curtain of blond hair hiding her reaction. She ate everything on her plate, not tasting the food, but happier than she'd ever been—and more frightened than she would ever have thought possible.

"What if Noonan plays rough?" Sarah asked Wolf later as he got ready to leave to make out a report.

Wolf shoved his billfold in his back pocket. Today, since he was off duty, he'd dressed in jeans and a blue plaid cowboy shirt, the sleeves rolled up to his elbows. Sarah sat on the couch, worry reflected in her face and voice.

"If Noonan or Summers starts playing for keeps," Wolf said as he turned to face her, "I've got an ace up my sleeve."

"What's that?" How darkly handsome Wolf looked, Sarah thought. He was more cowboy than forest ranger. She could easily envision him astride a horse.

"My friends."

"Your team from Peru?"

"Yeah." Wolf walked over and sat down next to her. Sarah deserved a full explanation. He didn't want to cause her any more worry than necessary, but it was hard not to get distracted. She had left her hair down instead of putting it up in braids today, and he ached to sift his fingers through it.

"Sean Killian and Jake Randolph are my best friends. Jake was in the Marine Corps, like me—we got out at the same time. Killian was in the French Foreign Legion, along with Morgan Trayhern, my boss, and that's where they met, a long time ago.

"I need to give you some background on my work, Sarah," he continued, "and the people I work for. Morgan Trayhern is a Vietnam vet who got shafted by the Marine Corps. They had him up on treason charges for leaving his company when it was overrun by the enemy in Vietnam. Everybody in the States swallowed the cover-up story, except for his family and the woman he fell in love with, Laura Bennett. She began investigating Morgan's past, and together they found out a CIA boss had framed him. It's a hell of a story, and he's a hell of a man.''

"Sounds like Laura isn't too bad herself," Sarah said.

Wolf nodded. "She's a fighter, just like you.''

Eyeing him, Sarah added, "So Perseus could bring their troubleshooting skills here?''

"That's right." Wolf scowled. "I may ask them to fly into Philipsburg if I can't handle this situation on my own." He reached out and caressed her pale cheek. Her eyes were as huge as those of a child being told a scary story. "They're good men, Sarah, not killers. If I can settle this thing with Summers and his men peacefully, I will. No one hates fighting more than I do.''

She released a breath of air. "I am glad you have a backup plan," she admitted.

He grinned, even though it hurt like hell. "If I didn't learn anything else in Peru, I learned to rely on my team, to ask for help. I'll be back by noon, and I'll take you to lunch." He pointed to her feet. "Soak them in hot epsom salts and then pack them in ice.''

Sarah felt absolutely bathed in his undeniable caring. "I will." She reached forward and gripped his hand. "Wolf, be really careful, okay?''

"For you, I will be," he promised huskily, forcing himself to leave. It was that or sweep her into his arms. Rising, he said, "I'm leaving Skeet here with you. My rifle is in the bedroom. Keep the doors locked, and don't answer the phone. Understand?''

Sarah nodded, the reality of her situation burying the joy of having discovered so many things about Wolf. "I promise," she said solemnly.

When Wolf entered the jail, a man dressed impeccably in a gray silk suit, white shirt and navy tie was talking to Noonan. Noonan gave Wolf a squinty look. The man next to him turned with a calculating glance.

"Looks like you ran into a Mack truck," Noonan drawled.

Wolf closed the distance, his intuition screaming a warning about the man in the suit. He had gunmetal-gray hair, cut short and neat, dark brown eyes that were like bottomless caves, and ramrod-straight posture.

"It wasn't a truck, Sheriff." Wolf threw three photocopies of hospital reports down on the officer's desk. "I want you to make out a warrant for the arrest of these three men. They jumped me last night at Sarah Thatcher's cabin. They made the mistake of going to the emergency room to get treatment after leaving me unconscious on the cabin floor."

Noonan's mouth dropped open. He snapped it shut just as quickly. Glancing at the man in the suit, he hesitantly reached for the hospital records.

"Well, now..." He slowly perused each set of copies.

"You must be Ranger Harding," the other man said smoothly.

Wolf held his cold gaze. "That's right. Who are you?"

"Gerald Summers. I'm a local mine owner."

Wolf didn't extend his hand, and neither did Summers.

"You say three men jumped you?" Summers coaxed in a cultured voice.

"That's right." Wolf wanted to add, *Three of your men.* But it was too early to indict Summers. He shifted his focus to the sheriff, who was scowling.

"More than likely these three have left town by now," the sheriff told him testily.

"I don't care. I want warrants made out for them. Just give me the papers to sign so that you can put the legal end in motion," Wolf ordered.

Summers smiled slightly. "Sheriff, I'll leave now. Ranger Harding, nice meeting you."

Wolf nodded but said nothing. Summers reminded him of a weasel, as sleek and oily-looking as that bastard Ramirez.

"Like I said before," Noonan repeated, "these boys have probably left town."

"As *I* said before, I don't care, Sheriff. I want them caught."

Noonan's eyes hardened. "No one tells me my business, Harding."

Wolf stared back into the sheriff's belligerent eyes. "And no one gets away jumping me from behind—or trying to steal from Sarah Thatcher."

Leaning forward, resting his palms on his desk, Noonan looked Wolf over. "Kinda chummy with her, ain't you?" he asked finally.

"That has no bearing on this," Wolf growled, pointing at the copies.

"Yep, she's got you wrapped around her little finger. She did that once to a guy name Philip Barlow, you know. Poor fella was all the worse for it. He had to leave town once she got done with him. A real viper, she is."

Gritting his teeth, Wolf leaned across the desk. "Noonan, I don't want to hear one more thing out of that filthy mouth of yours about Sarah Thatcher. Got it? Your job is to track down these bastards. If you don't do it, I'll make sure it happens. Do we understand each other?"

Noonan's eyes grew large, then squinted in fury. He came bolting around his desk and clutched at Wolf's shirtfront.

Instantly Wolf grabbed the sheriff's soft white hand with his own. "Don't do it if you want to live, Noonan," he ground out softly.

Releasing Wolf's shirt, Noonan straightened, his face white with anger. "Get outa here, Harding. You're bad news, just like that Thatcher woman. A cold wind follows you, mister. A real cold one."

"I'm coming in here tomorrow to find out what you've done about apprehending those three men, Sheriff."

"Don't threaten me!"

Wolf walked slowly to the door, then stopped, his hand resting lightly on the doorknob. "It's not a threat, it's a promise."

"No one tells me my job!"

"I'll be here at 1:00 p.m.," Wolf snarled. He jerked open the door and left.

Outside, the weather was warming quickly. It was eleven o'clock and he had enough time to get home, pick up Sarah and take her someplace special for lunch, Wolf thought. He was looking forward to it. Every minute was precious when it was spent with Sarah. He frowned as he got into his truck. As he drove away from the jail, Wolf wondered who this Philip Barlow character was. Momentary jealousy stabbed at him, and he had trouble shrugging it off. The idea of any man making love to Sarah made Wolf uneasy. His grandmother had always said he had a bit of a jealous streak, but it had never surfaced—not until now. Then Wolf recalled the rest of his grandmother's words—that his jealousy would only rear its head when he fell in love with the woman who would walk with him as his wife.

Rubbing his brow, Wolf replayed his medicine-woman grandmother's prediction. He'd never been jealous of Maria in any way, he had to admit. He'd known that she'd had two lovers before him, and it had never bugged him. But this Philip whoever-he-was bothered the hell out of him. Was he an ex-lover? An ex-husband? Wolf knew so little about Sarah, and suddenly he wanted to know everything.

Chapter Ten

The noontime trade at Francey's Diner consisted mostly of tourists, and for that Sarah was grateful. She didn't want locals who worked for Summers to see her with Wolf or possibly eavesdrop on their conversation. As it was, she and Wolf were seated in a vinyl-covered booth at the rear of the diner, as far from the other patrons as possible, and they kept their voices low.

Wolf sat opposite her, their knees brushing beneath the narrow table. Sarah was hungry, finishing off a hamburger platter with relish, but she noticed that Wolf had left his hot beef sandwich practically untouched.

"What's bothering you?" she asked, blotting her mouth with a paper napkin.

Wolf shrugged. "Not much." He'd told her about the incident with Noonan, but not about Philip Barlow. There was no sense in making Sarah suffer because the sheriff hated her. She'd had enough nasty words flung at her.

Tilting her head, Sarah smiled. "You're brooding. You look like a thunderstorm ready to split open and pour down rain."

Wolf attempted to return her smile. "Good analogy," he told her. Moving his fork absently around the table-top next to his plate, he added, "It's nothing." It was something, all right, and Wolf was becoming angry with himself, because it seemed that he could hide nothing from Sarah's perception. Jealousy ate at him, although he knew it shouldn't.

"Oh." Sarah sat back and picked up her mug of coffee. "I thought friends could share problems and concerns."

"They can."

"I'll listen if you want to talk," she said softly.

Wolf glanced up at her, on the verge of asking about Philip. He knew he was behaving like some immature sixteen-year-old kid—and it was making him mad. Swallowing, he shook his head. "It's nothing," he repeated.

"For once, I'd like to help you," Sarah whispered. "I'm not a world traveler, and I don't have more than a high school education, but maybe all you need is a set of ears."

"Sarah," he said, scowling, "stop putting yourself down."

"Was I?"

"Yes. You've got so much going for you. You've got drive, energy and brains. You handle a career like gem mining all by yourself. And," he said, "successfully. I've seen college grads and Ph.D.s who were worthless at running a business."

Grinning, Sarah said, "Okay, so I'm a good business-woman. Thank you."

"You're welcome." Wolf saw a slight flush come to Sarah's cheeks. What she needed was a little care, a little pampering—a focus on her strengths.

"So," he said, moving aside his platter of uneaten food, "how did you manage to get half this town angry at you?"

With a laugh, Sarah said, "It wasn't hard, Wolf. My dad bucked Summers, and after he died, so did I."

"You had a reputation as a troublemaker even back in high school," he said, baiting her.

Frowning, she agreed. "Yes, I did. As my mom said, I don't suffer fools gladly." Sarah brightened. "My mom was always quoting different passages, things that made sense to me." Her happiness faded. "That's one of the things I miss about her since the stroke. She always had the right saying for any occasion."

Wolf hurt for her. "At least she's alive, and there's a part of her left," he said gently. Maybe he should take Sarah to the nursing home to see her mother. "And you love her. She knows that."

Sarah shrugged unhappily and sipped her coffee. "Maybe she does, maybe she doesn't. I just wish . . ."

"What?" Wolf said softly, absorbing her sad, pensive face.

With a sigh, Sarah forced a slight smile. "I just wish Mom was still here. I really miss talking to her and getting her advice. She sure helped me get through some tough times."

"Such as?"

Sarah gave him an arched-eyebrows look. "My reputation in this town was bad news after the FBI investigation, Wolf. A lot of locals wouldn't have anything to do with me—of course, a lot of them work for Summers. But even those who don't are afraid of him." She gave him an apologetic look. "See what happened to you because you've sided with me? They almost beat you to death."

Raising her hand to his lips, Wolf kissed her fingers gently. The need to give her some solace burned hotly through him, and he watched as her eyes widened at the touch of his lips on her skin.

"I wasn't beaten to death, Sarah. You have a tendency to blow things out of proportion."

Sarah's fingers tingled pleasantly. For a moment, she sat in shock from Wolf's unexpected kiss. Scrambling to find words, she said, "I know."

Smiling, Wolf reluctantly released her hand. "That's one of the many things I like about you, Sarah Thatcher." How much heartbreak Sarah had endured. The look in her eyes was one of warmth mixed with desire. Wolf wondered if it could really be desire for him.

Sarah's heart wouldn't settle down. She had watched his strong mouth gently graze her hand, and the sensation had shone like sunlight through her until she ached to love him. But did he like her enough to want her? She sat digesting those thoughts as she finished her coffee.

Wolf pulled his platter back in front of him and began to eat the now-cooled beef sandwich, potatoes and gravy. Sarah smiled.

"What brought back your appetite?"

"Talking with you."

She gave him a rueful look. "Noonan must have mentioned my name when you went to see him."

"Yes. And not in very pleasant terms."

"I'm sure." Sarah fingered her sweat-beaded water glass. "I'm not a mean person, Wolf, although part of this town may paint me that way. I'm a fair-minded person. And I'm easily touched by sad stories.'' She gave a little laugh.

"You bluster a lot, but underneath you've got a soft heart, honey,'' he agreed.

Sarah blushed at the endearment, drowning in the burning gray of his gaze. "Mom always called me feisty,'' she admitted wryly with a widening smile. "I'd get my hackles up at the drop of a hat, but then, I'd cool down just as quickly.''

"You're a woman of fire. I like that.''

The words, gritty and low, made Sarah quiver with a hunger she'd never experienced. "Y-yes, I guess you could say I am.'' The powerful intimacy that had sprung up between them frightened Sarah badly. Each time she held Wolf's tender gaze, more of her trust reached out to him. It just couldn't happen! Inwardly she began to panic. When she was around Wolf, she automatically surrendered to him, to the emotions that blossomed in his presence. Summers posed a physical danger to her, but Sarah felt the danger of being around Wolf becoming even more frightening.

"After lunch I'll take you to see your mom at the nursing home, if you want.''

Desperate, Sarah jerked her chin upward and met his gaze. "I—No. I called the nursing home when you were gone, and she's doing fine. She really doesn't miss me.'' Nervously she moved the water glass around between her hands and tried to prepare herself for the explosion she knew was coming. "Wolf, I want to go back to the cabin today.''

Her pleading tone tore at him. Frowning, he muttered, "You're not ready to go back there, Sarah.''

"I have to! You know I've got to mine enough sapphires to pay the bills coming up."

Wolf stopped eating and again pushed his plate aside. Sarah had both elbows on the table and was leaning forward, her eyes intense and stubborn-looking. "I can't protect you if you're up there, Sarah."

"I can protect myself. Wolf, take me home—please." Sarah had other reasons for leaving. She knew that if she remained with Wolf she might do something embarrassing and stupid.

Leaning back in the booth, Wolf held on to his patience. "Why can't you work at the house?"

"It's impossible," Sarah said, spreading her hands. "I've got to dig more sapphires."

The conversation was getting too heated. Wolf looked around and dug money out of his billfold. "Come on," he growled. "We'll talk about this on the way home."

Sarah glanced around, realizing she'd become a little too loud. Wolf was right: The diner was no place to discuss the situation. She remained silent until they were on their way home, Skeet sitting between them.

Wolf broke the silence. "Look, if it's the money worrying you, I'll give you whatever you need, Sarah." Holding her pleading stare, he added, "I'll pay your bills. I'd rather have you safe than out on that mountain alone."

Desperation filled Sarah. "No, Wolf. I've never taken anyone's money, and I'm not starting now. Thanks, but—"

"Make it a loan, then."

Tensing, Sarah whispered, "No."

His mouth tightening, Wolf lowered his voice as he pulled into the driveway of the house. He slammed the truck into park and turned to Sarah. "All right, level with me. Why do you suddenly want to leave?"

Blinking, Sarah whispered rawly, "Because I'm drawn to you, Wolf, that's why." She watched him rear back as if he'd been struck, surprise written all over his harsh features. "Well, you don't have to act like that," she said bitterly. "Don't worry, I'll keep to myself." She climbed out of the truck and nearly ran into the house, Wolf following close behind.

Once they were in the living room, Wolf gripped her by the shoulders. "We need some straight talk," he rasped. He realized how tightly he was gripping her, and eased his fingers a bit. "You're afraid if you stay around me that something will happen?"

Hanging her head, Sarah nodded. Wolf's hands were like brands on hers. "I can't trust myself. It's not you...."

Wryly Wolf said, "Don't kid yourself. This is a two-way street, Sarah. But we can deal with this like adults. You don't have to run away from me, from the protection I can give you." He watched Sarah's head snap up, her eyes huge.

Sarah forced herself to meet and hold Wolf's gaze. There was such tenderness in his eyes that she felt her breath escape in response. As a lover, Wolf would be cherishing with her, Sarah realized instinctively in that moment. All the more reason to leave. But she saw the set of his jaw and knew that Wolf wouldn't let her go—at least not yet.

Driven to a point of desperation she'd never thought she'd feel, she twisted out of his grip. Taking several steps back, she lied to him. "I need time to think this over, Wolf. I—I want to go see my mother and think about it."

Wolf raised his eyebrows. She'd said she didn't want to visit the nursing home. Sarah's face was flushed, and there was fear in her eyes. Wolf wrestled with the knowledge she'd shared with him. He knew that she was scared. He nodded. "Maybe that would be better," he agreed thickly. Inwardly he breathed a sigh of relief that Sarah was going to remain under his roof.

"Come on," he said, all the emotion draining from his voice. "I'll take you over there."

"Fine," Sarah rattled. "Just let me get my purse." Her mind was racing with alternative plans. Somehow she would find someone—perhaps Pepper Sinclair, the closest thing she had to a friend in this town—to drive her up to the cabin. Once she got there, Wolf would realize too late that she'd meant what she said. She had to get away from him. He moved her as no man had ever done, and Sarah couldn't risk losing the last of her disintegrating self-reliance to Wolf.

Part of her was relieved, but another part was crying out that she would miss Wolf's company, his presence. The feelings she'd had for Philip and those she held for Wolf were chasms apart. Her mother had told her what real love was like, how it felt, and what it meant. Did she love Wolf? The thought was pulverizing, sweet and unsure.

In front of the nursing home, Sarah turned to Wolf. She ached at having hurt him. Dragging in a breath, Sarah said, "I want to meet Pepper Sinclair when I'm done seeing Mom."

"Who's Pepper?"

"She's a smoke jumper for the forestry department. I'm surprised you haven't met her yet. She's the only woman on the team."

Wolf roused himself from his unhappiness that Sarah wanted to leave. "No...I haven't met her, yet. I heard her name mentioned once."

Sarah forced a small smile. "She's a lot like me—independent and a fighter."

"Are you two friends?"

With a shrug, Sarah said, "I guess Pepper is a friend to me—but I haven't been a very good one to her."

"Because of the trust issue?" Wolf guessed grimly.

"Yes." Sarah licked her lower lip. "I'll call her from here, Wolf. I . . . I need some time away from you—from everything."

"How are you getting home?" he asked, trying not to feel the smarting pain of her honesty.

"I'll have Pepper drop me off. It'll be a couple of hours, so don't worry, okay?" She looked up to see the torture in his eyes and felt terrible for her dishonesty. More than anything, Sarah wanted to avoid subjecting Wolf to an argument over her leaving. This way it would be cleaner, less hurtful to both of them.

"Just keep your eyes open, Sarah. I don't trust Summers at all."

Without meaning to, Sarah reached out and grazed his puffy cheek. "I'll be careful because you care," she told him, her voice quavering. And she would.

The tingling dulled the pain in his jaw. Wolf watched her leave the truck. Unhappy, he sat with his hands resting on the steering wheel. There was nothing he could do to stop Sarah. He'd lost Maria through a very stupid mistake; he didn't want to lose Sarah the same way. He tried to tell his hammering heart that she would be safe enough at the nursing home. And he'd heard that Pepper Sinclair was a woman warrior in disguise.

Sighing, Wolf put the truck in gear and backed out of the asphalt parking lot. His entire body ached, but, worse, his heart was in utter turmoil. Sarah had admitted some of her feelings for him. He tried to understand the terrible pressures that must put on her. She didn't want to trust him, didn't want to like him, but she did. Exasperated, Wolf left the nursing home. He'd go take a nap, and maybe, by the time he awoke, Sarah would be home.

Sarah moved guiltily around her cabin. Pepper had just left, and she was alone for the first time in nearly a week. The silence of the cabin was nerve-racking; something it had never been to her before. Nervously, Sarah looked at her watch. Two hours had passed since Wolf had trustingly left her at the nursing home.

Staring at the phone, Sarah knew she should call him. She didn't want Wolf to worry. Perhaps she'd wait another half hour... She dreaded calling him—dreaded his reaction. The cabin needed to be dusted and mopped. She noticed that Wolf had all the lapidary equipment back in place after Summers's henchmen had tried to steal it. One chair—her rocker—was broken. Moving over to it, sadness stole through Sarah as she gently touched the back of it.

Forcing herself to get to work as the evening light began to steal through the cabin windows, Sarah tried to focus her energy on housecleaning. She should be happy to be home, but somehow she wasn't. The vacuum cleaner was a noisy old machine, and Sarah ran it over the burnished cedar floor. Brushing strands of damp hair off her brow, she finally finished cleaning the living room and shut it off.

A car door slammed in the driveway. Sarah jerked up, her heart pounding. Summers? Or Wolf? She froze, the vacuum in hand. She saw the shadow of a man pass the kitchen window, heading for the door. Gulping, Sarah dropped the vacuum handle. Sharp banging on the door made her jump.

"Sarah?"

Her mouth dropped open. Wolf stood at the kitchen door.

Crushing her hand against her breast in relief, she hurried as fast as her healing feet would take her to the back door. She saw the agitation on Wolf's face and tried to emotionally prepare for his righteous anger. Opening the door, she muttered, "How did you know I came home?"

Wolf held onto his anger as he moved into the kitchen. He deliberately shut the door softly behind him. Sarah's face was riddled with guilt. "I got worried," he said, "and I called the nursing home. They said you left with Pepper. When you didn't come to my house, I figured you came up here."

"I—I'm sorry, Wolf."

"You didn't have to lie to me, Sarah," he said sadly.

"Yes, I did!" she cried, moving into the living room.

Wolf followed. "Don't you realize you're at risk?" he demanded hoarsely, stalking up to her until mere inches separated them.

Belligerently, Sarah raised her chin and met the fierce thunderstorm of his eyes. "Risk?" she cracked. "Being with you is the biggest risk of all, Wolf! Don't you realize that? I tried to tell you earlier . . . I tried . . ." And she took a step back, choking on the words.

Blindly Wolf made a grab for Sarah. He thought she was going to run from him—again. His hands closed

around her upper arms, and he drew her against him.
"No," he rasped. "Don't run, Sarah. You make yourself a target, and I can't... I can't let you be killed!"

With a whimper, Sarah tried to pull away. Wolf was
too close, too overpowering, and his masculinity was
undoing her in every way. Raw emotions flowed through
her, ribbons of need entwining with heat and longing.
Tears stung her eyes as she lifted her hands to push at
him.

It was impossible!

Instinctively Wolf cupped Sarah's face with his hands.
There was such love radiating from her eyes—mixed with
her fear of her feelings for him—that he couldn't stop
himself. His breathing suspended as he barely grazed
Sarah's parted, waiting lips. A soft moan came from her.
His hands tightened imperceptibly on her face, and he
made contact with her again, feeling her lips move shyly
beneath his. There was such uncertainty coupled with the
need in her kiss. Her mouth opened as a flower opens to
the sun's rays, lush and questing. This time, Wolf's control disintegrated, and he met and melded hotly with her
lips. A groan reverberated through him like thunder.
Sarah's returning kiss was hungry, inciting a fire within
him. Despite her awkwardness, her shyness, Wolf
drowned in the heat and fire of her offering. The spicy
scent of her hair and velvety feel of her skin filled his
senses, dizzying him.

Sarah drowned in the splendor of Wolf's fiery kiss. His
mouth was strong and coaxing. Her nostrils flaring, she
drank in the scent of Wolf, a combination of pine and
fresh air and pure male. Her fingers tensed against his
barrel chest, and she felt one of his hands slide down the
length of her spine and tightly capture her hips against

his. The contact was shocking, pleasurable. Gasping, Sarah broke the kiss, gulping for air.

Instantly Wolf released her. She swayed. He caught her gently by the arm and allowed her to lean against him. They were both trembling.

"Sweet," he breathed against her hair, his arm going around her shoulder as she sank weakly against him, "you make a man tremble like a willow in a thunderstorm."

Sarah couldn't talk, she could only feel. She burrowed her head against his chest, hearing the wild beating of his heart. His arms swept around her, and she surrendered to his superior strength. After a moment, Sarah lifted her head and gazed up into his stormy eyes— and what she saw there was a combination of savage hunger and tenderness.

The kiss should never have happened, her mind screeched at her. But, somehow, Sarah couldn't fight herself any longer. Wolf was just as stunned by the kiss as she was, she was sure. It had happened like lightning striking them, leaving them shaken in its wake.

Wolf gently eased just far enough away from Sarah to see her flushed features. As her lashes lifted to reveal lustrous blue eyes, he groaned silently. Her lips were glistening from the power of his kiss, and he reeled with need of her. Trying to grapple with the situation, he rasped, "I never want to share anything but honesty about how we feel about each other." His voice was low as he lightly removed strands of golden hair from her cheek. "You give me hope, Sarah. I felt dirtier than hell before meeting you, and you make me feel clean inside." He continued to stroke the crown of her hair, marveling at the way the light changed and danced across the strands. "I'm still carrying a lot of guilt about Maria, about what happened. When you started living with me, I started feeling differently about myself, maybe about the world in general.'' He gave her an embarrassed look. "You have that kind of effect on me, honey. You're one of a kind, a special woman. Magical.''

Sarah clung to his words. They were spoken with such reverence. "It shouldn't have happened, Wolf.''

"We both wanted it.''

Wincing, Sarah bowed her head. "I felt so terrible lying to you, Wolf. I'm scared . . . so scared . . .''

The tremor in her voice deeply affected him. "I know, honey. So am I—for different reasons.'' He grazed her cheek. "You're afraid to trust outside yourself, and I'm afraid I can't protect you well enough to deserve that trust.''

Sarah nodded, but she knew Wolf was questioning his own ability to love, too. "Let me stay here, Wolf. Give me the time I need,'' she pleaded.

"Sarah—''

"No, hear me out—I have a gun. I know how to use the thing! I'm a crack shot, and believe me, I've shot at Summers's men before.'' She pulled out of his arms, hating herself for it, hating the loss she saw in Wolf's eyes. "You've got to understand, Wolf. Being around you is a special kind of hell for me! I—I can't keep my mind on Summers while I'm trying to deal with the emotions you pull out of me.'' Opening her hands, her voice dropping, she whispered, "Please, let me stay here. I'll be okay. I know I will.''

Wolf's gut warned him that Sarah wasn't safe at all. But what could he do? He couldn't kidnap her. He wouldn't force himself on her in any way. The hot memory of their explosive kiss seared him. Maybe Sarah was right: The emotions that leaped to life between them were too much for either of them to deal with right now. Maybe they needed a cooling-off period.

"Okay," he growled, finally. "I'll go back to the house and pick up your clothes and the faceter."

Relief tunneled through Sarah. "I know how hard it is for you to let me go...."

Grimly Wolf held her tearful gaze. Words choked in his throat, and all he could do was nod.

Drowning in his lambent gaze, Sarah whispered, "It's nice having someone in my corner who believes in me."

"I've got to get going," Wolf heard himself say. "Are you sure you want to do this?"

Sarah nodded and took a step back from his imposing height. "I have to, Wolf."

"I'll be back in about two hours," he promised. Fear for her safety ate away at him. He felt completely helpless. "Be careful," he warned, and then he left.

It was almost nine in the evening when Sarah got ready to take her shower. Wolf had been gone almost an hour, and she knew he'd be home by now, packing her clothes. The kiss still hovered hotly on her lips, she caught herself touching them, feeling the power of Wolf's mouth molding against her own. Never had she been kissed like that. She'd tasted him, felt his heart thudding in unison with her own. Most of all, she'd felt as if she were merged with him, all the way to his tired, wounded soul.

Absently Sarah touched the broken rocking chair, caught up in her escaped feelings for Wolf. The kiss had ripped away her pretenses, her lies to herself about not trusting Wolf. Standing there, she shut her eyes and felt a new kind of pain drift through her vulnerable heart. Did she know what real love was? She wished she could talk to her mother about the wildly fluctuating feelings

she had for Wolf. In comparison, the relationship she'd
had with Philip had been tame.

Opening her eyes, Sarah chastised herself for thinking
too much. Her mother had always told her to flow with
her feelings and not let her head interfere. But if she allowed her feelings to flow, they would wrap around Wolf
in every way. It wasn't that she couldn't live her life
without Wolf's presence; it was simply that her life was
better with him around. He somehow enhanced her, and
it made her feel awakened as a woman, made her feel that
she possessed sensual longings she hadn't known existed.

As she walked across the living room toward the bathroom, Sarah glanced up. She jerked to a halt, thinking
she must be imagining things. Out of the corner of her
eye she saw the shadow of a man cross the darkened
window. Her heart started a slow, uneven pounding. Was
it her overactive imagination playing tricks on her? Ever
since Wolf had left, she'd felt nervous and vulnerable.

Licking her lower lip, Sarah stared hard at the curtained window. There! Another shadow! A small cry
broke from her. It wasn't her imagination. It was Summers's men! Because her feet were healing, Sarah
couldn't turn quickly. Awkward in her movements, she
lurched toward the bedroom to get the rifle that sat in the
corner. Hurry! The door in the kitchen was being jim-
mied. Her throat constricted.

A cry broke from Sarah as she saw three men with
bandaged faces rush through the door into the cabin. The
cedar floor was highly polished, and she was in her
stocking feet. Rattled, she slipped in the hallway and fell.
She heard one man grunt as he came closer to her. Sarah
scrambled to her knees. Forgetting the rifle, she lunged
to her feet and ran toward the front door of the cabin.

Jamming her hand around the doorknob, she tried to pull the door open. Escape! She had to escape!

"Hold it!" a man snarled, settling his hand on her shoulder and gripping her hard.

Blindly Sarah lashed out with her elbow as she was dragged backward. Pain and light exploded along the side of her face and jaw. She slammed against the door and crumpled to the floor.

"Don't move."

Gulping for breath, Sarah opened her eyes. Three men dressed in cowboy shirts, jeans and boots were hunkered over her. They moved aside when a fourth man entered the cabin.

"Summers," Sarah hissed.

Chapter Eleven

Shakily Sarah pressed her hand against her smarting cheek. It was bloody. Trying to steady her breathing, she glared up at Summers as he approached. He wore a suit, and, as always, he appeared freshly groomed. In his hand he held a sheaf of papers.

"Sign this."

"Like hell I will."

Summers's mouth curled. "It's an agreement, Sarah, that you're turning over the mine to me for the tidy sum of fifty thousand dollars. Now, that's not a bad profit for a quarter of this mountain, is it?"

Sarah pushed herself to her feet, using the door as a support because her knees were wobbly. Looking around at the hardened faces of Summers's men, she realized that two of them were the same men who'd attacked her before. One grinned at her. She shrank back against the door.

"You can kill me, Summers, but I'll never turn this place over to you. Never!" she cried.

Summers gave a one-shouldered shrug. "Billy here said he owes you for cold-cocking him with that prospector's hammer." Summers smiled evenly. "You've always been wild, Sarah. Your reputation precedes you. Billy, wouldn't you like to even the score?" He turned to the man, who nodded, his angry gaze riveted on Sarah. Summers smiled a little more. "If you sign, we'll leave right now, Sarah."

Her heart pounding in her chest, Sarah crouched, fear overcoming her. Billy's large nose was bandaged. Wolf must have broken it the day before.

"What if I don't sign?"

"Well, first I'll let Billy even the score with you, and then we'll leave. But we'll be back tomorrow night. The boys might get bored fighting you and want some other kind of fun." Summers looked around the cabin. "Be a shame if this place went up in smoke..."

"No!" Sarah's voice cracked with fury and disbelief.

He lost his smile. "And if you refuse even after you've got cinders at your feet, Sarah, we'll keep harassing you until you do sign. Understand?" He held out the paper and pen once more. "Make it easy on yourself. Sign now."

Rage exploded violently within Sarah. Without thinking, she pushed away from the door and lunged for Summers. He barely dodged her flailing fists, knocking over the other man as he stumbled backward to dodge her attack.

"Get her!" Summers roared as he fell to the floor.

Sarah scrambled toward the kitchen. Throwing herself out the back door, she dug her toes into the pine needles and dry soil, disappearing into the darkness. Pain shot through her feet and ankles, but she ignored it as she raced away from the cabin. No one knew this mountain more intimately than she did. Two of the men were coming after her. The night was bathed in black. Sarah swerved to the left. There was a ten-foot drop-off just ahead. If she could make it without breaking an ankle or her leg, she could lose her pursuers.

Wind tore past her as she stretched her stride to the maximum. Both men were bearing down upon her, and she heard them cursing and gasping for air. Just a few more feet! The edge of the rock ledge was coming up fast. Sarah threw herself off it, bending her knees to take the impact of landing.

She hit the ground hard, automatically flexing and rolling to absorb the jarring shock. Quickly she scrambled to her hands and knees, then pushed to a standing position. A scream lurched from one of the men above her. There was no time to take satisfaction in the thought of the two men falling over the cliff. Sarah ran to the right and crouched down, pushing through several bushes. Behind the shrubbery was a small cranny in the rock, a cavelike depression.

Sarah pressed her hands across her nose and mouth to try to soften the sound of her breathing. She heard both men strike the forest floor, one groaning loudly. The other cursed. She sat very still, her knees jammed against her chest and chin. Rock wall bit into her back, but she ignored the discomfort. Anything was better than being beaten or raped. Anything. Shaky with adrenaline, Sarah concentrated on trying to breathe quietly.

The cursing grew louder. Sarah hunched down as one of the shadowy figures came close to her hiding spot.

"Son of a bitch!" Billy yelled. "She got away!"

"Screw the bitch," the other one groaned. "Come back here and help me. I think I busted my ankle, Billy. Dammit to hell!"

Sarah's eyes had adjusted to the darkness, and she saw Billy hesitate near the bushes where she hid, then turn back to help the other man. Burying her head in her arms, Sarah breathed through her mouth, trying to stay quiet. Both men hobbled off, and in a few minutes the forest had grown quiet again.

How long Sarah waited, she didn't know. Finally, the urgent need to warn Wolf that Summers and his men were at the cabin got the better of her. Disregarding her painful feet, she slowly extricated herself from the depression and carefully moved along the cliff wall. A deer path led back toward the cabin and the road, she knew. She had to warn Wolf before he ran into Summers and his gang!

By the time Sarah made it back to her cabin, Summers and his men were gone. She stood just inside the tree line, wondering if it was a trick. No trucks were in her driveway. It was quiet. Deathly quiet. Beginning to tremble in earnest, Sarah wrapped her arms around herself. The summer nights were always cool in the mountains, and sometimes chilly. Her keen hearing picked up the sound of a truck being driven at high speed down the dirt road toward her cabin. Was it Wolf, or was it Summers returning?

Sarah waited, positioning herself so that the headlights wouldn't flash over her and give away her position. As the truck drove into the driveway and braked to a halt next to the cabin, she realized it was Wolf.

With a little cry, Sarah lurched out of the forest. Sobbing Wolf's name, she ran toward him, her arms open.

Wolf emerged from the pickup and heard Sarah's cry. Startled, he jerked around toward the sound. His eyes widened enormously. Sarah's shadowed features were twisted with fear, and blood was smeared along her cheek. Wolf grabbed his rifle off the rack and loaded a round in the chamber. Skeet leaped down, remaining at his side. His breathing was strangled, and his heart was beating hard in fear. Terrible flashbacks of finding the Peruvian villagers slaughtered slammed into Wolf as he stood frozen for that moment.

"Sarah!"

A cry broke from her as she staggered into his arms. Instantly she was surrounded by Wolf's strength, by the protection of his arms and massive body.

"Summers was here!" she sobbed.

Wolf's senses were screamingly alive. He held Sarah as she collapsed against him, but his gaze never stopped roving around the area.

"What happened?" Wolf rasped. "Honey, are you okay? Talk to me! Are you okay?"

Sarah nodded, burying her face in his shirtfront, shaking so hard that her knees were threatening to give out from under her. "It was Summers. He came when you left, Wolf. I—I'm all right. I was so scared . . . so scared . . ."

Getting a better hold on Sarah because she appeared faint, Wolf guided her toward the cabin and the open kitchen door. "Hang on," he growled. "Are they gone?"

"I—I think so." The light hurt Sarah's eyes as Wolf led her up on the wooden porch and into the kitchen.

Wolf placed her against the counter. "Stay here," he ordered tightly. "If you hear firing, drop to the floor and then get the hell out of here. Understand?"

Sarah looked up at him. This was a side of Wolf she'd never seen before: the mercenary. His face was impassive, covered with a fine sheen of sweat, and his eyes were merciless. The ease with which he held the rifle made her tremble with fear. She gave a jerky nod of her head, and he turned away to search the rest of the house.

Unable to move because she was afraid she'd fall, Sarah leaned against the counter until Wolf returned. Skeet had remained at her side, guarding her fiercely.

"It's safe," Wolf announced as he returned to the kitchen. All his attention swung to Sarah, and he placed the rifle on the counter. The blouse she wore had been torn open, her jeans were dust-covered and she wore no shoes. His gaze moved up to her face. A long scratch had bloodied her cheek and temple. The terrible realization that he'd failed to protect Sarah from danger sheared through him. He'd left her undefended for two hours, and Summers had capitalized upon the opportunity. Anger surged through Wolf.

"Come here," he ordered tightly, "and sit down." He pulled a chair out from the table.

Sarah collapsed into the chair as Wolf moved to the sink and wet a cloth. When he returned, he moved her and the chair so that she was facing him. Kneeling down, he placed the cold cloth against her cheek and gently began to clean away the blood.

"Tell me what happened," he said gruffly. Sarah's eyes looked haunted and shocky. Her pupils were dilated and black, and her flesh was cool and translucent.

Stuttering and stammering, Sarah told him everything. When she mentioned Billy and told him he'd intended to beat her up, Wolf winced visibly. His hand tightened momentarily on her arm. Then, becoming aware of the pressure, he released some of his hold.

"I—I had to escape, Wolf," Sarah rattled as he continued patiently cleaning her face, neck and arms.

"They could have killed you," he agreed in a shaken tone.

Miserable, Sarah held his tortured gaze. "You were right," she whispered, "I was wrong to come back here alone. This was my fault, Wolf. I'm so sorry...." And she reached out to him, because right now she needed to be held more than ever before.

Wolf pulled Sarah out of the chair and into his arms. He shakily pushed the hair away from her eyes and face. "It's okay, honey. It's my fault. All my fault. I shouldn't have left you alone...."

Sarah slid her hands upward to frame his bruised and swollen face. "No," she choked out. "Don't do this to yourself, Wolf. I was the one who tricked you, who lied to you." She saw the haunted wildness in his gaze. Tears glittered on his short black lashes. A small cry escaped her as she threw her arms around his broad shoulders and held him as hard as she could. Sarah understood his tears; they were for the past, which had come back to haunt Wolf in this very moment. He had loved Maria, and despite her shock she knew he was vividly recalling that time in his life. To lose her as he had Maria would have been too much.

Wolf buried his face in Sarah's hair and felt all her woman's strength go around him, holding him, caring for him. Tears leaked from his tightly shut eyes. His mouth moved into a tight line, fighting back a sudden and unexpected deluge of emotions that tunneled up through his chest. How many times had he ached to have Maria come to him and hold him like this. After the rape, she'd tried to sleep with Wolf, as she had before, but it was impossible. The six months following her terrible ordeal had been agonizing, the nights spent tossing sleeplessly, knowing she lived in her parent's hut and not with him. They'd carved a scar on Wolf's heart he'd thought would never disappear.

The driving need to give Maria solace against the fears that stalked her day and night had nearly driven Wolf insane. He'd fall asleep for just a little while, then jerk awake, his arms wrapped around him, as if Maria had been there, as if he'd been holding her as he had before the rape.

Tears trickled down Wolf's face, and he tightened his embrace around Sarah's slender form. He'd failed abysmally, and he was once again overwhelmed by the grief he'd never released over Maria's murder. As Sarah's arms held him, a sob worked its way up and out of Wolf. His entire body shook, his focus narrowing on the pain rushing up through him.

"It's all right," Sarah whispered brokenly, caressing Wolf's shoulder. Tears touched her eyes. She'd never seen a man cry before, and it tore her apart. Sarah understood the source of Wolf's weeping, and she had never wanted to help someone as she did him. He hadn't left her since that day he'd found her. He'd been loyal and unswerving in his devotion to her, and to her safety. Pressing small kisses against his cheek, temple and neck, Sarah allowed herself to trust Wolf as never before. He deserved nothing less.

A soft groan issued from Wolf as Sarah's small kisses grazed his flesh. The moment was exquisite as the internal anguish dissolved and freed Wolf. He'd never been able to console Maria. Now, with Sarah holding him with all her strength and courage, he released the woman he'd loved and lost so long ago.

Sarah felt the emotional storm within Wolf diminish. She felt his entire body lose its tension. All she wanted to do was console Wolf—the touch of her hand upon his thick black hair, a reassuring embrace with her arms, or the soft whisper of her voice near his ear. At least that she could do. After what she'd put him through because of her own fears and lack of trust, Sarah hoped her presence, her care, would be enough.

Feeling gutted, Wolf slowly loosened his hold on Sarah.

"Let's go into the living room, to the couch," Sarah urged softly, and led him through the cabin to the cedar couch. Sitting down close to Wolf, she felt her heart burst with compassion as he raised his hand and dried the tears on his face. His gray eyes looked wounded, and Sarah framed his face with her hands, gazing deeply into his dark eyes.

"I didn't mean to hurt you like this," she choked out. "It's my fault. I put you through your past all over again, Wolf. I'm sorry... so sorry..."

Wolf took in a deep, ragged breath as he drowned in her blue eyes, eyes that were swimming with tears. He was wildly aware of Sarah's small hands on his face, of the care she was giving him so unselfishly. Despite a roller coaster of emotions he'd been through, Wolf understood what it cost Sarah to extend her care to him. She hadn't wanted to trust again, to give her love to another living human being.

Removing her hands and putting them in her lap, Wolf nodded. He brushed the tears coming down her pale cheeks. "You didn't do it on purpose," he rasped, then managed a lopsided smile.

Sarah bowed her head, feeling guilty. "The only thing to come out of my stupid decision was that you got to release so much grief from the past.'' She raised her head, and when she spoke again, her was voice scratchy. "You needed to cry for Maria. For yourself. I understand, Wolf."

And she did. He gazed at her, unable to believe that anyone could see that far into his scarred, tortured soul. "I did," he admitted brokenly. "This whole thing tonight triggered it, Sarah. I got scared when you came running out of the woods. I saw the blood on your face." He groaned and shut his eyes. "Everything from the past was suddenly superimposed on the present, and I was back there again. A flashback."

"But I'm alive, Wolf, and I'm fine." Sarah tried to smile and failed. "At least you cried. That was important." Shyly she added, "I never saw a man cry before. I—I didn't know what to do. I felt so useless, but I knew crying was healing for you." Sarah sniffed, closing her eyes and pressing her cheek into the palm of Wolf's hand.

"You did everything right," Wolf said hoarsely, continuing to graze Sarah's cheeks. "Everything." He slid his hands around her shoulders. The driving need to kiss her, to reassure her, forced him forward. As his mouth met and moved against Sarah's, he took her hungrily, starved for her taste, her texture. The grief of the past evaporated beneath Sarah's equally hungry response, her lips moving, molding to his.

Sarah was drowning beneath the searching heat of Wolf's mouth, aching to find a way to tell him how very much he meant to her. His hands, roughened by outdoor work, moved upward to capture her face as he deepened the kiss. As his tongue seared her lower lip, she drew in a gasp of air. Sensation was moving through her like lightning. Following pure instinct, Sarah placed her hands on Wolf's chest and felt the powerful beating of his heart beneath her palms. His breath was hot against her face as she responded guilelessly to his needs.

Wolf broke their kiss gradually. Sarah was in his arms, resting against him, her lips wet and pouty from his exploration of her. With a trembling hand, Wolf smoothed her mussed hair. Her eyes were the color of a foggy morning sky in North Carolina. Molten heat burned through him as the corners of her soft mouth pulled into a shy smile.

"You're healing," Wolf whispered, and pressed a kiss to her brow. *And I love you for your unselfishness. I know what it cost you.* Wolf looked deeply into her eyes, never wanting to say those words to anyone but Sarah. "I thought they'd shot you or something," Wolf said in a strained tone. "I care deeply for you, honey. I don't know what I'd do if you'd been hurt."

His words moved Sarah to silence, and all she could do was stare up at his rugged features, which were awash with grief. "I—I care for you, too, Wolf."

He pressed his finger to her lips. "Shh... You don't have to say anything, Sarah. I know what it cost you to reach out to me."

She captured his bruised and scarred hand and kissed it gently. "I'm not saying it because you want to hear it. I'm telling you how I feel, Wolf."

He nodded, absorbing her quavering admission. "Look," he said with an effort, "we need to get cleaned up and go to bed." Looking around, Wolf added, "I don't think Summers will try anything more tonight. I'll stay with you. Skeet will alert us if anyone tries to get within a mile of this place."

With a sigh, Sarah nodded. "Let me get a quick bath." She looked down at her dirty clothes. "I smell like fear."

"You're in good company," Wolf mused.

Sarah had just changed into her cotton nightgown when Wolf knocked lightly at the bedroom door.

"Come in."

Wolf walked in, narrowing his gaze on Sarah. She looked small and vulnerable as he approached. He missed nothing, from her distraught features to the shadowed darkness lingering in her eyes as she put a damp towel across the back of a wooden chair. He'd just taken a hot, cleansing shower himself, but before he climbed onto the couch to sleep, he wanted to make sure Sarah was all right.

"How are you feeling?" Wolf wanted so badly to reach out and pull her into the safety of his arms.

Sarah stood uncertainly by her bed. "I feel like I could fall asleep on my feet."

Wolf nodded and crossed to the bed, pulling back the covers. "Get in," he ordered softly.

"Where will you be?"

"I'll sleep on the couch," Wolf promised. Sarah was slurring her words with fatigue. "Come on, climb in and I'll tuck you in." Wolf wanted to do much more than that. He wanted to lie beside Sarah and hold her.

Stumbling to the bed, Sarah slipped off her robe and set it aside. "Thanks," she whispered wearily, getting into bed. She no longer questioned her heart, which was clearly ruling her fuzzy brain. She reached up and caught Wolf's hand. "Come to bed with me? Hold me?" She saw surprise flare in his darkened eyes and feared he'd say no. "Please, Wolf. I—I don't want to be alone to-night...."

He squeezed her hand, shattered by her honesty. "Okay," he rasped. "Let me make one more tour of the cabin, and then I'll join you."

Nodding, Sarah moved over in the double bed and brought the sheet and blanket back. She watched as Wolf turned and left. Skeet came in and lay down on the braided oval rug, his chin resting on his crossed paws, his eyes and ears alert. When Wolf returned, he carried the rifle in his hand. He shut the bedroom door and locked it. Then he placed the rifle on his side of the bed, where he could get ahold of it in a hurry. The lights were already off, but a slice of moonlight filtered through the lacy curtains at the east window.

Sarah's heart pounded briefly as Wolf divested himself of his shirt. He gave her a sheepish look.

"I'll wear my briefs," he said.

Sarah nodded, her mouth going dry as he pulled off his jeans, dropping them in a heap on the floor near the bed. The moonlight accentuated his powerful build. Sarah had never felt such a keen longing.

Wolf got into bed, bringing up the sheet and blanket. It was so easy to turn onto his side, slide one arm beneath Sarah's shoulders and draw her against him. She nestled her head in the crook of his shoulder, her arm going around his waist. With a sigh, Wolf closed his eyes, the exhaustion torn from him. The cool cotton of Sarah's nightgown was such a thin barrier between their bodies. Yet he controlled his need of her. Tonight he could give Sarah the protection he'd never been able to give Maria. It had nothing to do with sex. It had to do with unselfish love.

He pressed a chaste kiss to her damp hair. "Go to sleep, honey. I'll hold you."

Wolf's deep, vibrating voice drifted through Sarah, and she felt safe. All the panic died within her as Wolf grazed her arm with his hand, as if to reassure her. His lips against her hair stirred her senses, but the exhaustion and shock of the attack overwhelmed her.

"Thank you..." She fell into a deep, spiraling sleep.

Wolf kissed her temple. The words *I love you* wanted to escape. He whispered instead, "Sleep, honey. You're safe...."

His rough, low voice lulled Sarah to sleep almost immediately. She vaguely remembered his lips pressed to her temple, and the gentle strength of his hand on hers.

The sun was shining brightly into the bedroom when Sarah awoke. She sat up, groggy and disoriented. Looking at the clock on the bedside table, she saw that it was nearly ten in the morning! The odor of sausage frying heightened her senses as she scrambled to get out of bed. Every muscle in her body protested, and she groaned.

"Slow down," she reprimanded herself, standing. Touching her cheek where she'd been slapped the night before, Sarah found it puffy. It hurt to open and shut her mouth. First she'd wash up, then she'd get dressed. Sarah could hear Wolf moving around in the kitchen, and she relaxed.

After a hot shower to take away some of the soreness, Sarah chose a short-sleeved white blouse and pair of jeans. Although her feet were getting better, she still couldn't put on her mining boots, and she had to settle for a pair of sandals instead. She brushed her hair, then headed for the kitchen.

"Hi," Sarah whispered, halting at the entrance. Wolf wore the same jeans and shirt he had the night before. When he lifted his chin and met her eyes, Sarah saw how bloodshot his were. Hadn't he slept?

Wolf looked up, stunned by Sarah's natural beauty as she stood uncertainly in the doorway. He smiled tenderly, remembering last night, remembering the softness of her against him, of her shallow breath against his chest. "Come on in. I'm fixing us pancakes and sausage." He transferred a stack from the oven to two plates on the table. Placing the links in a basket between them on the table, he asked, "How'd you sleep?"

Self-consciously Sarah shrugged. She was hotly aware of the light burning in Wolf's eyes. It made her feel a keening ache that centered in her lower body, as if she were missing something and didn't know what. Yet Wolf's gaze made her feel whole, made her feel like a woman. "Like the dead," she said, then grimaced as she sat down. "Scratch that. I slept like a log. 'Dead' sounds terrible to me right now."

Wolf poured them coffee and joined her. The color had returned to Sarah's face. Her blond hair was freshly washed and dried, falling about her shoulders like a golden frame. He wanted to say so much, yet didn't know where to begin. Or end. He loved her. It was that simple, and that complex. But Sarah appeared so tentative, so fragile, after last night's attack that he didn't know what to say. "I understand."

"You look awful."

"I kept watch last night," Wolf said gruffly, handing her the maple syrup.

"Watch?"

"Yes. I'm treating this situation like a wartime one. One person sleeps, the other stays awake in case the enemy comes around."

Shivering outwardly, Sarah set the syrup down on the table. "This is like a nightmare, Wolf."

"It's getting messy," he agreed. "This morning I called Morgan and filled him in on the situation."

"What do you mean?"

"I wanted to put him on alert and let him know what was happening out here." Wolf saw the color drain from Sarah's face. "I intend to handle this, but just in case, I want someone from outside this area to know what the hell is going on."

Sarah felt her stomach shrink in terror. "What can he do?"

Wolf tendered a smile to ease her fear. "Honey, they're professional soldiers. We've got a sheriff who's in cahoots with Summers. And he's got a lot of men on his payroll if he wants to attack us. If I can't handle this, then we're going to need help, and the only help I can count on is from Perseus."

"Summers wouldn't like that. Wolf, he's got a lot of men."

"I know that," he said patiently. "And don't worry, I'm not going to drive into Philipsburg like a posse, shooting up the town. I'm going into town this morning to try and negotiate a settlement on this with Summers."

Fear shot through Sarah. Wolf could be killed—just like her father. An icy coldness bathed her. "I never thought it would come to this. I thought Summers would just harass me off and on."

Wolf shook his head grimly. "He'll never lay another hand on you. That's a promise."

The words, spoken in a low, menacing growl, made a chill work its way up Sarah's spine. Her world was coming apart at the seams, and Wolf was all that was keeping it from completely collapsing around her. "If you weren't here, Summers would already have the mine," she murmured.

"And you might possibly be dead."

The thought was sobering. She gave Wolf a sideways glance. For a few awkward minutes, she pushed the pancakes around on her plate, forcing herself to eat. Who knew what lay ahead today? Keeping up her strength had to be primary, so she forced the food down.

Wolf watched Sarah through hooded eyes as he ate. He didn't taste the food. All his senses were focused on her. Her brow was drawn in a frown, and he saw the tension around her soft mouth. A mouth he wanted to worship, to kiss reverently, for the rest of his life. He knew he didn't deserve this kind of second chance—not with someone as courageous as Sarah. She was a match for him in every way—proud, independent, unselfish, and generous to a fault. What had last night meant to her? His mind returned to Sheriff Noonan's remark about Philip Barlow.

His mouth tightening, Wolf put his fork and plate aside. He had to know. "Sarah?"

She raised her head. Wolf's entire demeanor had become dark and serious. Her heart started a dreadful pounding. "Yes?"

"Maybe I don't have any right to ask you this, but I need to know about a guy named Philip Barlow. Noonan said he was your boyfriend?"

"Oh." She pushed the plate aside and opted to slip her fingers around the ceramic mug filled with coffee. "I imagine he didn't have anything good to say about me in relation to Philip, either?"

Wolf shook his head. "No."

With a slight shrug, Sarah whispered, "When I turned Ricky Noonan in to the FBI, my boyfriend, Philip, got really furious with me."

"Why?" Wolf's heart beat a little harder.

"I didn't realize Philip was tied up with Noonan, too. He was selling drugs for him. When I found out, it just tore me apart. I thought—" She grimaced and avoided

Wolf's probing gray eyes. "I thought Philip loved me. I sure loved him...."

"First love?" Wolf ventured softly.

"Puppy love was what Mom called it," Sarah said with a slight, pained smile. "When the FBI finished their investigation and indicted Philip along with Ricky Noonan, I was heartbroken. Philip accused me of setting him up, of... so many things. The evidence against him wasn't that strong, so the FBI let him go, and he left town. I haven't seen him or heard from him since. He said I'd ruined his life."

Relief rushed through Wolf. Reaching over, he captured Sarah's work-worn hand. "Honey, you didn't ruin his life. He ruined it for himself."

Wolf's touch was so right, and Sarah shyly returned his squeeze. Her hand was engulfed by his, and it gave her an overwhelming sense of protection. "I know that—now. Years ago, I didn't. My mom really helped me get through the heartbreak." She held his warm gaze. "I thought I loved him, Wolf." Then, quietly, she added, "He was the first and only boy to ever like me."

"I don't believe that," Wolf said, and he meant it. Couldn't they see beyond Sarah's clothes and her mining job? They were all crazy, Wolf decided. Clothes and a career didn't make a woman.

Sarah frowned. "My reputation in this town was bad news after the FBI investigation, Wolf."

Raising her hand to his lips, Wolf gently kissed her fingers. The need to give back to Sarah some of what had been cruelly taken from her burned through him. He watched her eyes widen beautifully as he brushed the kiss over her skin.

Wolf grinned and reluctantly released her hand. Now that he knew the truth about Philip Barlow, his jealousy had subsided. The look he saw in her eyes was one of warmth mixed with desire. Wolf wondered if it was desire for him. He'd never wanted a woman more than Sarah, but it had to be her decision; he'd never force her into bed with him.

Her hand tingled, even after Wolf let it go. Was it possible? Did the care he spoke of last night mean he might love her?

Sarah considered while she finished her coffee in the comfortable silence of the kitchen with Wolf. The robins chirping their songs outside the window eased some of the tension she unconsciously held in her shoulders.

"When will you see Summers?" she asked.

Wolf got up and put the dishes in the sink. "I'm going in now," he said grimly.

"May I come with you?"

"No." Wolf turned and faced her. He leaned against the counter and crossed his arms against his chest. "The safest place for you is here. You'll keep Skeet with you, and you've got a rifle." His brows fell. "I don't think Summers will try two days in a row. He's probably going to wait to see if you're going to run into town to sign those real estate papers of his."

"He said he'd come back tonight, Wolf." Her voice was hollow with fear.

"If I get to him today, he won't be back," he promised darkly.

"Why can't I come with you?"

Wolf didn't want to say, but he didn't know how to evade Sarah. "You're safer here," he repeated with more authority.

"Because if Summers sees your truck he could have his men fill it with bullet holes?"

Wolf's mouth tightened. At least Sarah was a realist. Unwinding from his position at the counter, Wolf straightened. "Exactly. Better a single than a double target."

Sarah winced, her hands tightening around the mug.

Wolf came around behind her and placed his hands on her shoulders. He gently kneaded her tight muscles until she began to relax. "Look, I know this is tough on you, but you're safest here. You already evaded Summers's men once, and you know this area, honey. Once I find Summers, I'll settle this thing with him once and for all."

"How?" Sarah twisted a look up at him, glad that he was standing behind her, glad that his hands were on her shoulders.

"I'll tell him about Perseus and our connections with the FBI and the CIA, and I'll tell him that if he doesn't leave you alone once and for all we'll have him investigated." Satisfaction rang in Wolf's voice. "He's the kind of slimy bastard who wants to avoid public notice and a trial at all costs."

Sarah couldn't help but shiver. She tried to be brave, not only for Wolf but for herself. "I—I just worry about you, that's all."

Wolf leaned over and placed a kiss on her cheek. "Your worry isn't for nothing," he told her huskily. "I'll be all right." Straightening, he forced himself to move. The last thing he wanted to do was to leave Sarah for any reason. "What I want you to do is form an escape route in case Summers does come back. Tell me where I might find you if you have to make a run for it."

"I'd rather be out on the mountain working, not here at the cabin." Sarah gave him a narrow look. "I'll work at the new mine site. That way, I'll have a chance to hear them coming. Besides, there's a series of caves down on the other side of Blue Mountain,'' Sarah whispered, her hand touching her throat, where a lump was forming. ''I could hide there and they'd never find me.''

''Good. I know the area you mean.'' Wolf glanced down at her feet. ''Are you sure you can work?''

''I want to work, Wolf. I'll go crazy if I have to sit here waiting for you to come home. You know that.''

''Yeah, I guess I do.'' Wolf felt more sure now that Sarah had a plan in place. ''Draw me a map of the cave area, and I'll take it with me when I leave.'' He gave her a slight smile meant to buoy her. ''We'll get out of this alive and together,'' he promised her.

Together. Sarah nodded jerkily and got to her feet. She wanted to cry, because she'd just discovered Wolf—the first man she'd truly loved in her life. And now he was going into a town bristling with enemies who carried weapons that could all too easily be aimed at him. Everything was moving too quickly for Sarah. Her emotions were in shreds, and she knew they didn't have time to sit down and talk about all the new discoveries cascading through her.

Forcing herself to think, she went into the living room and picked up a notebook to draw Wolf a map of the caves.

Chapter Twelve

Sarah waited tensely at the cabin. It was exactly noon, the time Wolf promised he'd be home. Her heart rate rising, Sarah gasped as she saw the dark green forest service truck turn into the driveway. It was Wolf, and he was safe! Moving off the porch, Sarah met him as he parked the truck and shut off the engine. She tried to read his rugged, closed features as he opened the truck door and stepped out. Skeet rushed up and wedged between them.

"How did it go?" Sarah asked. What she wanted to do was throw her arms around Wolf in welcome. She wasn't sure what to do, or how to act; her nerves were stretched to the breaking point, her emotions frayed by the hourly unknowns of her life.

Wolf absently patted Skeet, then devoted his attention to Sarah. He heard the fear in her voice, and saw it in her eyes. Automatically he placed his arms around her. The softness of her parting lips made him ache with need as she came against him without resisting.

"Summers couldn't be found," he told her as he walked with her to the cabin. "I talked to Noonan."

Sarah pressed her head against his shoulder, content, a feeling of safety enveloping her once again. "Is that good or bad, Wolf? You look worried."

Wolf released Sarah once they entered the kitchen. "I don't feel good about it, honey." He scowled and settled his hands on his hips as he studied her. "Summers is playing a game. I think he'll be back here again. Maybe tonight, if not sooner."

Gulping, Sarah's eyes widened. "What are we going to do?" Her voice was strained.

Wolf smiled, but the smile didn't reach his eyes. He saw the sandwiches on the table and motioned for her to join him. "When I was in Philipsburg, I called the airport at Anaconda." He held her frightened gaze. "I'm taking you out of here, tonight. You've got an airline ticket to Washington, D.C., Sarah. I've talked to Morgan, and he's agreed to put you up at one of the condos the company owns until this thing gets resolved."

"We're leaving?"

"No, you are. I'm staying." Wolf saw stubbornness come into her face. "Sarah, please, don't argue with me on this. I want you safe. I'm not going to keep you here in the line of fire."

"I'm not going anywhere if you're not going with me, Wolf!" Her voice was strident and off-key. Sarah suddenly stood up and gripped the back of her chair as she held Wolf's weary gaze. "This is my fight!"

"It's our fight," Wolf agreed, trying to calm her down. Didn't Sarah realize he loved her? That he wanted her safe and out of harm's way?

"But this isn't fair, Wolf! You're in danger, too! It isn't just me!"

He held up his hands. "Honey, I'm more equipped to deal with it than you."

"How?" she demanded, shaken. "I've been shot at, Wolf. I've been beaten up by Summers's goons. I've shot at them to scare them off."

"But you've never killed, Sarah."

Stunned, Sarah heard the haunted quality of Wolf's voice. His eyes were tired-looking, his mouth was a tight line. There was such pain mirrored in his face that Sarah froze.

"You think it's coming to that?" she asked hollowly.

Wolf rubbed his face gently. A lot of the swelling had gone down, but the dark bruises remained to remind him of Summers's way of dealing with situations. "I do."

"Oh, God." Sarah sat down. She clasped her hands on the table and stared at Wolf. "Did Noonan say that?"

With a twist of his mouth, Wolf said, "Noonan turned white, red, and then plum-colored. I told him about Perseus, and the fact that Morgan would call in a head honcho from the FBI to begin investigating Summers if he didn't leave you and your mine alone once and for all."

"What did he say?"

"He got angry and accused me of threatening him." Wolf shrugged and pushed the plate bearing the sandwiches around and around with his fingers. Finally he looked up at Sarah. "I know what's going to happen. Summers is hiding out—for now. Noonan will take the information to him, and I know in my gut that Summers will hit us either tonight or tomorrow."

Trembling, Sarah sat down again. "Then that's all the more reason for you to come with me, Wolf. You can't stay here and fight it out alone."

"You're a gutsy lady," Wolf said, "but there are times when you need to know when to retreat. This is one of those times. The only flight out of Anaconda to Washington is at midnight. I wish it was sooner. It's not exactly a hub airport, so I don't have any choice in the matter." Worriedly Wolf held her blue eyes, and saw them shimmering with unshed tears. "I need you to leave, Sarah. I lo—I care for you too much to keep you here." He reached out and gripped her hand. "I can't let what happened to Maria happen to you," he told her fervently. "I can't lose you." Wolf sat tensely. He'd nearly slipped and said he loved Sarah. Her face had blanched white, and he wondered if she'd caught his faux pas.

Love? Sarah sat there, very still, very much aware of Wolf's warm, strong hand around hers. She was sure that was what he'd stopped himself from saying. Her mouth grew dry. As she clung to his darkened gaze, Sarah realized that Wolf did love her. The tenor of his voice shook her as nothing else could have. The desperation in his eyes verified his fear for her life.

She pulled her hand from his grasp. "Wolf, I'm not leaving you here alone to fight it out with Summers," she began in a low voice. "I'm sorry, but I'm not abandoning you. I can't—" And her voice cracked.

Wolf unwound from the chair and came around the table. He placed his hands around her arms and pulled her upward, emotionally devastated by Sarah's tears. "Now listen to me," he rasped thickly. "You're not abandoning me. No argument on this, Sarah. I'm taking you to Anaconda tonight. Now, I don't care if you agree with my plan or not." His hands tightened on her arms, and his voice became hoarse. "*I won't lose you. And I don't care if you curse me, hate me, or never want to see me again—you're leaving.*"

Tears blurred Sarah's vision, and her lips parted. She couldn't stand the agony in Wolf's eyes. "You don't understand!" she cried. "You just don't understand!"

Grimly Wolf pulled Sarah against him. He'd needed her closeness, her warmth, all morning. With a groan, he buried his face in her hair. As her arms twined around his waist, he released a shuddering sigh. "I understand a lot more than you'll ever know," he rasped, and he held her as tightly as he dared.

The inky cape of night had fallen across the valley by the time Sarah was ready to leave the cabin. Wolf had helped her pack, extraordinarily tense and hyperalert to any sound that seemed out of the ordinary. He kept his rifle nearby and watched Skeet for warnings.

Sarah closed her only suitcase, a small one, and Wolf took it out to the pickup. She stood in the center of the living room, torn. When Wolf appeared, she was startled; he'd come back without her having heard him. His face looked grim as he approached her.

"What about my mother?"

He placed his hands on her small shoulders. "I know you're worried about her," he said soothingly.

"Summers has gone to her a number of times in the past, Wolf, and tried to get her to sign papers that would give him our mine. If I'm gone, he could try it again."

He shook his head. "I've talked to Jean Riva, the owner of the nursing home, and told her to call me if anyone wants to speak with your mother." Wolf saw the anguish in Sarah's eyes. "She'll be fine," he told her. But would she? He couldn't promise Sarah anything except safety for herself—once he got her out of this hellhole.

"Look at it another way," Wolf said, gently caressing her shoulders, "if Summers did get her to sign over the mine, you could contest it in court and win. Your mother isn't of sound mind, and the doctor would make it clear that because of her stroke she wouldn't really know what she'd been coerced into signing."

"Maybe you're right," Sarah murmured. She placed her hands on Wolf's powerful chest. "Please let me stay."

Just the touch of her hands upon him sent a hot longing through every level of Wolf. He leaned down and kissed her wan cheek. "I can't..."

It was time to go, and Sarah eased out of his hands. Fighting back tears, she turned to him as he followed her out the door. "What if you're wounded? Who would care for you, Wolf? You're one man against all of Summers's men."

"If I need help, I'll call Morgan," he told her, capturing her hand as they walked to the truck. "I just think we need to get over the next couple of days and we'll be okay. You've got to trust me on that, Sarah."

She did trust him—with her life. With her heart. The words begged to be torn from her, but she swallowed them. Wolf opened the passenger side of the truck. Skeet jumped in first, and Sarah followed. The silence was ominous as she watched Wolf looking around, alert and wary, as he moved around the truck. Before getting in, he placed the rifle on the gun rack across the back seat.

He got in and started the truck. His gut was screamingly tight. This was a bad time of night to be leaving. He couldn't drive without lights on the twisting, turning dirt road. The moon was concealed by the thick clouds overhead. It looked as if it might rain. Wolf backed out and put the truck in gear, gravel crunching beneath the wide tires. He glanced over at Sarah's strained face.

"You'll be safer away from here," he told her.

She shyly slid her hand across Skeet's broad back and touched Wolf's shoulder. It was Wolf's past that was making him react this way. "I feel as if you can't trust me to hold up my end of this fight, Wolf. Just because I'm a woman."

Wolf winced, his mouth tightening. Sarah had a good point, but he didn't dare capitulate to her rationale. "Honey, one thing I learned the hard way was to retreat instead of just charging blindly ahead. When Maria was murdered, I lost it. I wasn't thinking clearly, for myself or my men. I got myself captured, and Killian, too. And for what?" He glanced over at Sarah's shadowed features. "This has nothing to do with you being a woman. This has to do with me trying to deal differently—better—with the same situation all over again. Do you see that?"

Torn between what she felt was right for her and her all-too-clear understanding of Wolf's past, Sarah shrugged. "Yes," she whispered, "I know what you're trying to do. What if you just got me a hotel room in Anaconda and stayed a few days? Wouldn't that be good enough, Wolf?"

He shook his head. "What if Summers's men are tailing us? What if they found out where you were staying?"

The grimness of the scenario Wolf outlined made Sarah realize he was right. "I worry for you...."

"I'm worried for me, too." Wolf tried to smile for her benefit. He placed his hand across hers momentarily, keeping his eyes on the road. The headlights stabbed through the night. "Maybe because I've got a woman who takes me as I am. You've allowed me to open up and talk, Sarah. I've never done that before, and I've got to tell you, it feels damn good. You've taken away a lot of the load I carried.''

Her throat constricted. ''It's because I care for you, Wolf. Mom always said love makes carrying a problem less.''

Surprise at her softly spoken admission sent Wolf's heart skittering. Just as he opened his mouth to speak, he saw the winking of rifle fire to the right, on Sarah's side of the truck. His words turned to a croak of warning, and he jerked Sarah down off the seat just as the bullets slammed into the truck.

Hitting the brakes, hearing glass shattering and flying all over the cab, Wolf ducked. Son of a bitch! They were being bushwhacked! He knew why, too. The threat of an FBI investigation had gotten to Summers. This was his answer to the problem: Kill Wolf and Sarah, the two eyewitnesses, and there could be no trial. Noonan and Summers would be free.

''Stay down!'' Wolf yelled, jerking the wheel of the truck to the left. The pickup shrieked and skidded down the loose gravel road. More rifle fire poured into the cabin. Skeet howled. Sarah screamed.

Jamming his foot down on the accelerator, Wolf kept low. The bastards! They were out in the middle of nowhere, too far from the main highway, from Philipsburg, from civilization, for anyone to report gunshots. They were alone.

The truck coughed and strained. The gunfire stopped. They were out of range for now. At the top of small knoll, the truck's engine coughed, sputtered and quit. Cursing, Wolf pulled over onto the berm of the dirt road.

"Sarah, are you okay?"

"Y-yes." She raised her head, realizing what had happened. Skeet was squeezed in beside her on the floorboards of the passenger side of the truck. "I—I think Skeet's okay, too."

"Good." Quickly, Wolf pulled the rifle down off the gun rack. "Get out! Hurry! They'll be coming to see if we're dead!"

Bailing out the door, Sarah fell, her knees giving way out of fear. With a little gasp, she forced herself to stand. Skeet leaped out of the cab, growling deep in his throat. The night was black, with no moonlight to help guide them. She squinted, unable to see what Skeet must either see or hear.

Wolf came around the truck, putting a bullet into the chamber of the 30.06 rifle. "Come on," he rasped, gripping her by the arm, and they hurried down the embankment and into the fir trees below. Luckily, there was little brush to hamper their escape, and Wolf kept Sarah at a steady run back toward the cabin.

"Who?" Sarah gasped.

"Noonan and Summers," he ground out, jogging alongside her. Skeet moved ahead of them, his tongue lolling out the side of his mouth. "We're lucky they didn't kill us."

"Wh-what are we going to do?" Sarah gasped between breaths, not used to such violent exercise. Wolf moved fluidly, as if running were the easiest thing in the world for him. Although her feet were healing, Sarah could already feel them beginning to throb from the exertion.

"We're three miles from the cabin. I don't remember any houses along the way where we could stop and make a phone call. I want to try to make it back to the cabin so we can call for help.''

Sarah gasped when car lights about a mile away suddenly flashed on and headed toward them. Wolf saw them, too. He gripped her arm and propelled her more deeply into the woods. She stumbled, caught herself, and ran on.

''They'll kill us, Wolf.''

''Only if they catch us.'' Worriedly Wolf realized that Sarah didn't have the physical stamina to outrun Noonan and his bunch. She was already gasping loudly, sucking in huge drafts of air. Dammit! He loved Sarah, and there was no way she was going to be taken from him. No way in hell! Keeping a firm grip on her arm so that she wouldn't fall, he rasped, ''Run as far as you can, and then we'll stop and rest, Sarah.''

The headlights flashed through the dense fir. Sarah heard several vehicles screech to a halt. Men's voices, loud and angry, punctuated the air. They were still at least a mile ahead of them. Skeet had dropped to the rear, as if to protect them. But nothing could protect them from bullets.

''How many bullets have you got?''

''Two boxes. Enough to take them out one at a time if I have to,'' Wolf told her. ''No more talking, Sarah. They might hear us. Just concentrate on running.''

Tears jammed unexpectedly into Sarah's eyes. She sobbed for breath, her legs beginning to feel like strings of rubber. Wolf jogged easily at her side, strong and seemingly impervious to the harsh conditions. She'd admitted her love to him in the truck and had seen the surprise, and then the tenderness, in his face. There was no question in Sarah's bursting heart that Wolf loved her, too. Now Noonan and Summers were out to kill them. And how could one man with a rifle and an injured woman stop them?

Chapter Thirteen

Sarah was running hard, occasionally slipping on the pine needles only to be caught and steadied by Wolf, who never left her side. She knew she was slowing him down with her injured feet. Behind her, she could hear men crashing through the underbrush, not far behind them. Flashlights stabbed through the blackness toward them. Her lungs were burning. Her throat was raw and felt as if it were going to tear apart.

The level floor of the valley was starting to slope gently toward the mountains ahead, where her cabin was situated. Each foot flung in front of the other made her labor harder. Then her toe caught on a small rock and she was thrown off her feet.

Wolf caught her before she slammed to the ground. Gasping, she clutched at his arms as he dragged her upright.

"Wolf...go on without me. I...I can't run any-more!"

Looking around, his eyes now adjusted to the dark-ness, Wolf glared back at the men following them, real-izing there must be three to five of them.

"Hold on," he rasped, sliding his arm under her arms and supporting her. Taking Sarah to a depression be-hind a huge black boulder, he placed her there. "Get down on your belly, Sarah, and don't move."

"What are you going to do?"

"I'm going to try the wounded-bird-with-a-broken-wing routine." He gripped the rifle in one hand and forced her to lie down. "Cover your head with your hands. I'll lead them away from you. Whatever you do, don't move. Don't speak. Understand?"

Sobbing for breath, she nodded. "B-be careful!"

"Don't worry, honey, I will." He gripped her shoul-der hard. "I love you. I'm not about to lose you."

Sarah jerked her head up. Wolf was gone like a silent shadow, and Skeet with him. Had she heard wrong? Wolf loved her? Her heartbeat wildly erratic, she hugged the rock with her body. Luckily, she wore dark clothes and couldn't be easily seen. Cries and curses drew closer. What if they found her? What if they shot Wolf?

Concentrating on being silent, Sarah opened her mouth and breathed through it. She pressed against the boulder, hugging it like a snake. Blond hair was a detri-ment, she thought suddenly. Its color standing out in even the worst darkness. If the men didn't come around the boulder, she'd be safe. If they did... Sarah gulped, not wanting to think about it.

As the group grew closer, the flashlights were like floodlights to Sarah. She recognized Noonan's raspy voice and that of the red-haired man who had attacked her previously. Adrenaline plunged through her when she recognized Summers's voice.

"She can't run that far. Not with those feet in the condition they're in," he growled.

"Well, hell," Noonan exploded. "Where are they, then?"

"I don't know. Fan out! Thirty feet between each man," Summers ordered, out of breath. "We can keep track of one another by watching where our lights are."

"Anything makes a sound, shoot!" Noonan added angrily. "I want them dead!"

Sarah heard a distinct rustling in the distance, as if someone were bulldozing through a heavy patch of brush. All five men stopped talking. It had to be Wolf deliberately making noise to get their attention.

"It's them!" Noonan exploded harshly.

Within seconds, all five men were running toward the sound. Sarah crumpled wearily against the rock. She was safe—for now. Lifting her head, she slowly got to her hands and knees. The men were crashing through the forest, not even trying to be quiet. A far cry from Wolf's stealthy retreat, Sarah thought as she got to her feet.

Her knees were still rubbery, and she was shaking with fear. Pushing the hair off her face, Sarah remained by the boulder, waiting . . . waiting.

A hand snaked around, jerking her backward and off her feet. A scream caught in her throat. Sarah stumbled, off balance, and fell against the hard body of a man. The smell of sour sweat struck her nostrils. Closing her eyes, she bit down as hard as she could on the fingers clamped over her mouth.

"Ow! You little bitch!"

It was Noonan! Sarah managed to twist around. She kicked, hit and bit, blindly striking out at the sheriff. His hand caught her by the neck, his fingers sinking deeply into her flesh. With a small cry, Sarah felt herself being slammed to the forest floor.

Noonan was breathing harshly, his hand splayed out across her chest and collarbone. He shoved his face down into hers and grinned.

"Not too smart having blond hair, Sarah." He grinned and put his rifle next to him on the ground. "Don't move." He reached into his back pocket for handcuffs.

Sarah saw the handcuffs and struggled wildly. "No!" she shrieked. If he got those cuffs on her, she was dead, and she knew it. Lashing out with both feet, she connected solidly with Noonan's chest. The sheriff grunted, rolling over backward.

Scrambling to her feet, Sarah dived into the darkness.

"Come back here!" Noonan roared.

Sobbing, Sarah struck a tree, bounced off it and hit the ground. She had to think! She had to stay calm! Noonan was after her! Get up! Get up!

Rifle fire suddenly split open the darkness. Bark from a nearby tree exploded, flying in all directions. Sarah ducked and cried out. She had to remain silent! Getting to her feet, she concentrated on avoiding the trees in the darkness. Noonan was close! The rifle fired three more times. Bullets whined around Sarah.

To her left, she heard a shout. The night suddenly flared with the muzzle blasts of several rifles. Wolf! Oh, God! Sarah dived headlong up the slope, climbing hard, tripping and catching herself. Had Summers found Wolf? Tears squeezed from her eyes. Sarah knew she had to reach the cabin. She had to get to Wolf's friends to get help. Was Wolf injured? Dead?

Cresting another hill, Sarah found a huge boulder and hunched down behind it. She'd lost Noonan long ago, and had maintained a steady walk or trot for another hour, even as the pain in her ankles increased. The watch on her wrist read midnight. Shaking from fear as much as from the drop in temperature, Sarah felt her heart breaking into pieces. Had Wolf been captured? Wounded? What had happened back there? Tears came, this time in earnest. Wolf loved her. He'd said words she'd never thought to hear.

Shakily wiping her dusty, damp face, Sarah looked up through the shadowy firs at the sky, which was lit with stars now. Meager light shone from pinpoints that looked like tiny white sapphires to her. Trying to think where she was in relation to the road, and which way was north, so that she could find her cabin, she continued to study the stars. Long ago her father had taught her to navigate at night by them alone, without a compass.

Sitting there for a good fifteen minutes, Sarah began to relax. Still trembling from the chilliness of the mountain air, she wrapped her arms around herself. The thin nylon windbreaker she wore wasn't enough. Sarah realized she had strayed off in a northeasterly direction and would have to make a correction. How many miles out of the way had she come? In her hysteria to escape Noonan, she'd become disoriented and had run to save her life.

A twig snapped. Inhaling sharply, Sarah tensed, her fingers digging into the soft, fir-needled ground. Who? What? Her heart was beating so hard that she couldn't hear anything else in her ears. Frustrated, fear crawling up her spine, she slowly eased to her hands and knees to look around the rock. The light was practically nonexistent, but she prayed she would be able to see what had caused the sound. Maybe something had dropped from a tree. That was possible.

Nearly paralyzed with fear, Sarah peeked out from behind the rock. Probing the darkness, she could see nothing, but that didn't mean no one was there. She remained crouched by the rock, ready for flight.

A dog whined.

Sarah's eyes grew huge. It was Skeet! Or was it? Coyotes regularly prowled the mountains. She tried to ferret out some movement in the direction of the sound, her mouth dry. She was torn. Should she call out Skeet's name? What if Summers had a dog along with him?

Another whine.

Shaking, Sarah got to her feet, her fingers digging into the boulder. The sound was much closer this time. A rustle came from the right. Sarah whirled around.

"Skeet!" she cried out softly.

The dog stood there on three legs. He whined once more.

Sarah dropped to her knees and carefully touched the dog's massive head. His right front leg was lifted up. She spoke in a crooning tone as she used her fingers to trace the injured leg. The dog winced.

Warm, sticky blood met her touch. Skeet sat down, panting heavily as Sarah tried to find the extent of damage to his paw.

"You're okay," she whispered in a trembling tone. Taking off her jacket, she quickly tore off one sleeve, then took several strips of nylon to wrap his paw in a makeshift bandage. The work took her long, tortuous minutes, because her hands were shaking so badly that a knot was impossible.

Looking around after dressing Skeet's paw, Sarah choked back tears. "Where's Wolf?" she asked the dog. The animal whined soulfully, as if he understood her question.

Just the feel of Skeet's thick, soft fur gave Sarah a faint sense of safety. Skeet would protect her. Wolf had trained him to attack, and he'd taught Sarah the commands. If Skeet was shot, there was a good chance that Wolf had been similarly injured. Man and dog had left her together.

Sarah couldn't contemplate such an awful thing. Yet she knew Summers and his men played for keeps. Killing was perfectly acceptable to them. Patting Skeet, she peered down at the animal.

"Find Wolf!" she whispered. "Go find Wolf!"

Instantly Skeet raised himself to his three good legs and began hobbling off in the direction he'd come from. Sarah followed, as quietly as possible. From time to time, the dog would stop, turn his head to check on her progress, then continue. The slope was steep, and Sarah slipped and fell a number of times on the pine needles. With every step she took, Sarah prayed that Wolf was alive.

Wolf bit back a groan of pain. He lay beside a fallen fir twice his height, his hearing keyed for Summers and his henchmen. Sticky wetness spread across his shirtfront, where a bullet had grazed him an hour earlier. The stray shot had knocked him off balance, and he'd fallen over a fifteen-foot cliff. Looking up, Wolf knew he was lucky to be alive after tumbling over that ledge. Careful not to make a sound, he tested his limbs and his reflexes. Nothing was broken.

His mind returned sluggishly to Sarah. He'd heard her scream. Did Summers have her? If so, where were they? Wolf lay on his side, hugging the fallen tree for safety, as well as for camouflage. There were no sounds to indicate that Summers was still in the area. Had they captured Sarah and left? Wolf felt a cry welling up from deep within him, begging to be released. It was a cry of pure rage and denial. If Summers had captured Sarah . . . Vignettes of Maria, of her raided village, pummeled Wolf's senses.

From his left, he heard a whine. Skeet! When he'd fallen over the ledge, he'd lost his dog. Getting shakily to his hands and knees, Wolf saw the animal appear out of the darkness, limping toward him. His eyes narrowed. *Sarah!* Her name nearly tore from his lips as he rose unsteadily and turned to meet her. An incredible avalanche of relief shattered through him, ripping away at his raw feelings and exposing his love for her.

Sarah jerked to a halt as a hulking shadow rose from the darkened ground. A scream nearly left her throat. And then she recognized Wolf. With a little cry, she flung herself forward, her arms open.

The instant Sarah hurled herself into Wolf's awaiting arms, she realized he was injured. She heard him groan her name close to her ear, his arms going around her like tight bands of protection. He held her close, and she pressed her head against his chest wall, a sob coming from her.

"It's all right," Wolf rasped thickly. "It's all right...." And it was. Just the special scent of Sarah, and the feel of her thin but strong arms going around his waist in welcome, was enough. Wolf pressed a series of hungry, quick kisses against her tangled hair, her cheek, then searched wildly for her mouth. The instant she turned her face upward and their lips met, Wolf hungrily claimed her.

The world, the danger, ceased to exist, if only for a few moments. Sarah lost herself in Wolf's searching, heated mouth. Immersed in a kaleidoscope of surprise and pleasure, she sank against him.

"I love you," he said hoarsely, pulling back and drowning in her tear-filled eyes. There was no need for further words, Wolf realized humbly as tears streaked down Sarah's grimy features. He framed her face with his shaking hands, touching her as if he didn't know whether she was real or a fevered figment of his tortured imagination.

"You're alive...." Sarah choked out. "Oh, Wolf..."

He touched her lips with his fingers to silence her. Holding her tight, he lifted his head and began to search the darkness. Wolf was relying on his dog's acute hearing and smell more than anything else. Skeet sat nearby, alert, through his silence telling them they were safe—if but for a moment. Removing his fingers from her lips, Wolf touched Sarah's hair. There were so many pine needles in the fine golden strands that they'd have to be removed by hand, not with a comb.

The moment Sarah's hand came to rest on Wolf's shirt, she gasped. The wet, sticky stuff was blood. Her eyes widened enormously as she drew away from him and saw the dark stain across his belly.

"You're hurt...."

"Just a graze. I'm okay. Sarah, we've got to get out of here."

Shaken, Sarah couldn't tear her gaze from his wound. A graze? Half the shirt was bloodied, and it was torn where the bullet had ripped into the fabric. She remembered that Wolf was a mercenary by trade, that his soldiering instincts were finely honed, but nevertheless he was surely in pain.

Taking Sarah's hand, Wolf squeezed it to get her attention. "Your feet?"

"Th-they're fine."

"Sore?"

"A little."

"What do you mean, a little?"

Wetting her lips, Sarah tried to think coherently. "I— They hurt, Wolf, but I can walk on them."

Convinced she was telling the truth, Wolf looked around. "I don't know where Summers and his gang are anymore. I blacked out after I fell over that ledge."

Sarah eyed the jagged rock far above them. A chill swept through her. Wolf was far tougher, and far luckier, than any man had a right to be, and she was grateful for that. Holding his hand tight, she whispered, "I don't know where Summers is, either. I haven't heard them for over an hour."

Nodding, Wolf checked out Skeet. The dog remained passive, and he was sure none of their enemies were close. "Are you hurt in any way?"

Sarah shook her head. "No... Noonan jumped me from behind, but when he tried to cuff me I broke free." She gave a wobbly smile. "I was never so scared.... But I was more scared for you. They were firing those rifles in your direction, Wolf."

Relief came on the heels of Wolf's terror over Sarah's trembling admission. More than anything, he wanted to hold her and keep her safe. She was shaking like a leaf. But then, so was he. There were several small scratches across her brow and cheek, plus a bruise on the side of her neck. He wanted to kill Noonan. Realizing that he was gripping Sarah's small hand too tightly, Wolf released her.

"We have to get to the cabin."

"Yes."

"I don't know how far we are from it," Wolf admitted.

"It doesn't matter. We have to make it."

His mouth pulled into a sour grimace. "We'll go slow and quiet, honey. Skeet will be our ears and nose." Stroking her hair, he saw her rally at his barely whispered words. Sarah had courage, true courage.

"Let's go," she said, and gripped his large hand once again.

Wolf swiveled his head and caught Skeet's attention. Instantly the dog was on his feet and hobbling out in front of them. There was little brush between the huge Douglas firs, so it was relatively easy to walk hand in hand with Sarah. Slowly Wolf's heart settled down into a steady rhythm again. He still had his rifle and ammunition. The odds were against them, but they definitely had a chance.

As Wolf guided Sarah through the maze of darkened trees, his thoughts moved back in time. Back to Peru, to the fact that Maria and her people hadn't stood a chance against Ramirez and his men. At least Sarah was alive and had escaped. A resolve more powerful than any emotion he'd ever felt in his life tunneled through him. Even if he had to die in the process, he was going to make sure that Sarah wasn't hurt or captured by Summers. This time, things were going to work out.

They were resting beneath a huge tree when the muted sound of gunshots echoed in the distance. Sarah stiffened, and instantly she felt Wolf's arm tighten around her shoulders. Both of them looked toward where the sounds had originated from.

"What do you think?" Sarah asked in a low voice. They'd taken a break from their walking to catch their breath. She knew Wolf had done it for her, not for himself.

Wolf stirred. "Probably Summers. His men are jumpy, and a deer might have made them start shooting."

Hope sprang through Sarah as she leaned forward on her crossed legs. "How far do you think we are from the cabin?"

Wolf shrugged. "I don't know." He gazed down at her uplifted features. Exhaustion was written across Sarah's face. "Could be a mile or so. We scattered and ran, so it's hard to tell. I want to get to the road, because it'll be easier going." He added grimly, "We can't walk on the road, though, because Summers and his men might be waiting to ambush us again. We'll parallel it from the safety of the tree line."

With a sigh, Sarah relaxed against Wolf's body and pressed her brow against his shoulder. "I wish we could sleep...."

Leaning over, he pressed a kiss to her hair. "I know."

"But we can't." Sarah slid her hand around his waist. The bleeding from the bullet that had grazed his torso had finally stopped, much to her relief.

Getting to his feet, Wolf growled, "No." The last thing he wanted to do was leave. After admitting his love to Sarah, all he wanted was to know her reaction. Had she even heard his words? Wolf felt terribly unsure, and he was trying to combat the feeling of panic deep within him. Gently he helped Sarah stand.

"By the time we get back to the cabin, it's going to be dawn," he told her in a hushed tone. Picking several pine needles from her mussed hair, he smiled and held her shadowed eyes.

Then he placed his arm around her shoulders, drew her near and whispered, "Let's go. Dawn will shed new light on the situation."

Sarah nodded, feeling numb inside. The shots worried her. Who had fired them? Were Summers and his men hanging around, waiting for them to appear? Everything seemed so tentative, so extraordinarily fragile.

Sarah halted, her heart beating in triple time. "Wolf?"

He frowned and halted. Automatically his hand went to her arm. She looked forlorn. Frightened.

"What? What is it, honey?"

Just the endearment gave Sarah the courage she needed. "Wolf...I...I'm scared, and I love you...." There—the words were out. She stared up into his craggy, drawn features, her breath jammed in her throat. Croaking, Sarah forced out the rest of what had been begging to be said. "I—I know it's too soon, that we haven't known each other very long, but I have to tell you how I feel. I didn't want to trust you, to care about you, but I couldn't help it. I was afraid to admit I loved you, because I was so afraid I'd lose you...." Sarah looked down at the ground and bit her lower lip. "I still might," she said with a sob. "Inside, I feel so vulnerable and frightened that we could die at any moment." Afraid that she'd said too much, or hadn't said it right, Sarah halted. It took every last bit of her courage to lift her head to see the effect her words had on Wolf.

Trying to steel herself against possible rejection, Sarah lifted her lashes to meet and hold his hooded stare. In that instant, she knew that even if Wolf rejected her she would never love another man as she loved him. No one could possibly match Wolf in stature, in his understanding and complete acceptance of her. But was the love he'd professed to her earlier a fleeting thing? An affair? Sarah couldn't stand that thought. Her feelings ran too deep, and she looked at commitment as a long-term thing.

Wolf raised his hands to Sarah's face. There was such hope and anguish in her eyes. Tears jammed his, and he didn't try to hide his reaction to her low, unsteady admission.

"It's me who should be down on his knees to you, Sarah, not you to me."

Confused, tears brimming her eyes, Sarah whispered, "What are you talking about?"

His smile was tender as he caressed her temples and cheeks. "I'm scarred and wounded, Sarah. I have huge chunks of myself that still aren't healed, but you love me anyway." Unshed tears blurred her face in front of him. Choking out the words, Wolf rasped, "Sarah, I love you. I meant what I said tonight. I'd been feeling that way ever since I met you. And, yes, it hasn't been a long time, but it doesn't matter. What matters most is that you gave me your trust and I gave you mine."

Blindly Sarah moved into his arms, a small cry escaping her lips. "We could die at any time. I—I just wanted you to know, Wolf, to know I love you."

With a groan, he took Sarah's full weight against him, holding her, holding her love forever. "I don't deserve a second chance," he said thickly, his lips near her ear, "and I certainly don't deserve you."

"Yes, you do," Sarah said with a little laugh that was partly a sob of relief. She looked up, his glistening eyes melting her heart. "I just wanted you to know, in case something happened to me—to us."

"We'll get through this—together." He leaned down, capturing her tear-bathed lips. "Together . . ."

Chapter Fourteen

"Wolf, look!" The words escaped Sarah as they neared the cabin. Dawn had come and gone, and the strong morning light was now sending blinding shafts through the fir trees on Blue Mountain. Beside the cabin were several cars, among them a black Jeep. In addition, there were three state police cruisers, and another black car Sarah hadn't seen before. She saw two men in expensive suits, and two other men, in jeans and short-sleeved shirts, who looked dangerous and alert.

"It's Morgan!" Wolf said, coming to a halt, disbelief in his voice. "And Killian. And Jake."

She twisted a look up at him and saw the joy leaking into his exhausted features. "Your boss?" she croaked.

A slow grin started across Wolf's mouth as he looked down at Sarah and brought her hard against him. "Yes, and my team. I'll be damned," he whispered, and kissed her long and hard. As he broke free of her lips and saw her stunned expression, he said, "Morgan must have sensed all hell was going to break loose and decided to come after I called him. If I'm not mistaken, the other guy in the dark suit is a top FBI official. Come on, honey, we're saved!"

Sarah needed no coaxing. She knew they both looked disheveled, and the blood on Wolf's shirt gave the appearance that he'd been wounded much more seriously then he had. The first to sense their approach was a cougar-lean man with black hair. He swiveled around, instantly on guard.

"Wolf!" Killian called to the other men and then trotted toward them. A quarter of a mile separated them. The rest of the men raised their heads, stopped talking and looked with amazement in their direction.

Realizing just how tender Sarah's feet were, Wolf decided to halt on the slope and give her a well-deserved rest. He watched his friend's approach. Although Killian never smiled, Wolf could see his friend's green eyes dancing with silent welcome as he trotted up to them. "We're okay," Wolf said, extending his hand in greeting.

Gripping Wolf's hand, Killian's narrowed eyes swung from Wolf to Sarah, then back to Wolf. "Thank all the saints, you're alive. We were worried. Summers wasn't talking after we apprehended him and his men earlier this morning down the road from the cabin. We figured, with the arsenal they were carrying, that they'd been hunting you."

Wolf nodded. He kept his eyes on the group of men at the base of Blue Mountain. "That's exactly what happened. Who's with Morgan and Jake?"

Killian briefly turned his head. "State troopers, and FBI agent Kyle Talbot."

Relief plunged through Wolf. "Good. When did you arrive? And what the hell's happening? You said you nabbed Summers?"

"Morgan can fill you in on the details, but after you called him yesterday, he rounded us up. We caught the first flight out to Anaconda and rented a car. Kyle came with us. Morgan pieced things together. He figured you'd be at Sarah Thatcher's cabin, so we came up here. We met Summers and his men, running around like idiots with rifles in their hands, about three miles from here. Kyle arrested them, and then after we checked out Ms. Thatcher's cabin, we figured they'd been hunting you." His mouth pulled into the slightest of smiles. "Morgan said if you were still alive you'd eventually show up here at the cabin. He was right."

Sarah sagged against Wolf, dizzy with relief. "It's over," she murmured.

Wolf studied her anxiously and kept his grip firm around her waist. He glanced over at Killian. "Sarah, this is Killian, one of my men."

Killian nodded. "Ms. Thatcher."

Sarah tried to smile, but she was incredibly exhausted. "Hi, Killian. Thank you for coming...."

"Then Summers and his men are in jail?" Wolf demanded.

"That's right. All of them, including Sheriff Noonan."

Sarah pressed her hand against her heart, relieved. "I'm so glad...."

Concerned for Sarah, Wolf glanced at the rest of the men coming to greet them. "We're going to make some fast introductions, and then I want to get Sarah cleaned up. We both need to rest," he told Killian.

"Looks like you may need to go to the hospital," Killian warned, pointing at the rust-colored blood staining Wolf's shirt.

"Just a graze," Wolf muttered. "Right now, I need a hot bath, bed and—" he smiled down at Sarah "—this lady at my side."

Sarah fought grogginess as she emerged from the shower and wrapped herself in a thick, fluffy towel. Outside the door, she could hear the Perseus men talking in low tones in the living room of her cabin. It was over. All over. Meeting Morgan Trayhern and the other men had been little more than a blur in her spongy state. She remembered shaking hands, but that was all.

As she pulled on her cotton gown and donned her robe, she heard the men leaving. Glancing out the bathroom window, she saw Morgan and his men climb into the black Jeep. The FBI agent stood talking with Wolf for a moment before he got into his dark sedan. With a sigh, she opened the door and stumbled toward the bedroom. What she needed was Wolf to hold her. The need to be in his arms was overwhelming.

Sarah pulled back the covers and lay down. Before she could even pull the sheet over her, she fell into a deep, spiraling sleep.

Wolf rubbed his eyes. They were burning from lack of sleep. His steps echoed through the cabin. Spotting the bathroom door open, Wolf moved slowly toward the bedroom door. At the entrance, he hesitated, a slight smile tugging at his mouth. Sarah lay on her side, curled in a fetal position, her hands beneath her cheek. She was fast asleep. Just the soft parting of her lips stirred him, made him want to love her as he'd never loved another woman.

Quietly he tiptoed into the room and pulled the sheet and blanket across Sarah's sleeping form. Her hair, still damp from being recently washed, framed her face. Gently Wolf touched her cheek and felt the velvet firmness of it beneath his fingers.

Forcing himself to move away from her, Wolf knew he desperately needed to bathe before joining Sarah in bed. As he left the room and closed the door, nothing had ever seemed so right to him. He was drained in a way that left him weaving across the floor to the bathroom, and he knew he'd be lucky to make it to bed and gather Sarah into his arms before he keeled over from sheer exhaustion.

The impertinent chirp of an upset robin outside the raised bedroom window awakened Sarah first. Evening light filtered in the window, telling her it must be close to nine o'clock at night. She'd slept a long time. Wrapped in a sense of being protected, she groggily turned and realized that she was pressed against Wolf's entire length. His arm was wrapped around her shoulders, and her head lay in the hollow of his shoulder. Just his soft breathing, the rise and fall of his massive chest, stirred her. Wolf was alive. She was alive. How close they had come to dying less than twelve hours ago, she thought.

Tentatively she slid her hand across the massive breadth of his darkly haired chest, allowing all of her senses to absorb the exploration. There was such latent power to Wolf, and yet he had been nothing but gentle and sensitive to her, to her needs.

Raising up on one elbow, Sarah gazed down at Wolf's sleeping features. The beard lent his face an even more dangerous quality. She rested her palm against his heart and felt the slow, powerful beat of it beneath her hand. His hair was tousled, and it gave his face a vulnerable look. Her heart expanded with such joy that she blindly followed womanly instinct and leaned forward.

The first, tentative brush of Sarah's lips on Wolf's mouth eased him out of deep slumber. Was he dreaming again? But this was too real. He barely opened his eyes as he lifted his hands. Her mouth was warm and inviting, softly exploring his. A groan rumbled through him as Sarah artlessly pressed herself to him, a signal to his spinning senses that she wanted much more than just a kiss from him.

Sleep was torn from Wolf as he eased Sarah onto her back against the bed covers. The evening light through the window was muted, giving the room a quiet sense of surrender to the coming darkness. The gold of Sarah's fine, silky hair as he ran his finger through the strands satisfied Wolf even more. Her eyes were lustrous with allure, and his body hardened in response.

"Sarah..." he rasped, cradling her cheek. "Honey, wait..."

Sarah's hand skimmed Wolf's bearded cheek. She took pleasure in his sweetly sleepy state. There was such unexpected vulnerability in him. "We've waited long enough," she whispered.

Wolf saw the longing in her blue eyes, eyes that were drowsy with desire. Every fiber of his being wanted to love her. With his thumb, he traced her parted lips, lips he wanted to ravish. "I love you," he rasped, his heart pounding in time with the urgent throbbing of his need.

Her hands skimmed his arms, shoulders and neck like a tantalizing breeze.

She framed his face with her hands. When she spoke, her voice was low and quavering. "I love you, Wolf. I trust you. I was so afraid about how I felt toward you." She smiled a little. "I know your love can help me across whatever fears might be left." Sarah felt the sting of tears and blinked them away. She felt the massive, potent power of his barely controlled body above her, felt a fine trembling shudder pass through him as she spoke those words.

Love. Wolf pressed his brow against Sarah's. He tried to find the words, but couldn't. Only her hands, moving across his body, brought him out of the turmoil within him. Finally he eased back enough to hold her shimmering gaze.

"I love you, Sarah. When I told you that last night, in the heat of battle, I meant it."

"I was scared then, and I'm scared now," Sarah quavered, "but in a different way."

He nodded and closed his eyes. "That makes two of us." When he opened his eyes again, he added, "I'm afraid that I'll go too far too fast and scare the hell out of you, or make you push me away. And," he added sadly, "I'm afraid I'll see fear, see fear of me, come into your eyes . . ."

Whispering his name, Sarah eased upward, grasping his shoulders. Wolf had taken a terrible emotional beating in many ways, and as she pressed a kiss to his jaw, Sarah knew she could help him. She would welcome his advances, reassure him with herself, with her body and, most of all, with her heart. It was thrilling to discover that she could give Wolf back a huge piece of himself that had been crushed by the events in Peru.

"You can't hurt me," she whispered. "Just love me, Wolf. Please . . . I want you . . ."

Wolf nuzzled her cheek, found her mouth and gently trapped her against the bed as he claimed her. There was such lushness to her eager, exploring lips against his.

It took real courage to reach out and live life, Wolf realized, to love despite the possibility of rejection. As he drowned in the splendor of Sarah's welcoming mouth and touch, Wolf knew he had to risk himself, and place his damaged hope once more on the line. As Sarah came willingly into his arms, her strong, loving body pressing urgently against his, Wolf surrendered to his heart as never before.

As he drew the flowery printed nightgown off Sarah and gazed down at her, Wolf transcended his own fear; perhaps it was Sarah's fearless approach to wanting to love him. Wolf wasn't sure, and in that golden, heated moment it no longer mattered.

Sarah closed her eyes as she felt Wolf's strong hands caress her shoulder, her waist, and on down to outline the shape of her hips. There was such tenderness in his exploration of her that she felt herself unraveling. His touch was like sunlight skimming silently across the land. When he leaned over, his mouth capturing hers at the same moment that his hand caressed her breast, she moaned.

The world spun to a halt as Sarah drowned in the heat, the fire, of Wolf's mouth, and when his lips settled on the peak of her breast she gave a small cry of pleasure. Her fingers kneaded his broad, damp shoulders as he drew her deep into his arms, pressing her hotly against him, his mouth bringing a new kind of fire that raced through her.

The ache centered in her lower body, and as she moaned, Sarah lost herself in all the sensations of Wolf as a man.

She tasted the perspiration of his taut shoulder, felt him tremble as she caressed him intimately. Her boldness, her need to show just how much she loved him, broke through whatever barrier continued to hold him a prisoner of the past. As she lifted her lashes, she saw his burning gray eyes meet and hold her own as he covered her with his body.

The moments suspended. Sarah held her breath as she felt Wolf's knee guide her thighs apart. His hands framed her face, and she clung to the hooded, heated look in his eyes, to the tension mirrored in his rugged features. There was still a thread of fear in Wolf's eyes, and instinctively Sarah allowed her feminine heart to guide her as she arched upward to meet him, capture him, pull him deeply within herself.

She immediately felt Wolf's fingers tighten around her face, and she not only heard, but felt, a deep animal growl come from within him as she enclosed and held him within her molten, silky confines. It was as if something snapped within Wolf as he arched and tensed within her, and Sarah smiled softly as she felt him surge forward, taking her, claiming her for the first time.

In those golden, spinning moments, moments that seemed so far removed from the real world, Sarah surrendered herself to Wolf in every possible way, for the first time in her life. As he slid his hand beneath her hips, giving back the same pleasure she was giving him, she understood what real love was all about. It was about sharing—giving, taking, allowing the fear to fall away in order to love fully. Whatever issues of trust she'd had also dissolved beneath the cherishing strength of his mouth, the worship of his hands across her body that made it sing like the most beautiful bird she'd ever heard. There was such beauty being shared, such care and love, that tears matted her lashes.

The lightninglike heat grew deep within Sarah as he moved with her, making her his own. The sudden current of release shot through her like a lush explosion, catching Sarah by surprise. Arching into Wolf's arms, pressed against his length, absorbing his strength, she cried out and threw her head back as the waves of sensation overwhelmed her. The intense pleasure went on and on, and Sarah could only helplessly sponge up the wild, fiery feelings that Wolf prolonged for her.

As Sarah began to slide back into the molten fire afterward, she felt Wolf tense and grip her hard to him. In those moments, as she held him, her face pressed to his shoulder, Sarah willingly received Wolf's gift of himself to her. All she was aware of was his damp, hot skin, his ragged breath against her face and neck, and his hands wrapped lovingly in the length of her blond hair.

Opening her eyes, she smiled up at Wolf. All the tension and fear had been drained away from him by her vessel of a body, by her love fearlessly reaching out to him. Extending a hand, Sarah gently caressed his darkly bearded cheek.

"I love you with my life," she told him, her voice quavering.

Much later, they stirred in each other's arms. The small night-light on the wall broke the hold of darkness in the bedroom as Sarah roused herself. She realized that Wolf was already awake, at her side, his hand resting against her as he studied her in the silence. There was such peace and serenity in Wolf's face that Sarah was stunned by the change in him. She smiled sleepily up into Wolf's rugged, shadowed features.

"I slept again," she whispered, her hand moving across his chest, luxuriating in the soft, dark hair there.

"We both did," Wolf murmured, running his hand slowly up and down the length of her strong spine. "I woke up first, though." He tendered a slight smile to show her how much he loved her. Wolf caressed Sarah's shoulder and arm, feeling like a thirsty sponge absorbing everything about Sarah. Earlier, she had been damp and slick against the hard planes of his body. Now her skin was like velvet beneath his touch.

"You were wonderful," Sarah told him as she sat up facing him. The covers pooled around her hips, and she captured his hand. "We were wonderful."

Wolf nodded, absorbing the shining luster in Sarah's eyes as she smiled. She fed his soul. Reaching out, he sifted strands of her gold hair through his fingers. "You weren't afraid like I was," he told her. "You had the courage to go all the way. I knew I was holding back..."

Leaning forward, Sarah laughed softly and captured his mouth to let him know how much she loved him. Wolf's response was instant and heated. As she reluctantly broke the kiss and gazed into his molten gray eyes, she whispered, "Maybe because we love each other so much, that helped us get past our own fears."

He gave her a lazy smile and eased her upward until she lay over him. Instantly he saw the change in her eyes and felt the heat of her stir the fires within him again. "I feel like life is going to start getting good again," he confided. "For both of us, honey."

Sarah delighted in her contact with Wolf. "We have the time, don't we?"

Sarah leaned down and nuzzled Wolf's cheek, then gave him a swift, hot kiss on the mouth before laying her head on his shoulder. "All the time in the world," he said. He brought his arms around her. He wanted to discuss marriage, but it was too soon. Or was it?

"Wolf?"

"Hmmm?"

Sarah smiled tentatively and brushed his short, dark hair away from his furrowed brow. "Will you stay here until Summers goes to trial?"

Wolf stilled and held her serious look. "Sarah, I'm not the kind of man who does well at one-night stands or even living together." He scowled and pushed his fear of rejection aside. "Loving you was a commitment," he told her gravely. "I don't want to stay just for Summers's trial. I want what we have to be the start of a commitment that works toward marriage."

His words were like a sweet dream flowing through her. Sarah swallowed against her tears. "I wasn't sure, Wolf.... I don't want a one-night stand, either. And I'd like you to come and live with me, if that's what you want." She saw his face become gentle with emotions, and it gave her the courage to dive headlong into what really lay in her heart.

"I know we haven't known each other very long, and I know we need the time. With Summers going to jail, we'll have it. I just need you to know how much I love you. It's not a passing thing, Wolf. You opened yourself up and let me give you my trust. It was something I never thought I could do again, but you made it easy." She leaned over and kissed him.

"I love the hell out of you, Sarah Thatcher," Wolf whispered thickly, fitting his mouth against her parted lips. He loved her fiercely, for her goodness, her thoughtfulness toward others—and for the fact that she moaned and returned his kiss with all the womanly fire she possessed. He cupped her cheek and held her lustrous blue gaze. Her eyes were shining with love for him alone. "I'd like to move in here, to live with you."

"Good..." Sarah sniffed and gave him a trembly smile.

Smiling softly, Wolf pressed a kiss to her salty, wet lips. So much had been taken away from each of them, and yet, as they held one another, he realized that despite their individual scars, together they achieved a wholeness that would give them a new lease on life.

Wolf eased Sarah into his arms and wiped the tears from her cheeks with his fingers. "We'll have the time now," he told her, "to grow and know each other. We've got some tough times ahead with the trial, but we'll take that together." His voice went deep with raw feeling. "When the time's right, I want to marry you, Sarah. I want you to carry our children, if that's what you want. We're going to take life together, on our terms. You hear me?"

She did, and she closed her eyes as she uttered Wolf's name. As his arms closed around her, Sarah knew, at last, that with love, anything was possible.

* * * * *

Silhouette

S P E C I A L   E D I T I O N ™

It takes a very
special man to win

That **SPECIAL** *Woman!*

She's friend, wife, mother—she's you! And beside each Special Woman stands a wonderfully *special* man. It's a celebration of our heroines—and the men who become part of their lives.

Look for these exciting titles from Silhouette Special Edition:

April   FALLING FOR RACHEL by Nora Roberts
Heroine: Rachel Stanislaski—a woman dedicated to her career
discovers romance adds spice to life.

May   THE FOREVER NIGHT by Myrna Temte
Heroine: Ginny Bradford—a woman who thought she'd never love
again finds the man of her dreams.

June   A WINTER'S ROSE by Erica Spindler
Heroine: Bently Cunningham—a woman with a blue-blooded
background falls for one red-hot man.

July   KATE'S VOW by Sherryl Woods
Heroine: Kate Newton—a woman who viewed love as a mere fairy tale
meets her own Prince Charming.

Don't miss THAT SPECIAL WOMAN! each month—from some of your special authors! Only from Silhouette Special Edition! And for the most special woman of all—you, our loyal reader—we have a wonderful gift: a beautiful journal to record all of your special moments. Look for details in this month's THAT SPECIAL WOMAN! title, available at your favorite retail outlet.

TSW2

Silhouette
SPECIAL EDITION™

Once there were seven...

Seven beautiful brothers and sisters who played together,
and weathered adversity too cruel for their tender ages.
Eventually orphaned, they were then separated. Now
they're trying to find each other.

Don't miss Gina Ferris's heartwarming

FAMILY FOUND

Sunday's child may be fair and wise but she has a lot to
learn about love and trust. And who better to teach her than
a sexy, mysterious man from her past? Read all about
Lindsay, as this youngest Walker gets her own story in
FAIR AND WISE (SE #819).

Be sure to catch the other members of the Walker clan in FULL OF GRACE (SE #793) and
HARDWORKING MAN (SE #806) by sending your name, address, zip or postal code along
with a check or money order (please do not send cash) for $3.39, plus 75¢ postage and han-
dling ($1.00 in Canada), payable to Silhouette Books, to:

In the U.S.	In Canada
Silhouette Books	Silhouette Books
3010 Walden Avenue	P.O. Box 609
P.O. Box 1396	Fort Erie, Ontario
Buffalo, NY 14269-1396	L2A 5X3

Please specify book title(s) with your order.
Canadian residents add applicable federal and provincial taxes.   SEFF-3

WHERE WERE YOU WHEN THE LIGHTS WENT OUT?

SILHOUETTE

SUMMER Sizzlers '93

This summer, Silhouette turns up the heat when a midsummer blackout leaves the entire Eastern seaboard in the dark. Who could ask for a more romantic atmosphere? And who can deliver it better than:

**LINDA HOWARD
CAROLE BUCK
SUZANNE CAREY**

Look for it this June at your favorite retail outlet.

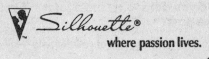

Silhouette®

where passion lives.

SS93

Relive the romance...
Harlequin and Silhouette
are proud to present

by Request™

A program of collections of three complete novels by the most
requested authors with the most requested themes. Be sure to
look for one volume each month with three complete novels by
top name authors.

In June: **NINE MONTHS** Penny Jordan
                              Stella Cameron
                              Janice Kaiser

**Three women pregnant and alone. But a lot can
happen in nine months!**

In July: **DADDY'S**   Kristin James
             HOME   Naomi Horton
                              Mary Lynn Baxter

**Daddy's Home...and his presence is long
overdue!**

In August: **FORGOTTEN**   Barbara Kaye
           PAST   Pamela Browning
                              Nancy Martin

**Do you dare to create a future if you've forgotten
the past?**

Available at your favorite retail outlet.

HARLEQUIN®   Silhouette®

REQ-G

New York Times Bestselling Author

Sandra Brown

Tomorrow's Promise

**She cherished the memory
of love but was consumed
by a new passion too
fierce to ignore.**

For Keely Preston, the memory of her husband
Mark has been frozen in time since the day he was
listed as missing in action. And now, twelve years
later, twenty-six men listed as MIA have been
found.

Keely's torn between hope for Mark and despair
for herself. Because now, after all the years of
waiting, she has met another man!

**Don't miss TOMORROW'S PROMISE by
SANDRA BROWN.**

**Available in June wherever Harlequin
books are sold.**

TP

MORGAN'S MERCENARIES
Lindsay McKenna

Morgan Trayhern has returned and he's set up a company
full of best pals in adventure. Three men who've been to hell
and back are about to fight the toughest battle
of all . . . love!

Be sure to catch this exciting new trilogy
because you won't want to miss out on these
incredible heroes:

Wolf Harding in HEART OF THE WOLF (SE # 818),
available in June.
Appearing in July is Sean Killian, a.k.a. THE ROGUE
(SE # 824).
And in August it's COMMANDO with hero Jake Randolph.
(SE # 830)

These are men you'll love and stories you'll
treasure . . . only
from Silhouette Special Edition!

SEMM-1